SUPPLANT

SHANE M TOMAN

Printed in the United States of America
Print ISBN: 978-1-953910-58-5
eBook ISBN: 978-1-953910-59-2

Library of Congress Control Number: 2021908830

Published by DartFrog Plus, the hybrid publishing imprint of DartFrog Books.

Publisher Information:
DartFrog Books
4697 Main Street
Manchester, VT 05255
www.DartFrogBooks.com

Join the discussion of this book on Bookclubz. Bookclubz is an online management tool for book clubs, available now for Android and iOS and via Bookclubz.com.

For Dad.

Contents

A BRIEF HISTORY

1935: German scientists synthesize testosterone, the first injectable anabolic steroid.

1954: Professional athletes infamously begin using anabolic steroids for performance enhancement in the Olympics as the Soviet weight-lifting team wins gold or silver in every weight class.

1971: The genes of two different species, namely viruses, are successfully combined for the first time by Dr. Paul Berg of the Stanford University School of Medicine.

1976: Anabolic steroids are banned in sports but continue to be used to greater and greater effect as more testosterone derivates are created.

1978: The Belgian Blue cow is introduced to the United States for the first time, known for its extreme musculature due to natural genetic repression of myostatin, a muscle growth inhibitor.

1981: Dr. Thomas Wagner of Ohio University creates the first transgenic animal by inserting rabbit genes into a mouse.

1996: Dolly the Sheep becomes the first fully cloned animal, rapidly leading to new frontiers in the understanding of genetic code.

2003: The entire human genome is mapped for the first time in history after thirteen years of analysis.

2012: The CRISPR method of gene editing is unveiled to the world, leading to innovations in the manipulation of livestock and plant genes for higher quality and quantity food yields.

2015: The first human embryo is unethically edited with CRISPR, creating controversy and huge delays in human CRISPR testing.

2018: The first human gene editing trials begin, using CRISPR technology to target blood disorders.

2020: The entire coronavirus genome is mapped in a single day as technological advances have allowed the genome of any organism to be mapped in fewer than two days.

2031: With medical gene editing now widespread, genetic risks and precursors for cancer and other diseases have been brought to zero in the developed world.

2035: With a one-billion-dollar grant, scientists successfully edit the genes of a single volunteer, an amateur bodybuilder, by supplanting his genes with the myostatin-repressing genes of the Belgian Blue cow, exponentially increasing muscle growth.

2036: The bodybuilder easily wins Mr. Olympia, the greatest bodybuilding event in the world. Unfortunately, he dies during the awards ceremony from starvation due to vastly increased caloric needs brought on by the edited genes. As a fallout from this event, animal-human gene combination, or supplantation, is banned by the US government and the World Health Organization.

2041: Operating in utmost secrecy, the US Department of Defense awards Dr. Larry Needleman, head of genetic research at the Harvard University School of Medicine, a blank-check grant to supplant the genes of volunteer Army cadets with the echolocation genes of a fruit bat.

2043: The supplantation completed safely, and without side effects, the cadets successfully pull off a night capture of a known international terrorist, Hans Schlemmer, without the use of infrared goggles or other equipment. News of this quickly leaks, leading to an outpour of public demand for further supplantation research.

2047: Using select genes from various animals, supplanting reaches public consumption for cosmetic and performance enhancement. Within a year, going "under the needle," named after Dr. Needleman, becomes the world's most sought-after form of elective procedure, albeit with tightly controlled approved supplanting options.

2048: The first child of a supplanted human is born with massive birth defects. In the ensuing years, all offspring of supplanted people are born with horrible disfigurements, many dying soon after birth, and others living as grotesque examples of a failed experiment. Supplantation is quickly banned and criminalized throughout the world, gradually leading to an underground market of supplanters, people willing to perform these procedures on customers at great risk and great cost.

CHAPTER 1

RUNNING LATE

JULY 22, 2071

The screen played a little musical tune and displayed ARRIVED AT DESTINATION in bold yellow letters. Zen placed her palm on it. It read her fingerprints and prompted her to scroll through the various payment options. When she selected one, the divider window between the driver and the back seat went from opaque black to perfectly clear. The driver waved and gestured with a thumbs up.

"Thanks for the ride," she said and got out. She would have driven herself to the hospital, but her license was still pending as it had been for over six months. All cars had been self-driven for the past thirty or so years, but the entire system went haywire a couple of years back. They had only recently finished tallying the death toll from that day. Cab drivers and other specialized personnel, along with the super-wealthy, of course, were top priority for licenses. Everyone else was waiting in an endless backlog.

Her shoes seemed to melt as she stepped onto the pavement. It was absolutely sweltering—104 degrees—and the closeness of the buildings only served to trap that heat into an unbreathable stew. Nevertheless, downtown Chicago still held some of the charm it had in her childhood. Her life had improved drastically since then, growing up a poor black girl in Roseland on the South Side, just before corporate districting had started. She now lived in Hinsdale, an affluent suburb thirty minutes west of the city, and worked on the road a lot, so she relished her opportunities to come back. Roseland was unrecognizable, but the expanded downtown area, which stretched north to Lincoln Park and Lake View with Wrigley Field, hadn't changed as much. Sure, buildings were built and destroyed, and the zoo and stadium had become abandoned historical landmarks, but the streets and especially the smells were extremely familiar.

In front of her stood a massive white structure, the main building of the east campus of Barack Obama Memorial Hospital, built twenty years prior to honor the former US president. She was just on the cusp of running late for her appointment, so she hastily walked through the automatic doors into the lobby. If she moved any faster, the sweat would start. It was early in the afternoon on a Wednesday, and luckily there wasn't much of a crowd waiting to pass the security station. Two armed men stood on either side of the station desk, and a woman in a white lab coat sat behind it. The line moved quickly, and she soon found herself at the front. At the desk was a small machine with a black pad and notification lights, a sensor that read the patient's genetic code and fed it to a computer that quickly interpreted the results.

If someone were found to be supplanted with genetic code from unapproved non-human organisms, they would be denied entry and could be subject to something much worse. Although it wasn't technically illegal to have supplanted genes, it was near impossible to get into any reputable establishment if the person had any code that wasn't on the approved list from 2047. And there were always people who were out to get those supplanted people for whatever reason, be it political, religious, or personal.

"Hello," the woman said with a polite smile. "First and last name and date of birth, please."

The retina scanner at the hospital entrance had already identified Zen, but in places that required surgery, it was customary to double-check.

Zen smiled back instinctively. "Zen Thomas. Five, fifteen, thirty-seven."

"Thank you. Please put your right index finger on the pad when the light turns green."

Zen stretched her fingers, suddenly realizing how tense they were. The light flashed green, and she placed her finger on the pad.

"Please hold it there until the light changes color," the woman said. Clearly, she went through the routine hundreds, if not thousands, of times per day. The light changed to blue, and within ten seconds, the monitor flashed CLEAR. The security guard on the left gestured for Zen to enter the main area of the hospital.

Zen pulled out her phone to check her appointment. Although a small fraction of the older generations still used smartphones, most people had small removable chip implants called HUDPhones that allowed a rudimentary augmented reality system that had features like GPS mapping, business reviews, and vital signs that overlaid normal vision. She had an old-school kind of attitude when it came to technology. Important things were better dealt with in person. That was why she was here at the hospital after all and not doing a virtual appointment as was customary for anyone not coming in for a procedure. Plus, she was an executive for a private security firm, and it didn't hurt to mitigate the risks of hacking or something like that self-driving disaster with a chip in her head.

Third floor, OB/GYN. Five minutes. That HUDPhone walking GPS would have really come in handy in a maze like this. After taking the stairs up, she half-jogged down the hall to the right, hoping it was the correct decision. She felt her anxiety taking over, not even noticing she was slowly getting winded. Internal medicine, surgical specialties, and there it was. She exhaled deeply, slowed her pace, and walked into the small OB/GYN waiting room. There was no receptionist here, only another retina scanner. It identified her, and a small screen confirmed her arrival. She sat down in one of the chairs in the waiting room, and her right leg immediately started nervously jimmying.

Barely a minute later, she felt her phone buzz in her pocket. She pulled it out and saw the invitation to enter the office. She got up and walked over to the door, which was now automatically unlocked, and walked in.

"Good afternoon, Mrs. Thomas!" a short, balding man with glasses greeted her. "Thanks for coming in. Please—" he gestured with a sweeping arm motion, "—follow me." He sounded happy, but his mannerisms were at odds with his voice. Slumped shoulders, shuffling walk. He motioned to a leather chair in his office.

"Thanks for seeing me, Dr. Kohn. I know this is usually reserved for procedures. I—" she paused for a moment. "I just like to talk in person. It feels a hell of a lot better than online, you know?"

"No problem at all, Mrs. Thomas. Let's get to it, shall we? Sorry for the curtness, but I'm a little pressed for time." Dr. Kohn typed a few keys, and a transparent screen on his desk transformed into an internal image of the female reproductive organs. THOMAS, ZEN 05/15/37 was displayed in the upper left-hand corner. "Here is your uterus." He pointed with his finger. "And here is your cervical wall." He smiled awkwardly. "Notice the shape here. The wall is broken, in layman's terms, which prevents a fetus from ever reaching viability. Unfortunately—" He paused again, attempting another smile. "It's a structural issue, a congenital defect. And likely why you have had, let me see—" He typed a few more keys and looked at his private monitor. "Two miscarriages."

He's definitely not a people person, Zen thought. His clinical approach to something so personal and raw pissed her off, but he had been willing to see her in person, so she waited quietly. She knew what he was going to say before he said it.

"I'm sorry," Dr. Kohn said. "It is simply impossible for you to have children." He attempted a frown, but it looked absurd. She had heard it before, but she wasn't here for it to end like that. There had to be something they could do.

"Impossible? And what do you mean, it's congenital? I thought that wasn't even a thing anymore." She was consciously trying not to let emotions take over. The doctor wasn't the kind of person to appreciate that kind of approach.

"The structure of the cervical wall is compromised. Sure, you can conceive, but the fetus will never reach term. And yes, it is congenital. Infant genes are edited to remove disease precursors, but there is nothing that can be done for structural defects. They generally occur during fetal formation, in the womb."

Zen felt her frustration start boiling up again but inhaled and exhaled deeply to calm herself down. "What about surgery? Isn't there a procedure or something that can fix it?"

"I'm sorry. In certain cases, we're able to strengthen this wall, but yours can't be improved without a real risk of causing severe internal problems."

She had come ready to fight but suddenly just didn't feel like it anymore. It was over. She felt her fingers untensing. Her anger dissipated. It was replaced by overwhelming sadness. Sadness and emptiness.

"It's time for my next appointment, Mrs. Thomas," Dr. Kohn said. "I'm sorry I couldn't be of more help."

Zen barely heard this. She was already halfway out of the office. She felt tears welling up in her eyes and didn't want the doctor to see it. He didn't deserve to see it. She exited the waiting room into the fluorescently bright hallway. She walked over to an area that was set up for patients and families to do work as they waited. She sat down at one of the tables and pulled out her phone. She pressed it twice. Her husband's face and phone number stared back at her. Her hands trembled, and a tear muddied the screen.

CHAPTER 2
RIBEYE

Mik's hands and forearms were killing him. He had been unloading the trucks for at least three hours now. His buddy, Ollie, was out sick today. Well, "sick" was more like it. Mik had picked up on the pattern of absences a long time ago, and he didn't think Ollie had any idea that he had caught on. Every fourth or fifth Wednesday like clockwork. It was always strange how Ollie suddenly felt fine to come into work the next day, well, at least with his HUDPhone on dimming mode. He dreaded these days because he had to do two different jobs, and there was no one else to fill in. Plus, it wasn't like he didn't go out drinking the night before as well.

Normally, his duties were limited to chopping and preparing the cuts of meat in the butcher shop. He had been working there for ten years, first as an apprentice as soon as he got discharged from the Army, and then as the full-time butcher. The owner of the shop, Filip, was really getting up there in years and was around less and less as time went on. Sitting home, collecting checks, probably slowly going senile. The bastard always smelled like almonds anyway. He was an old neighbor and friend of his father's from way back in the day. He gave Mik the job at the shop and helped him out with a lot of things, especially with the transition back to society. Business was always steady, if not booming. Most meat was now raised in a lab from stem cells. You know, why kill an innocent animal when you could eat a perfectly good artificial abomination that tasted like hell paste. In the area of northwest Chicago where Mik lived and worked, however, there was a good market for the traditional meats—steaks, chops, and sausages like kielbasa and bratwurst made from the real thing.

Corporate districting had taken over, as it had most of Chicago proper, but Tem Tem, the Singaporean manufacturing company

16

that owned this area, which encompassed the northwest portion of the city from Pulaski Park up to Portage Park east of the old O'Hare Airport, along with some other places he knew as a kid, pretty much left it alone. They hadn't destroyed apartments or houses, force-gentrified the area, or messed with rental rates, but it was quickly turning into a shithole because the company put next to zero money into infrastructure. On the bright side, at least he could afford to live there, and some of the Polish culture that he was raised in was still alive. After the Army, he had come back to live at his father's apartment, and he had left Mik the place after he passed away from chemical cancer back in 2064.

Mik finally finished unloading all the trucks. It was already four in the afternoon, and he was sweating buckets in the heat. He still had to prepare all the cuts for the morning, although he could put off the sausage-making until later in the week. He took a few moments after he wheeled the meats into the locker, so the freezing temperature could offer a bit of respite. After a good five minutes, he started cutting up the sides of beef and pork. Even though his muscles were past the point of fatigue, he worked quickly and efficiently, in pure second nature, as his mind thought of everything except the task at hand. He knew that he didn't need to concentrate for a second to get the job done to perfection. Never in his life did he have an issue delivering on results as long as he received clear orders and directions. It made him a perfect fit for the military, and consequently, a perfect fit as a butcher once he learned the ropes.

It was getting toward evening when he was finally done. Quick and efficient work still meant a lot of time when you had to cut up literally tons of the stuff. He put all the cuts in the freezer, washed his hands in the sink, and pulled a non-stick pan out from under the butcher's block. He was exhausted and absolutely starving. He hadn't eaten a single thing since his poor excuse for breakfast this morning. He turned on a portable electric plasma grill and oiled up the pan. The oil started lightly bubbling almost immediately, and he turned down the heat. He grabbed one of his freshly cut steaks, a juicy ribeye, pierced it with a fork, and laid it in the pan. It started sizzling, and the aroma made his stomach grumble loudly. He flipped the steak after a few minutes, and soon it had turned a beautiful medium-rare. He savored every tender bite, then washed it down with a cold beer from the fridge. With some food finally in his stomach, he locked up the shop and called a cab with his HUDPhone.

Mik had a license. He drove armored vehicles in the Army, so he was on the short list after the self-driving ban. He just didn't trust himself. He was going to get totally blitzed tonight, like every night, and after his last DUI, which landed him with a weekend in jail, a huge fine, and bonus legal fees, he figured a taxi might just be a touch cheaper. He plugged in his destination, Old Tom's Bar and Grille, a staple of the neighborhood for the last forty or so years. The name was a bit of a misnomer, as he didn't think they had ever served food. He probably could have walked there under normal circumstances, but the long day's work and the evening's still-present heat gave him a strong desire to just sit the hell down.

When the taxi arrived at the bar, he got out very slowly. Sitting down for even such a short period of time really tightened up his muscles and made them ache with every movement. On the sidewalk, he stretched his hands above his head and rotated his wrists and shook his arms out. Old Tom's was a dive bar to end all dive bars. The door was made of wood, which was a complete oddity these days. Amid concerns over deforestation and climate change, plus advances in material technology, there was a long-lasting national wood ban for construction. This was the original door, splintered and defaced with carvings and graffiti. The sign glowed neon above, and the music blared out onto the streets. He pulled open the door and entered. The music got even louder. No retina scanners here. No gene sensors. Even the dartboards were made of that crappy plywood and weren't electronic. He found a seat at the end of the bar on a stool with a ripped leather cushion. He signaled the bartender over and ordered a beer, quickly scanning the room as he did. Wait a second. Was that—?

"You motherfucker!" Mik nearly shouted to be heard over the music.

Ollie turned around. He had been standing at a table near the center of the room, talking to some other guys. He immediately smiled and laughed. "Ah, shit, Mik. You got me!"

Mik couldn't help but smile back. He already knew that Ollie was anything but sick, and the amusement of finally catching him in the act outweighed any leftover anger about having to do all that extra work earlier in the day. "Yeah, I did, you bastard. I can barely move now, thanks to you."

"That's what your mother said an hour ago." Ollie was always quick with the comebacks. His talents were wasted on unloading meat from trucks.

Mik laughed. It was funny, plus he never knew his mother, so the insult didn't exactly hit close to home. She had left when he was two years old, and he was raised by his father from then on. "Ah, you found her!" he said. "Where has she been all these years?"

"In my bedroom," Ollie answered. They both laughed. They ordered another round of beers. And then another. And another.

In what felt like no time at all, it was after 11:30. They had to get up for work the next morning, so they stumbled out of the bar onto the street. It was quiet out here, except for the music still playing inside. "Want me to order us a cab?" Ollie asked.

Mik thought for a moment. "Nah. No thanks. I'm gonna walk home." His muscles felt a lot better, helped by resting at the bar and undoubtedly by the eight or ten beers he had.

"All right, man. See you tomorrow," Ollie said.

"Yeah, you'd better show up," Mik answered.

He started walking down the street. The music slowly got softer and the night filled with a pleasant sort of low hum. He enjoyed taking walks late at night. There were few people or cars out on the streets. It allowed him to clear his head, and the beers gave him that sort of buzzed clarity that he relished. He continued walking, past all the bars and businesses that were still open to the residential area and its calming darkness. The streetlights were long ago broken, and with no corporate money coming in to fix them, no one had taken it upon themselves to install any replacements. Not that it bothered him. Not that he had any issue seeing just fine in the darkness. In fact, he didn't even need to open his eyes.

CHAPTER 3
THE VASE

Zen sat there for a while. She turned the phone off. She couldn't do it just yet. Not after the last two times. The first time she had a miscarriage, her husband, Aiden, did a moderately impressive job of making it look like he felt pity. He said things like, "I'm so sorry, baby," and "It's okay, we can try again." But even then, she could sense the contempt building up behind his eyes. The second time was much worse. Aiden had thrown a table vase into the living room wall. No, not in her direction, but she had felt like it hit her. He had started with the usual lines, but the mirage of pity was gone. His voice was dry and cold. And after he threw the vase, he said those lines that she could still hear, as loud as that day over a year ago. "What is wrong with you?" Still, she stayed with him, and after he calmed down and apologized, they agreed to try again. Third time's the charm and all.

They had met each other during her first year at the University of Illinois School of Law. She had completed her undergraduate degree at the Chicago campus, graduating with honors. She had been desperate to get out of Roseland ever since she was a child and made sure to put her everything into school so she could do just that. The university gave her a free ride and a choice of campus after placing in the top three percent of her class, but she was convinced by her parents to stay at home and go to the Chicago campus to save some money. With some money saved and another offer of financial aid, she started law school in Champaign, finally far enough out of the city to remove any of that old feeling and keep the memories of her childhood stowed away nice and deep.

Aiden was in his final year, a tall, handsome white guy who she thought wore a bowtie in just about the most stylish and sexy way a bowtie could be worn. They had only one class together, but it was an instant connection. She loved his little, sometimes-brutal jokes about the professors, and he loved her quick wit and gorgeous smile. He came from a respectable upper-middle-class family out in who-knows-where Minnesota, and his idea of urban life was a big college campus two hours from any major city. She found his naivete ridiculously charming, and he found her background fascinating.

When she finally introduced him to her parents at her graduation after two and a half years of dating, he put on that charm just like the day they first met. Her parents liked him immediately but were still apprehensive about the whole thing. They were tolerant people, but they had been black kids during Trump-era America in the heart of a dangerous neighborhood of a dangerous city. They had lived through the police beatings and false arrests. They had lived through the total joke that was the ensuing criminal justice reform, and then when Zen was in her senior year of high school, the redistribution of law enforcement and infrastructure to the corporations.

A biotech company called Oasis had bought up Roseland and some of the surrounding areas for pennies on the dollar with the promise to the government of bringing a strong police presence and a corresponding low crime rate to a formerly high crime area. At first, the police were overzealous, taking in people for the most minor of offenses or accusations, and then Oasis began building their own infrastructure. First, they built laboratories for their own research and then started destroying houses and apartment complexes they deemed eyesores. They built high-end condominiums and townhouses for the wealthy, pricing the poor out of the area, making them scramble for a place to live. Most of their neighbors became homeless or, at best, found low-rent housing in the areas that corporations neglected. Zen and her parents refused to end up like them. She started working as a waitress in her off time, and her mother and father both took second jobs. With the extra income, they negotiated the rental of half a condominium from a wealthy executive who was in Chicago for only three months out of the year on business.

Zen dated Aiden for four years after graduation, and his charm slowly ate away at her parents' misgivings. But when he proposed and Zen ran to her parents with the massive diamond ring on her finger, that fear snuck back into their hearts. Although anti-minority rhetoric had somewhat lessened over the years and was replaced with disdain of those who had been gene-supplanted, there was always the specter of what could happen when rich white men had control. She had pleaded with them for their blessing, and since she was their only baby girl, they relented, with the one condition that she keep the Thomas family name.

Only two weeks after the wedding, which was a substantial and elegant affair, Zen moved into Aiden's ultra-modern house out in Hinsdale. With accolades from her law professors and employers from the firm where she had worked since graduation, she landed a cushy job as a legal executive at Guardian Hill, a large company specializing in private security. The three years of marriage were going pretty smoothly, all things considered. Everyone fights. Relationships take work. All those sayings. But after her second miscarriage, that beautiful house had stopped feeling like home. Aiden had changed. Irreversibly.

And today, Zen didn't feel like calling. She didn't feel like going home. Sure, there was the fear of what could happen—would the vase be aimed at her this time and all that—but there was more of an emptiness than a fear. She put her phone back in her pocket. She left the hospital and walked down to a very fancy local bar called the Hazy Bee Parlor with a gene sensor on the door and plush leather lounge seats. She had a wonderful double of whiskey and a few more and decided to leave. She held the door for a very handsome gentleman with the most incredible blue eyes who just for a second made her forget about her husband. She pulled out her phone and called a cab. She was going to stay at her parents' place for the night.

CHAPTER 4
HAPPY HOUR

Autumn was having a real roller coaster of a day. She had been work-ing as a junior sales associate for five years at a small medical supply company. There was a rumor swirling around the office that they were going to file for bankruptcy at the end of the month and would be doing some heavy downsizing, especially of the sales staff. It was too bad. She liked her co-workers, and to be honest, she had a knack for sales. Her strikingly good looks and her bright orange-red hair that her parents had named her after didn't hurt when she had those virtual or in-person meetings with potential customers. The fact that most of those potential customers were older male doctors who worked too hard and were a touch starved for companionship made those sales even easier. It was frustrating that she could be losing her job, especially since they had removed the caps on commission a few months back, and she was bringing in good money.

Then, right before closing time, she got a call from the higher-ups offering her a promotion to sales manager. They were cutting part of the sales team, but they needed someone with an excellent record to help push the remaining staff to hit their quotas. Her best friend from the office, Maddie, got confirmation that she was keeping her job as well, so they planned to go out directly from work for happy hour to celebrate. Their office was right near downtown, so they decided to do a bit of a bar crawl. There were a bunch of nice places downtown because it was the only part of the city that the government still controlled, along with the historical landmarks, and they kept it very well maintained for the tourism money. Every bar and restaurant in the area had gene sensors and retina scanners outside. Some of the less classy ones had lighted signs on the windows that said things like SUPPLANTED? GO AWAY! or the slightly more eloquent PEOPLE

WITH SUPPLANTED GENES NOT WELCOME. After all, what sort of self-respecting tourists would want to visit a place that allowed supplanted people into the establishments?

Autumn and Maddie decided to start at the place with the best margaritas in town, The Magic Lime. Autumn immediately thought of how stupid the sign looked, animated LEDs of a lime jumping out of a magician's hat. The retina scanner identified them, they used the gene sensor outside the door, and when it cleared them, they sat down at the near-empty bar. It was just after five on a Wednesday, but it was happy hour, and they were going to do it right, whether the bar was packed or not. They agreed to order the same drinks as each other, starting with a frozen strawberry margarita with sugar on the rim. It was an unspoken competition between them to see who could hold their liquor better. The drink was amazingly refreshing, so Autumn started to drink it as fast as possible, but the sharp ache of brain freeze hit her, and she immediately regretted it. They savored that drink, and the next, a mojito filled with ice. They flirted with the bartender a little and got the second round on the house. They left, giggling, feeling just a little tipsy, and not bothered by the heat whatsoever.

The next stop was Dimwits, a kitschy bar with ancient arcade games. They even had originals from nearly a hundred years ago. The place smelled like stale beer and fried food, but apparently, that was part of its charm.

"This place is kinda gross, Mads," Autumn said. "I thought we were going to class it up tonight."

"Oh wow," Maddie responded. "You get a little promotion, and now suddenly you're too good for some terrible beer and food. I guess I overestimated you. Listen, we'll finish the night at a place with some amazing cocktails, I promise. This will just make us appreciate it a little more."

"Fine, fine. I probably should eat something, though. I don't particularly feel like throwing up in some fancy bathroom later. Nice, greasy fried food is perfect for absorbing all the alcohol, right?"

"Whatever you say. You still need to match me drink for drink. And I'm keeping count."

They ordered a couple of cans of beer—they didn't trust the taps to be particularly clean—and a whole bunch of chicken fingers and French fries. Autumn tried her hand at an old arcade game and failed miserably. Maddie tried next and beat her score but then accidentally spilled her beer onto the controls. They slowly walked away, yet again giggling and whispering, "Oh shit, oh shit," under their breaths. They figured they had better pay their bill and leave before someone caught on about what happened. One of the bartenders handed Maddie a palm pad, and she paid. She started pushing Autumn toward the door. They left, walked around the corner, and broke down laughing.

The sun had nearly fully set. It was after 8:30, but the heat was still borderline unbearable. Unlike the frozen drinks from earlier, the beers and fried food didn't help cool them down, so they were desperate to get inside to the next place before the sweat started messing up their makeup.

"Okay, so I know the perfect place. Best cocktails in Chicago," Maddie said.

"It'd better be close," Autumn answered. "I'm gonna start sweating in like a second, and I don't want to look like shit tonight."

"It's two blocks away. C'mon, follow me."

The Hazy Bee Parlor didn't have any anti-supplanted signs outside. It didn't have any stupid animated logos. It had a plain metal sign above the door that simply stated its name and nothing else. The place was known for its phenomenal whiskey selection and classic cocktails. It was on the pricey side, but the place had a decadent atmosphere.

"Umm, Mads? I'm still in my work clothes. I think this place might be a bit too fancy. How about we go home and shower and change? We can come back later."

"Absolutely not! You are so hot. If anything, you look too good for this place. And I really don't want to lose this buzz."

Autumn rolled her eyes and smiled. She didn't take much convincing, especially when compliments were involved. They placed their fingers on the gene sensor and entered. There were crystal chandeliers on the ceiling and large leather lounge seats with marble tables. It was starting to get busy, but they found the two remaining barstools. A bartender handed them drink menus and glasses of ice water.

"What do I even order here?" Autumn asked. "Everything on the menu looks so complicated. I don't even recognize most of the ingredients."

"Here," Maddie said. "This one has cherry liqueur and orange juice. I'm sure it's pretty sweet." She flagged down the bartender and ordered two.

The drinks were sweet and a little bit bitter, so they drank them slowly. Plus, they only had one ice cube in them, so they were quite strong. Autumn and Maddie were bordering on drunk at this point, so they agreed to pace themselves and have a glass of water between each drink. Feeling a little adventurous, they asked the bartender for a recommendation. What they got next was a smoky and spicy cocktail that was altogether different from what they were used to, but they kind of liked it. They nursed it for a good hour or so.

They finished up the drinks, and Maddie was feeling sleepy. "Hey, I think I'm done. That last one hit me really hard. And it's already after eleven. No idea how that happened."

"Yeah," Autumn responded. "Me too. Also, just checking, but we still have work tomorrow, don't we?" She laughed.

Before Maddie could answer, the bartender interrupted, "The man at the end of the bar—" He pointed to the far corner. "Got you these." He placed two Manhattans in front of them. Maddie leaned forward and back, trying to get a good look toward the direction he had pointed.

"No thanks," Autumn said. "I think we're ready for the check, actually."

"He's gorgeous," Maddie said. "I think you earned this one, sales manager. I'm gonna head out, but you should definitely stay. How long has it been, anyway, a year?"

"Shut up," Autumn said, mock angry.

"She'll accept," Maddie told the bartender. She winked at Autumn. "See you tomorrow. I'll cover for you if you come in a little late." She got up and started walking toward the door. She turned and smiled at Autumn and left.

Autumn immediately felt a pang of nervousness, but it was dulled by the alcohol. She leaned over to find the man who had bought her the drinks, but as she did, he was already there. He put his hand on her back to steady her. Maddie was right. He was gorgeous. Piercing blue eyes, shockingly perfect teeth, stone jawline. She was used to flirting a little to get her way, but now she felt like all those hapless men who gave in to her wiles.

"I hope you don't mind," the man said. *Wow, even his voice is amazing; smooth like honey.* "I saw you sitting over here when I came in. The drink was really meant for you, but it would've been rude to leave out your friend."

"Th-thank you," she stammered. She actually stammered. *C'mon, Autumn, that was pathetic.* She took a deep breath, and with the help of the booze, she regained her stature. "I think this might've earned you a seat." She patted the empty stool next to her where Maddie had sat.

They chatted for at least an hour, even ordering another round. The conversation flowed so well. The guy really had a way with words, and it was so refreshing that he wasn't completely flustered by her looks like so many other men were. "Want to get out of here?" he asked after they finished their last cocktail. Did they even exchange names? They probably did, but she was drunk and now felt too awkward to ask again.

Autumn thought for a moment. Even though it had been a while, like Maddie so rudely mentioned, and she was drunk on top of that, she didn't feel entirely sure about this. Then again, it couldn't hurt to at least see what happened. She could always make those important decisions later. Plus, she just got a promotion, and she was feeling adventurous. "Sure, why not," she finally answered.

They left the bar. "If it's not a big deal," the man started saying, then quickly paused. "Mind calling the cab? My HUDPhone broke a couple of days ago, and the new one hasn't come in yet. Don't worry. I'll pay you back." He smiled that disarming smile.

She nodded and called the cab to his address. Oasis District. Fancy. They hopped in, and he held out his hand for her to grab. She did, feeling giddy and drunk and wonderful. They didn't say anything, at least with words. They stared into each other's eyes.

A few minutes later, Autumn started feeling a little weird. She had a lot to drink tonight, and she hoped that she wasn't about to throw up or pass out or something that would totally ruin all this. She was feeling loopy and tired and weak. They arrived at their destination, a beautiful house in the heart of Oasis District with a palatial staircase out front. *He is gorgeous* and *filthy rich? Jackpot.*

She reached out her empty hand toward the palm pad to pay for the trip. Or at least she thought she did. But her hand was still by her side on the seat. She tried again. Nothing. "Everything okay?" the man asked and smiled. "Those drinks must have really hit you." She tried to shake her head, but she couldn't do that either. The man gently grabbed her by the wrist and directed her hand to the palm pad. Using her fingers, he selected a payment option. The divider window cleared up.

"Thank you," the man said. "She's a little tipsy, so I'm going to help her out." The driver nodded, no doubt well versed at the tribulations of drunk passengers. The man carried her out of the cab and up the staircase to the house. Autumn couldn't move a single muscle. She was even starting to have trouble looking in different directions. She was screaming with fear, but no sounds came out.

The man carried her to a large, beautiful bedroom on the second floor and dumped her on the bed. He started removing her clothes. She wanted to scream, to fight back. Her breath came in labored rasps. After she was naked, the man undressed himself. He smirked at her and mouthed the words, *I'm sorry.* His expression was evil. It was cruel. His piercing blue eyes looked like the pits of hell. When he thrust into her, she wanted to cry, but no tears came. She could no longer even look down or close her eyelids, just able to stare at the ceiling. She barely felt the physical sensations. No pain. Only fear and disgust and shame.

After he finished inside of her, he left her field of vision. Within a minute, her breathing stopped. She tried to gasp for air. Ice cold panic overtook her when none came. When the man returned and towered over her, she saw he was dressed again and holding a large, serrated knife. Just before she lost consciousness and her heart stopped beating, she had the strangest thought. *That was one refreshing margarita.*

CHAPTER 5
DUTY

Mik didn't think he had PTSD. Sure, he had been diagnosed by the mandatory psychiatrist upon discharge from the Army, but in his opinion, he just fucking hated sudden loud noises. Then again, who didn't? It was a pretty natural human reaction to panic a little when a goddamn explosive goes off near you and pretty natural to panic when you heard something that sounds just like it, even back home in Chicago. His military service had put him in this place, after all.

When he had gotten back to US soil from his tour in Lebanon in 2060, where he mostly just drove a truck around the desert, Mik got the news from home that his father had been diagnosed with chemical cancer. That was just great. Locked up in Army duty for two more years and his dad had to quit his job at the Tem Tem plant. As much as the government lauded over The Troops, they sure as shit didn't care enough about them to pay them decently. The medical bills for the cancer were going to be massive, and Tem Tem offered about as good an insurance policy as they did infrastructure to the area where he lived, which was to say about zero.

He went to his commanding officer and told him the whole sob story. *Sorry, son* was the gist of the response, but then he received a confidential letter at mail call two days later. There it was, in plain black and white on a special one-use tablet, addressed to Corporal Mikolaj Jesko, an offer to pay for all his father's medical bills. The letter praised his performance and valor in the field, and it came with a promotion to a new special forces division. The only caveat was that he had to take part in a quick little experiment.

The date, time, and location of the experiment were sent to him upon his agreement. All he had to do was sign the tablet, and it would transmit his permission wirelessly back to the necessary people.

Three weeks later, he showed up at the lab at the scheduled time. It was to be a painless procedure with little risk to him, except that he would be unable to father children.

He remembered bits and pieces of the genetic supplantation craze back when he was a teenager and that it had been banned ever since the children came out all messed up or worse. When the researchers told him that he would be undergoing a supplantation procedure, he initially balked. He never wanted children to begin with, but he knew how supplanted people were viewed by everyday society. He was familiar with all the gene sensors outside places, and he knew about the witch hunts against those who had genetic code from other organisms. The only supplanted people who were accepted by society were those who underwent the approved procedures during the eighteen months that it was legal and regulated back in 2047 and 2048. And that was some pretty basic stuff like improved vision from hawks and improved tasting ability from rabbits. Nothing that could make anyone inhuman or anything. The people who went to black market supplanters, though, were the real deviants. They got genetic code injected in putrid back alley safehouses from god-knows-what sort of creatures.

Gene sensors outside any number of places would identify this stray genetic code and flash it on a monitor for everyone to see, potentially preventing any of those people from entering. This included bars and restaurants, but also hospitals and government buildings. And once identified by these sensors, there was nothing stopping some vigilante from following that person home or tracking them down and punishing them for being supplanted. Only genes from the legal supplantation era wouldn't trigger those sensors.

Mik asked the researchers about that once they told him the nature of the experiment. They told him that even though he would be receiving code from an organism that wasn't on the list, he wouldn't have any issues getting into any places. They would make sure that he wasn't flagged, you know, as a reward for his service. With promises of pay going to his father back home and of life as a free un-supplanted man at discharge, the researchers injected him with the new genetic code. He had to wait another few days for the changes to fully take effect, so he had to live and sleep in a special dormitory attached to the lab building.

A day or so after the injection, he started noticing some small changes. A heightened awareness of things. Increased sensitivity to temperatures. Upon completion of his time in the dormitory, the full changes were extremely evident. He could see—sort of—the heat signatures of the lab employees outside the door. It wasn't exactly vision because he still saw normally with his eyes, but it imprinted on his brain in a very similar way. He saw the heat of other people as infrared radiation in a thermal map of sorts. He immediately thought of that ancient movie *Predator*—still a classic. He felt no other changes in his body whatsoever. They were right all those years ago. This procedure really didn't produce any side effects, except, of course, if he had children; well, let's not think about that.

When he was given back his belongings, he was told to report to his commanding officer for new orders. He was to be reassigned. US Army Special Operations Command 121st Reconnaissance Division. The same division that started the supplantation craze, with the soldiers given the echolocation genes of fruit bats back in 2041. He would be part of a new company, Viper Company, and he quickly found out why. He and seventeen other men were given the same genetic code with the same promise: all men who desperately needed more money to be sent back home. They all received genes from pit vipers that gave them the miraculous ability to "see" infrared light even with their eyes closed through new undetectable pit organs on their faces.

The eighteen men were sent on assignment to China to scout a military compound said to contain weapons of mass destruction. China had become a major threat to the US. They publicly reverted to a communist government, and everyone knows how much the US hates communism. The US and China had fully cut their trade ties, which caused a slowdown in manufactured goods as the US struggled to build new international relationships. Sure, there were tons of new domestic jobs available in brand new factories, but they were dangerous, and few people wanted them. And only so much production could be sent down to Mexico.

The Chinese had developed electromagnetic pulse (EMP) defenses that would nullify any night-vision sights, along with any sort of vehicles, radar, phone, satellite, or radio systems, for nearly ten miles in every direction—including upward. Mik and the other seventeen men had to scout out the installation without troop support or communication. They had to travel across miles of enemy territory on foot in the dead of night, using only their newfound infrared vision.

They split into three six-man squads. Squad One attempted to sneak through a chain-link fence in the northeast border of the installation only to be met with a tripwire claymore mine that sent tiny little ball bearings ripping through them. Luckily, none lasted long enough to truly suffer. Squad Two was successful in breaching the compound wall, but they were unlucky enough to stumble right into a barracks room deep inside the main building. They managed to take cover and gun down ten men, but the other fifty or so quickly overwhelmed them.

The Chinese military had installed pure lead walls throughout the entire building, including the barracks, which nullified any infrared vision. The lead walls were there for two major reasons. One was that it prevented any scouting or surveillance if the EMP was damaged, and the second was that it allowed them to use electronic devices inside the compound without damaging them. The small price, of course, was the long-term health of their men.

Squad Three, with Mik on point, was successful in fully breaching the compound. They were almost shocked to see that the US military had been correct for once. In a giant hangar were hundreds of artificial-intelligence-driven warheads. Nuclear gravity bombs. Neutron bombs. Biochemical bombs. Enough to destroy the populations of nations. With this information stored only in their heads, they escaped to report back. Because of the first two squads, the troops at the compound were now aware of the infiltration. The troops poured out, sending gunfire and artillery in the general direction in which Squad Three had escaped. There was barely any moonlight but just enough to press a wild attack. Flak and fire surrounded them as they ran through the forest. Trees burst into flames and exploded. Two men to Mik's left were shredded by wood shrapnel from an artillery explosion. Not a minute later, his three remaining squadmates were vaporized by bellowing fire. Mik managed to hide long enough for the troops to assume they had killed the entire squad and could return to the compound.

Only Mik escaped and returned to tell them what he saw. He was responsible for the US military investing billions of dollars into a new stealth bomber plane that was hardened to prevent against EMPs. He allowed US politicians and military leaders to sleep at night, knowing they had prevented the largest coordinated bombing attack in human history. But he was sent back home to his father's apartment with only a medal, a stipend, and a kick in the ass. The only surviving member of the 121st, and they didn't even live up to their promise. He was flagged by the gene sensor as soon as he tried to walk into City Hall.

And three years after he got back home and started working at Filip's butcher shop, his father finally succumbed to the chemical cancer despite the stipend and state-of-the-art treatment. And a week after the funeral, the checks stopped coming. They knew about his father's passing, and they didn't want to give him a single extra red cent. Just another loose end. Just another rusty cog that was no longer useful to the machine.

CHAPTER 6
INVESTORS

It was just before midnight, and Albert was the only one in the conference room. He would have been on the verge of sleep if it wasn't for the nervous adrenaline coursing through him. The call was scheduled for midnight, and Albert had been at the office since 7:00 a.m. He didn't feel completely qualified for this. Well, he felt qualified but not confident. He had worked at Genovas for six years and had two degrees in finance and one in accounting. He knew numbers better than most. But he was a little lacking when it came to dealing with people, and quite a bit was riding on this. And to be entirely realistic about the situation, he was here because he was the only senior employee who spoke Japanese. He was a fourth-generation American, but his parents made sure to keep the household bilingual. So, he sat there in the stark, empty room at a huge white table with a HoloComm in the center and waited for the call.

The HoloComm was a relatively new invention that was making its way into the big corporations before it was tested in the smaller markets. It projected rough holographic images of the remote speakers as if they were seated at the table. It was ugly and imperfect, but it made virtual conferences a bit more personal as one could pick up on mannerisms and body language.

The call came in at the exact scheduled time. If clocks still had second hands, it would have absolutely been at the official stroke of midnight. Japanese investors were calling in crisis mode, and Albert was responsible for convincing them not to sell. The Genovas stock was not doing particularly well. They wanted assurances that it would rebound, and they wanted to know precisely how it was going to do that. Genovas had grown exponentially when supplantation became legal, becoming one of just a few major corporations that provided approved supplanters to consumers, and they quickly went public. When supplantation was banned, they quickly transitioned to infant gene editing. This helped them rebound temporarily, but competition there was getting fiercer all the time. As their market share slowly dwindled, so did their share prices. There were a few jumps here and there with new hospital contracts, but mostly the stocks showed no signs of recovering.

The images of three suit-wearing men appeared in the three seats opposite Albert. He stood up. "*Konnichiwa*, Mr. Hara. Mr. Sakai. Mr. Uchida," he said and bowed gently. "Thank you for contacting us. I wanted to let you know that your time is valuable, and I will do my best to answer any questions you may have."

"Mr. Murata, I'll be very direct," Mr. Uchida answered quickly. "We are genuinely concerned. We have been discussing our holdings in Genovas, and we need to know how you'll be protecting our investment. We have been staunchly loyal these years, but it's no longer financially feasible to retain our shares. Without answers, and soon, we will be forced to withdraw. I'm sorry."

"Mr. Uchida," Albert responded. He dabbed his forehead with his shirt wrist. He could feel the beginnings of perspiration. "Things will turn around, I promise. And soon."

"Soon?" Mr. Hara asked loudly. "We've been hearing that for a long time, Mr. Murata. Without something concrete, we have no choice but to put our money elsewhere. Gene supplantation is against the law, and your corporation has done nothing to adapt."

"I understand your concerns," Albert said again. He felt lightheaded. "We've been involved in infant gene editing for some time, and we are taking steps to increase our market share there. And—"

"Yet that is not happening," Mr. Uchida responded. "Your company was at the forefront of infant gene editing, and all I've seen is your market share decreasing slowly over the years. Apparently, you're always taking steps but going nowhere. I don't like to do this, but we are selling our shares as of tomorrow morning when the markets open."

"There is something else, Mr. Uchida," Albert said. He removed his glasses and wiped his forehead. He felt almost sick. *Damnit, what are you doing? You're going to lie to investors now?* "We have a signed government contract. It's official, on the books, but it won't be public for another two weeks. That's why I neglected to mention it until now. I was hoping I'd convince you to stay while keeping it under wraps." *Oh, you're a genius now, Albert. When the investors find out that this is total bullshit, the stock is just going to tank that much faster.*

"Hmm, a government contract?" Mr. Sakai finally spoke. He had been sitting silently until now. "What are the specifics?"

Albert was already in it this far. "I can't give out details just yet, but it's a ten-figure contract. And it's renewable."

"Very interesting," Mr. Hara said. "Please, Mr. Murata, give us a moment to discuss."

"Of course," Albert said. The image of the three men dematerialized. The adrenaline was the only thing keeping him from fainting on the spot. He felt the sweat trickle down the inner frames of his glasses and along his nose. This will be a clear cause for termination, and he probably wouldn't be able to work in any large corporation ever again once the news got around that he tried to pull this little trick. He quickly poured a glass of water from a carafe along the side of the conference room. It was warm, leftover from previous meetings, but his mouth was sandpaper, so it helped a little. He tried and failed at a breathing exercise.

When the three investors reappeared on the HoloComm, he did his best to appear calm and ready for their reply. There was no greeting. "We will hold off on our decision for two weeks," Mr. Uchida said. "If we do not see anything finalized publicly by then, we will pull our investment immediately. You have until the markets open on August 6. Do you have any questions, Mr. Murata?"

"No. Thank you very much, Mr. Uchida. Mr. Hara. Mr. Sakai. *Ki wo tsukete.*" He bowed deeply. They bowed in response and ended the call.

Albert collapsed into his seat at the conference table. He was so tired, but his mind raced to try to come up with possible solutions. He was left with only one option. He had to convince the executives to make a big, risky move. He finished the glass of water and passed out with his head on the table.

CHAPTER 7

THE REAR HALF OF A CONDO

JULY 23, 2071

Zen woke up in the same bed she slept in her entire childhood. Her parents had transported it from the old place to the new one they rented. She felt extremely groggy. Spending the night in alternating states of all-out crying and total numbness can do that to you, especially after a few whiskey doubles. Her face was squished against the pillow, and she opened her eyes slowly and carefully. The shades in the room worked quite well, so the light wasn't too offensive. She had gotten to her parents' place—the rear half of a condo—well after midnight, so she didn't want to wake them up. She still had the same key from high school, well-worn and slightly rusted, but it worked like a charm, and she had snuck up to her room, cried quietly into the pillow, and fallen asleep.

She pulled out her phone to check the time. Twenty texts and five missed calls from her husband, Aiden. She didn't bother reading any of them. She had slept most of the morning away and still felt like she got next to no sleep. With a deep sigh, she sat on the edge of the bed and started to get dressed in the same clothes she wore the night before. She walked into the bathroom, found a toothbrush brand new in a package, and washed up. She headed downstairs to the kitchen and rummaged through the fridge for anything that could resemble breakfast. She wasn't particularly hungry, but she thought a bit of food might give her some energy. She found a couple of frozen waffles, put them in the toaster, and poured herself a glass of milk. As she waited for the waffles to be done, she noticed the quiet of the house. It was at the same time comforting and lonely. She grabbed the waffles and walked to the window. A thunderstorm started suddenly, and the patter of rain against the windows and skylights cut the silence. She looked out toward the driveway as she munched on her breakfast. Two cars were there, one parked behind the other. *That's weird*, she thought. Her parents both still worked full-time and were usually gone by eight in the morning. They had gotten their driver's licenses prior to all cars being self-driving, and renewals were being sent out quicker than new licenses, so they had theirs for the last year or so.

She called her mother first. It rang a few times and then went to voicemail. She called her father and had the same result. She walked to the base of the stairs and called out. Nothing. If they were still home, she would have heard them by now anyway. She didn't have their work numbers on her phone, but a quick search gave her the number to the law firm where her mother worked as a legal aide.

"Gordon and Stern, this is Kate. How can I help you?" a high-pitched female voice answered.

"Good morning," Zen responded. "This is Zen Thomas. Is my mother in? Ada Thomas?"

"Oh, hi Zen!" Kate said excitedly. "She talks about you all the time. I haven't seen her today, but let me check. It's been crazy here. Please hold a minute." Zen waited on the line, listening to the horrible hold music. It had been, what, a hundred years, and they still had someone choosing the worst possible songs? "Hi, Zen? Yeah, I asked around, and she hasn't been in today."

"Oh," Zen said. She didn't quite feel nervous but more the inklings of confusion. "Thanks."

"Zen? Would you mind having her call in when you see her? Mr. Gordon has some scheduling questions for her."

"Sure. Have a good one." Zen ended the call. This was a little strange. She immediately called the shipping company where her father worked and got a similar response.

She hadn't even let them know she was coming over last night, so it was possible they had skipped work for a day to go on a little vacation around town or something. She instinctively called out for them again, louder than before. She didn't expect an answer, but why not. Nothing. Of course. She then called Guardian Hill, where she worked, to let them know she was coming in late today. She had a high enough status in the company to not get any flak for doing that from time to time.

She went upstairs to go pack her things. She guessed she could stay there another couple of days, but she was already late for work, and with the amount she had left on her desk yesterday, she knew she was in for a late night at the office. She would try calling her parents again later in the afternoon, maybe after they came back from their boozy lunch or wherever they were. She entered her bedroom, and it immediately dawned on her to check her parents' room down the hall. The door was just barely ajar, and the lights were off. She pushed the door open slowly.

There they were. Her parents were lying in bed, still asleep. Her father snored like a jet engine. How had she not heard that from downstairs? They must have gotten totally drunk last night. She grinned. Light relief hit her, but she wondered if she was ever truly worried.

"Mom? Dad? Wake up!" Zen said in a voice best reserved for speaking with a deaf person. Groggily, her mother opened her eyes, at first confused for a split second and then happy. Her father grumbled but kept sleeping.

"Wake up, honey," her mom said, vigorously pushing her husband's back. He grumbled again, slowly turned over, and opened his eyes. He cleared his throat, coughed a couple of times, and weakly waved at Zen. "When did you get in?" her mom asked.

"I came in late last night. I didn't want to wake you. Why aren't you at work?"

"We had a long day yesterday, honey. We got some bad news, and then we got some gin and some olives. The condo owner is selling the place. He already has an offer at the asking price, and he didn't even let us know until yesterday." Zen's father grumbled again, this time totally awake. "We have a month to vacate the premises," she continued. "And we can't afford anywhere else in this area. Oasis District is absurdly expensive, and the prices have skyrocketed even from when we first rented."

"That's bullshit," Zen said. With what happened to her yesterday, and now this, anger boiled up inside her. Rich bastards always had a way of screwing you over, especially when you're most vulnerable. "There's got to be some law that allows you some say in all this. Or at least some extra time to find a place. Listen, I'll help. I'll chip in. I make enough to do that."

"Nonsense!" her father finally spoke. "We'll be fine. Why'd you come stay here last night, anyway?"

Zen told them what had happened. What the doctor said. Why she didn't feel like going home. She had admitted to her parents what had happened with Aiden after the second miscarriage, and they had implored her to leave him. She had been adamant before that they could work it out. He hadn't thrown the vase at her, after all. But now she said she didn't think it was possible. It was over. It was time to confront him and tell him what the doctor said. No matter what his response was going to be, it wasn't healthy to stay in that sort of relationship.

She kissed her parents goodbye, called a cab to work, and planned on heading out to her and Aiden's place in Hinsdale to have the talk when she got home.

CHAPTER 8

WRIGLEY FIELD

It fit into a relatively small bag, all things considered. It was kind of awkward to carry, but if you shifted your weight just right when you walked, it wasn't too much of a strain. Plus, it wasn't nearly as hot today as it was yesterday. That heat could have tired anyone out doing anything. The sun was slowly beginning its descent, and a pleasant breeze was starting to pick up. It was shaping up to be one of those perfect summer nights.

Wrigley Field was undergoing maintenance and was closed until tomorrow. It was always good to open on a Friday to take advantage of the most possible visitors. Wrigley had ceased operations after Major League Baseball decided to call it quits back in 2036, and now it was a historical landmark and a complete tourist trap. The government ran this area of Chicago and did its best to keep the attractions looking pristine. They allowed visitors to walk onto the field and take pictures and pretend they were the baseball players they grew up watching as kids or at least heard about from their parents. The maintenance team had replaced the entire field with new sod, and it took a few extra weeks of waiting for it to take root. When the MLB shut down, Wrigley had been one of the few stadiums that still used real grass—Kentucky bluegrass—just like the old days, and they wanted to keep it that way for tourists. The downside was that the heavy foot traffic did a number on it, and they had to close down a couple of times a year just to fix the field.

There were no maintenance men at the stadium today. They had the last few weeks off to enjoy themselves before the park reopened. There was, however, a tall man dressed in a maintenance uniform. He slipped under the locked chain at the gate. It would have looked a little funny if anyone saw him. Maybe someone did, but no one would have taken notice of a maintenance man, especially with the stadium opening its doors again the next morning. He was carrying a medium-sized black duffel bag, and the way he had to shift his weight under the chain looked a little unnatural. That bag must be heavy. The man walked from the gate through the concessions area. This was a neat area for tourists as well. The original awnings and equipment were still there. The man walked down the corridor to the field entrance along the first base line. Best seats in the house. It would have been funny to see him try to hop the short wall onto the field holding the duffel bag with both hands. There must be some fragile or important stuff in there if he didn't just throw the thing over first. He walked past the dugout onto the field. At the pitcher's mound, he laid the bag gently onto the ground.

The man pulled the zipper of the side compartment. He reached in and pulled out a bundle of green garden stakes, the type you would use if you're trying to grow tomatoes and you didn't want them to encroach on the other plants. He then pulled out a smaller bundle, this time of steel barbeque skewers, which would be perfect for making kabobs on the grill on a perfect summer day like today. Lastly, he pulled out a couple of tubes of quick-drying strong adhesive paste. He pushed three of the garden stakes into the ground right behind the pitcher's mound, spaced about a foot apart from each other.

He opened the main compartment of the bag. If someone else were there, they would have immediately been hit with a very pungent odor. The man didn't seem to mind, though. He rummaged in the bag for a few seconds and found what he was looking for. He picked up Autumn's foot, pale and slightly purplish. He double-checked to see which one it was. The big toe, with bright red nail polish beginning to chip off, was on the left side. He placed it at the top of the stake, the right one if you were facing home plate, and pushed down with most of his strength. If someone else were there, the sound would have been sickening, a combination of squishing and crunching.

He layered the top of the foot with a light coating of adhesive. He followed with the calf, cut off just below the knee, and then the top part of the leg. On the left stake, he followed this same routine. On the middle one, he placed the pelvic area. He adjusted it, so the pelvis nestled comfortably on the two legs. He then placed the torso, complete with a navel piercing, on top of the pelvis and followed with the chest up to just below the neck.

He grabbed a barbeque skewer and pierced it into the right shoulder girdle, making sure to apply extra adhesive there. He wasn't about to let something as trivial as gravity get in his way. He pushed the upper arm, cut off just above the elbow, onto the skewer. Pushing another skewer into the arm and applying more adhesive, he attached the forearm with a hand still dangling from it. Repeating this process on the left side, he was finished, except for the best part. He picked up the head with both hands. His eyes danced with happiness. He loved how Autumn's eyes were partially rolled back, and her mouth was enticingly agape. He lovingly pushed the head onto the middle garden stake and finished his masterpiece.

The man picked up the empty duffel bag and walked to home plate. He stared out at the pitcher's mound. It was glorious. The man could not stop beaming, his beautiful face lit by the waning sunlight, tears of joy gently falling from his piercing blue eyes.

CHAPTER 9
PENTHOUSE

Albert was on his eighth cup of coffee. By cup, more like a large-double-shot-whatever-latte-espresso thing. No matter how much he drank, the buzzing in his head wouldn't stop. The caffeine just seemed to change the buzz from a sleep-deprived low buzz to a wired, waking zombie, high-pitched buzz. It did, however, really help with the headache, so he counted that as a win, and he had that manic focus only a total lack of rest and a ton of stimulants can give you. He hadn't gotten to sleep until at least four in the morning due to the midnight meeting and the fact that his mind wouldn't get off the hamster wheel of anxiety. Then he had to get up at seven to start it all over again, and now he was about to meet with the big bosses upstairs to go over what happened with the Japanese investors.

Even with all the permutations running through his head last night, he still hadn't come to any solid solutions. He would basically just have to brute force the idea that the company had to take a risk in order to keep the investors on board and, well, really to have any future at all in the long run. Even if these investors weren't an issue, the stock still wasn't going anywhere positive after these years of futility. So, he braced himself and resolved to hold his ground on that idea. Risk was very necessary.

It was late afternoon when he entered the heavily air-conditioned elevator up to the top floor. The big, fancy penthouse. The building only had six floors, but it was still quite impressive up there. When he stepped out into the austere but expensive-looking foyer, a secretary greeted him to confirm his appointment. Albert's name was just about to leave his tongue when she said, "Hello, Mr. Murata. They're waiting for you in the room behind those wooden doors." She pointed to the end of the foyer. The double doors were oak or some other light-colored long-grain wood. Wood construction was illegal for everyone except the wealthy, apparently. As he walked by, the secretary said, "Sir?" and he stopped. She handed him a small cloth. "There's a smudge on your glasses."

"Thank you," he said as he cleaned them. That was some impeccable service.

He pulled open the door. The door looked heavy, and it was heavier than it looked. He was immediately slapped in the face with strong aromas of leather and tobacco. It even smelled rich up here.

"Mr. Murata, glad you could join us. Please, have a seat." A shorter heavyset man motioned to an extremely cushiony seat at the near side of the table.

Albert nodded, not totally sure if he should speak, and sat down. He smiled at the five men sitting at the table. He immediately realized just how ridiculous that smile looked. Just his mouth was smiling while the rest of his face looked like a nervous wreck.

"Tell us about the investor meeting. What did they say?" This was the big guy himself. He clearly didn't like sparing time for any sort of pleasantries. His expression was neutral, but he looked like a cobra ready to strike into anger at a moment's notice.

"Well, Mr. Colson, I'd first like to thank you for—" Albert immediately said, trying to defuse the tension.

"What happened at the meeting?" Colson was having none of it.

"Well, sir, they told me they were going to sell their shares as of this morning—"

"And they didn't. So how did you convince them not to?" Colson asked. Was that a smirk on his face for just a split second? "See, Johnson?" he turned to look at the man three seats to his left. "I knew it. I told you our good Japanese boy over here would do the job. They spoke in their own little language and came to an understanding."

Albert tried not to appear offended. "Umm." He cleared his throat. "Actually, it didn't happen quite like that, really."

Colson swiveled back to him. "What do you mean? What was it then? Well?"

"Well, sir. I told them—" Albert paused. There was no way this was going to be received pleasantly whatsoever, but maybe it was better to just rip the bandage off all at once. Colson eyed him impatiently as if every millisecond were a personal insult to him. "I told them that we had a government contract and that it hasn't gone public yet."

"What the hell did you just say?" Any appearance of pleasure was far gone from Colson's face. "You told them that we had a fucking government contract when I pray to God you know we don't have one?"

"Sir, I didn't know what else to say. They had made up their minds about pulling their investment. I was only looking out for the company, I promise! I told them it was two weeks from going public, so it gives us time to figure this out."

"Am I supposed to be happy with you?"

"Sir, I'm—"

"Shut up when I'm talking. You fucking—excuse my language—you fucking lied to investors because you couldn't get it through your thick little skull how to calm them down without blowing up the whole goddamn company. Thanks so goddamn much for the two weeks. We are saved now, thanks to you." His voice was dripping with sarcasm. He began to speak more quietly. "Now we are stuck with no options. They're going to pull out. The other investors will hear about this. We are done. You have ruined us, you fucking Japanese—"

The short, chubby man who had greeted Albert piped in. "Sir, what about the deal with Correc—"

"Johnson! Shut up, you idiot!" Colson swiveled back to the man with lightning speed. "There is no goddamn way we are considering that. I built this thing from nothing. From the fucking ground up. With something I like to call fucking ethics. And I'm not about to tarnish my pristine goddamn legacy, so a couple of fucking *foreign* investors don't get cold feet and fuck us over."

"Sir, it was your father's—"

"Get the fuck out. Right. Fucking. Now." Colson pointed at Johnson until the man sheepishly left the room.

He swiveled back to stare at Albert with a predatory look. "You're going to fix this, Murata. I swear to God, you are going to fix this, or you are out on your ass as of five p.m. tomorrow. And I am going to make goddamn sure that you will not work in this industry again. I know people, Murata. I fucking know people."

"Yes sir." Albert was in too much of a state of shock to be nervous at this point. "I'll do my best to—"

A man sitting to the right of Colson put his hand up. "Sir, may I speak?"

Colson nodded. "Why the hell not? It can't get any more incompetent in here."

"Johnson was right, sir. Correcticorp is technically a government contract. They contract with the government, and we contract with them. Sure, it's indirect, but it would save face with the Japanese investors and give us a huge boost in the market."

"What the hell did I just fucking say about ethics, you moron? There is no way in sweet hell that I would do that deal. That is off the fucking table."

"Sir, please, you need to reconsider—"

"Shut up. You know what? You can get the hell out, too. Why don't you and Johnson go out for a nice steak dinner together? God knows I pay you assholes enough. And Murata? Go the fuck home and come back tomorrow with a goddamn plan."

CHAPTER 10
BAD NEWS

The cab pulled up outside the house in Hinsdale. The place was gorgeous, although the lawn really needed a once-over with the mower. Zen was simply not looking forward to this. She knew that she had to tell Aiden about what the doctor said, on top of telling him that she wanted this relationship to be over. He never handled one bit of bad news particularly well, and now this would be the definition of doubling up. She put her key in but found that the door was already unlocked. She opened it and gave a total start, causing her to take a full step back down the few front stairs. Aiden was right there in the doorway. He never could grow a full beard, but there were at least a couple of days of patchy stubble on his chin.

Just as she was about to speak, Aiden asked, "Where have you been?" It didn't have the sound of genuine concern, more that of impatience. He looked at her with half-squinted eyes, but she couldn't tell if he was angry or just not used to the light outside.

"I was at the doctor. Then I went to my parents' place." She tried to sound as matter of fact as possible.

"Why didn't you come home?" Aiden was still standing at the doorway. Zen was still standing on the front steps. He seemed to realize that he looked like he was intentionally blocking her way inside and moved back into the foyer of the house.

Zen didn't go inside just yet. She took a deep breath. "I got some shitty news from the doctor, and honestly, I didn't know what your reaction would be." She prepared for an emotional change in Aiden but didn't notice any.

"Come inside. It's all right. What happened?" Was that the beginning of a kind expression on his face? The man was trying, at least. She cautiously entered. He turned and walked toward the kitchen. She followed more than a few feet behind. "Want a drink?" he asked. He took a bottle of scotch down from the liquor cabinet and placed it on the counter and grabbed two whisky glasses from the cupboard.

"Umm, sure." Zen was taken aback by his attitude. He was clearly trying to do the right thing.

Aiden handed her a filled glass and motioned toward the dining room. He sat down and took a small first sip. "So, what happened at the doctor?"

Zen sat down opposite him and took a sip herself. It was tasty, but she suddenly found herself very thirsty. She didn't want to seem rude by getting up again, so she decided to just tell him what happened. "I was a bit late for the appointment, but Dr. Kohn saw me. Honestly, the guy is a little bit of a jerk. Finally figured out why we are having so much trouble, though. I have something wrong down there, like a structural thing. The biology all works, but the way I'm built just won't let me give birth." Zen expected Aiden to get mad or frustrated or cold, but his face remained unchanged.

"So, there's like zero chance of ever having a baby?"

"Yeah."

Aiden sighed but smiled. "It's okay, baby. I get it. Look, I'm sorry for how I acted before. I don't know why I get so angry, but I've been working on it. On myself. I'm not mad."

Zen didn't know how to feel about this reaction. On the one hand, she knew that he was making a conscious effort to be better about how he reacted. On the other hand, she felt a little insulted. *Who cares if you're mad or not? It's my fucking body and my fucking issue.* She was worried about coming here today, not just because of his anger but because of what would happen if he wasn't angry. It would be easy to break up with him if he was the angry bastard that he was after her second miscarriage. She could walk out and never look back, hating him all the way. But the way he responded this time caused all the reasons she fell in love with him to come rushing back into her head. She came here to end it. She told herself and her parents that she was going to do it. Why did he have to make it so damn hard?

"So, I've been thinking," Zen finally said. "I feel like we really need to talk."

"About what?" Aiden asked. His mood almost indiscernibly shifted, but Zen picked up on it. "I said it was okay. We can move past this. Find another way to have a kid."

"I don't really know how to say this. I feel like this isn't going to work." Zen was trying to look as sympathetic as possible, but she had to be honest. The truth might not be the best way out of a situation, but it is surely the quickest.

"What's not gonna work?" Aiden looked positively distraught at this point.

"Us."

"What do you mean?"

"This. Us. Together. It's not like I forgot what happened last time I came home with bad news." Zen kept an even tone to her voice as much as she felt like raising it.

"We talked about that, Zen. I said I was sorry, and I meant it. Look, I'm so much better now. I was up all night worried sick about you. I didn't get mad at you for not texting or calling me back." Aiden's mouth was starting to quiver; whether with sadness or frustration, Zen couldn't tell.

"Aiden, I'm sorry. I've been thinking about it a lot. I was up all night, too. And this isn't an easy decision for me or anything."

"Then don't make the decision. You don't need to leave. I told you, I've changed." He was beginning to sound desperate.

"I can't do it anymore, Aiden. I'm sorry. I'm gonna go pack my things."

"Don't leave!" Aiden said loudly, not quite a shout. "How can I prove to you that I'm serious?" He tried to bring his voice back down to a conversational level.

"I'm sorry. My mind's made up."

Aiden started to tear up. "C'mon Zen, you're being fucking crazy."

"No, I'm not, Aiden." She was getting frustrated as hell herself. *Fuck his frustration, seriously.* "Please move out of the way so I can go upstairs and get my stuff."

"This is bullshit!" Aiden said loudly. "You can't just leave me after all this. This is total fucking bullshit!"

"Aiden. Move. Now."

Zen felt the hot sting on her face before she saw the hand. She reflexively put her own hand to her face, her eyes wide with shock. She felt the warmness on her skin and the tickle of blood rushing to the area.

"You fucking *bitch*! You think you can just leave me?" Aiden yelled, spit coming out of his mouth. "I dealt with all your problems, and now you tell me that you're done? *Fuck you!*" His hands were now balled up, his arms tensed.

Zen wanted nothing more than to get out of there as fast as possible. She pivoted back toward the front door. The wild left hook landed full on her shoulder. It exploded in dull pain. If she hadn't turned, it might have landed square on her jaw. Her legs found their strength, and she sprinted down the front steps and along the walkway. Aiden was still standing at the doorway, watching her. For a second, he didn't move. Then he started chasing her. He didn't have shoes on, so his pace was slower than it might have been otherwise. Zen tried to pull out her phone on the run, her fingers working desperately in the fabric of her front pocket, silently cursing herself for not having a HUDPhone implant. She managed to reach the sidewalk and ran across the cul-de-sac. Aiden followed behind, half running, half limping in his socks. She finally got her phone out and pressed the emergency button. As she put the phone to her ear, she took a quick glance behind. Aiden had stopped at the end of the walkway. She stopped running as well, waiting for the line to pick up.

"911, what's your emergency?" the voice on the other end of the line asked.

"My husband, he—" Zen said.

"I'm sorry!" Aiden yelled. He was now sitting on the grass at the end of the front yard near the sidewalk. "Please, Zen! Baby!"

"My husband, he hit me," Zen said.

"Are you in a safe place now?" the dispatcher asked.

"Yeah, I think so. He's sitting down now. He was chasing me before, but he's not anymore."

"Go to a place where you feel safe, where he can't reach you. We will send out officers to the location of this call. Is that where you are?"

"Yes."

"Officers are on their way. They have your phone location locked in and will come to wherever you are."

"Baby! I'm sorry!" Aiden yelled again. Zen could see that he was crying now, his hands on his knees, sitting cross-legged on the grass. "Please, tell them not to come. I'm sorry, I will make it up to you, I promise!"

The call had already ended, and even if she wanted to, the officers would still arrive. They knew better than to listen to someone suddenly telling them that everything was fine. Zen stood in the middle of the cul-de-sac, looking at the pathetic figure of her husband sitting on the grass and waited for the police to arrive.

CHAPTER 11
BAR FIGHT

Work was much easier today with Ollie actually showing up and on time, to boot. It also helped that the heat wasn't nearly as oppressive as the day before. Mik was able to get all the sausages made as well, something that he had to put off yesterday. They cooked up a couple of steaks and closed the place up.

"Old Tom's again?" Ollie asked.

"Of course," Mik answered. "But let's calm it down a bit tonight, all right? A little break until tomorrow. We can go all out then since it's the weekend, and I don't need to worry about you not coming to work."

Ollie smirked. "Just because you caught me once doesn't mean you're allowed to give me shit about it every day. You know as well as I do, I'm only sick on Wednesdays. But fine. We'll go easy tonight. Pussy."

"I'm the pussy? You're the one who has to skip work to sleep it off. I'm serious, though. My liver needs to breathe a little."

"Fine. Whatever you say, soldier." Ollie was well aware of Mik's military history, except for the whole supplantation situation. "I'll get the cab this time. I owe you that much for making you unload all the crap yesterday, anyhow."

"That's a start, asshole."

They pulled up to Old Tom's Grille and walked in through the old wooden door. No gene sensors. No retina scanners. Hell, there wasn't even a bouncer on duty tonight. They walked up to the bar. It was already completely packed, rare for this early on a Thursday. They got the bartender's attention and ordered two beers. The bartender, Eli, was an old, grizzled man with a white beard who was one of the few employees that had stuck around for more than a couple of months. One of the things this place always got right was the temperature of the beers. Always ice cold and damn refreshing. Eli popped the caps and handed them to Mik and Ollie.

They found a little room near one of the front windows, the glass of which was anything but clear, marked with misplaced paint, scratches, and unidentifiable stains. The neon light shone through from outside. Mik leaned against the wall, and Ollie followed suit. They clinked their bottles and took a nice, long chug.

"I just wanted to say, man," Ollie said, "You really have a way with sausages."

"Don't be jealous," Mik responded. "I'm good with my hands. Probably why I'm the butcher, and you're still unloading trucks. And still single."

"You're still single, too, asshole. Plus, I have my hands filled with your mom."

"Hey, that's your problem, not mine."

They joked around for another couple of rounds until two seats opened at the bar. They nearly sprinted over there to make sure they got them. Being on their feet all day added to their motivation. Mik still had half a bottle of his current beer left, but he made sure to order another round right away. He guessed his whole speech about going easy tonight was slowly going out the window. What round was this? Four? Five?

As soon as Eli returned with their beers and left to help other customers, Ollie got a tap on his shoulder. He quickly turned around.

"We were waiting for those seats." A young man, probably not much older than twenty, was standing there with a few of his buddies.

"So were we, my man. I'm sure a few other seats will open up soon. Be patient, young one." Ollie loved to push buttons, especially those of strangers.

"Those are our seats." The man's face was red, and he had a hilarious angry look on his face that, for some reason, made Mik think of a constipated mouse. Clearly, the guy had been drinking too much too fast. Always the young guys with their short tempers.

"I'm afraid they're not," Ollie said. "What with our asses sitting in them and all. Unless you want to sit in my lap?"

"Fuck you, old man. Get out of our seats."

"Old man? Damn, time really flies. Here I was, thinking thirty-five was on the younger side of the population. I guess when you're still in diapers, most people seem pretty old to you."

"Get the fuck up."

"My God, you seem ornery. Speaking of diapers, did you? Oh no, you didn't. In public? Wow, that is embarrassing. I know a lot of babies cry after they go pee pee because of the wetness."

The young man grimaced and grabbed the fabric of Ollie's sleeve and pulled. Ollie teetered on the barstool a little but retained his balance.

"Hey, man, I wouldn't do that," Mik chimed in. He was looking directly at the young man and smiling.

"Why the fuck not? What are you gonna do, you old fuck?"

Mik had stayed out of the exchange so far, but this was just getting ridiculous. "Here you go again with the old crap. How about you go home and have one of your buddies here change you before you do something you might regret?"

"Fuck you!" the young guy was visibly pissed at this point. He held onto Ollie's sleeve and yanked again. This time, he really put his back into it, and Ollie slid off the seat. Luckily, his feet were on the ground, so he basically just stood up.

Mik instinctively grabbed the guy by the shirt collar and pushed him away from Ollie and the bar. "Go home and get changed. This is a bad idea for you."

Eli noticed the commotion and jogged over. "Take it outside, guys. We don't need this kind of crap going on in here."

Mik let go of the young man's collar and turned toward the bartender. "All right, sorry, Eli." He turned back to gesture him out of there, but as he did, he was pushed sharply in the chest. The guy was clearly not heeding any warnings. "Goddamnit," he sighed.

Mik pushed him back, and one of the man's friends pushed Ollie back into the bar, where he unintentionally sat back down in his previous seat. Ollie grunted in pain as his elbow clipped the wooden edge of the bar. "Fucking babies," he said and got back up. The man who had pushed Ollie down swung for a looping right haymaker, which Ollie easily dodged, and Ollie came back with his own left jab, which hit the man squarely on the nose. It started bleeding.

"Motherfucker," said the man, who then swung back and hit Ollie in the ribs, only partially blocked by Ollie's forearm. The young man who had told them to get out of their seats lunged at Mik. Mik sprawled out to avoid being taken to the ground. After all, that was the last place you wanted to be during a street or bar fight. He then came back with a sharp right hook that sent the young man tumbling to the ground, where his head hit the metal legs of a stool.

The young man's other two friends joined in and started attacking Mik and Ollie. As soon as the fight was beginning to really ramp up, they heard sirens outside, quickly getting louder. The guy and his friends ran for the front door and down the sidewalk before the officers arrived. Mik and Ollie decided to stay around. That way, they could tell their side of the story and hopefully be allowed back into Old Tom's when everything was all wrapped up.

The public safety officers, as they liked to be called, arrived within another minute. They were contracted by Tem Tem to provide security to the district, and Tem Tem as a company didn't like to spend a lot of money, as evidenced by the shithole that the entire area was becoming. Cheapest bid. Not the sharpest knives in the drawer. Two young men in overly tactical-looking uniforms strutted into the place and asked what happened.

A woman, who was clearly the one who had called them, eagerly pointed at Mik and Ollie. "Those two were fighting some other men!"

"Listen, officer," Ollie said. "Some guys came in and tried to bully us and attacked us when we wouldn't give up our seats. That's pretty much the whole story."

Mik nodded in response. "Yep."

"Is that true?" one of the officers asked the bartender.

"That's exactly right," Eli said, nodding his affirmation. He knew Mik and Ollie well, and even if he didn't, he would tell them the truth either way.

The officer, a portly young lug of a man, sighed. What an inconvenience doing your job must be. "Fine. Listen, we have to take you down to the station. You two." He pointed at Mik and Ollie. "Come with us. You can fill out your statements there."

"That was the whole thing," Mik said. "It's all good now. It's over."

"Sorry, son. You have to come with us," the other officer said. *Son?* The officers were kids, basically. Probably watched too many movies and played too many video games.

"Seriously? The other guys attacked *us*," Ollie said. "This is a waste of time."

"Look, I don't want to be here doing this either," the officer said. At least he was admitting he didn't want to do his job. "Easier for everyone if we just go to the station and clear this up." Mik wondered what the motive was. Likely some bullshit quota for a promotion or some other nonsense.

"Fine," Mik said. "Let's just get this over with." He and Ollie followed the officers out to the street and to the car parked alongside, its siren lights silently flashing red and blue. They weren't technically police because they were under a private contract, so they had branded the car with *Tem Tem Public Safety*. One of the officers opened the rear door for them, and they sat down. There was no need for handcuffs or anything since it wasn't an official arrest.

The station was top-notch in terms of appearance and technology, one of the few places in Tem Tem District that was well maintained and very modern. While the security company clearly skimped on labor costs in order to provide such a low-cost contract to Tem Tem, they didn't skimp on the station. The retina scanner outside the door scanned Mik and Ollie, and they were immediately led to a desk with a gene sensor and another officer sitting behind it.

"Just go through the identification process," one of the officers who had brought them in said. "It shouldn't take more than a couple of minutes. Then meet us in room 3A so you can give us your statement."

"I thought we weren't under arrest," Mik said. "Why do we have to do all that ID stuff?"

"Routine procedure," the officer responded. "No big deal."

"I'd rather not then, if it's no big deal," Mik said.

"Please, sir, I don't want this to be difficult. It's just a quick process, and then we can take the statement. Sooner you do that, the sooner you can go home." This was the first time one of the officers addressed Mik as *sir*, and it sounded a hell of a lot better to him than *son*.

"Fine. Let's just do this, Ollie." He wasn't nervous about them finding the pit viper genetic code. He was in the military, so it was already in the federal database, and it had likely already come up during his past DUI arrests. Sure, they had screwed him over by not removing the red flag when entering government buildings or other establishments, but he was still on the list of legal enhancements for those who had the ability to look into it.

Ollie went first. "Sir, please state your name and date of birth for me," the officer behind the desk said.

"Oliver Stephen Pulaski, two, sixteen, thirty-six." Ollie had been asked his whole life if he was named after the old park in the city. Sometimes, to pick up women, he said he was.

"Thank you, sir; now, please place your right index finger on the gene sensor."

Ollie did.

"Thank you. All clear. Please proceed to room 3A. It's just behind you, two doors down the hall." He then looked at Mik. "Now for you, sir, same thing."

Mik nodded. "Mikolaj Jesko, eleven, four, thirty-two."

"And your middle name, sir?"

"Don't have one."

"Very well. Now please place your right index finger on the gene sensor."

Mik did, and within a number of seconds, a look of surprise took over the officer's face. "Wow. Sir. Thank you for your service." The monitor must have mentioned something about the genetic modification in the service of the Army, but the officer didn't give any indication that it went into any specific details.

"You're welcome?" Mik responded. He didn't know what else to say.

"Room 3A, sir."

"Yep."

Mik joined Ollie in the room, and the two of them were joined very shortly after by the same two officers who had driven them to the station. They gave their accounts of what happened at the bar, basically repeating what they had already said, and were quickly released from any sort of custody they may or may not have been in. One of the officers was even nice enough to call them a cab. They must have heard something about Mik's service and genetic enhancement through their earpieces from the officer at the desk. Kids like these really worshipped military guys, especially those in special forces, with something as interesting as a mandated supplantation. Must be all those movies and video games.

Mik and Ollie got into the cab. They dropped Ollie off first. "It always gets interesting with you, Ollie," Mik said.

"I aim to please." Ollie winked. "See you tomorrow, *son*."

"Yeah. See ya." Mik grunted a quick laugh. Ollie closed the door, and Mik was driven back to his apartment. He guessed they ended up going kind of easy on the booze after all with the night cut so short.

CHAPTER 12
LEGACY

JULY 24, 2071

After another restless night, Albert finished preparing for his meeting with Mr. James Colson, the CEO of Genovas. He wasn't sure if the same people as last time would be there or if it would be a one-on-one sort of thing. He had pretty much just given up on getting a full night's sleep at this point. Luckily, it was Friday, and if he happened to survive today's meeting, maybe he could catch up on at least a few hours over the weekend.

The cool air of the elevator was bracing, but it woke him up and gave him the tiniest jolt of energy. He said hi to the secretary on the sixth floor, who smiled and waved him on. He pointed at his glasses and looked at her questioningly. She gave him a thumbs up. Guess they weren't smudged today. Good start. He pulled on the large wooden doors of the conference room, this time really putting his back into it and bending his knees, knowing how heavy it was.

Colson sat at the table facing the door. He was alone. No Johnson, no anybody. Albert wasn't sure if this made him more nervous or less nervous. Either way, he figured he was as prepared as he was ever going to get.

"Good morning, Mr. Colson," Albert said, breaking the initial silence.

"Mr. Murata. Have a seat." Apparently, Colson wasn't a morning person either. "As I'm sure you remember, I am expecting you to have come up with a solution for our little investor problem."

"Yes, sir, Mr. Colson, please call me Albert. Actually, I don't have a solution for the investors per se, but—"

"Then, as I told you last night, Mr. Murata, don't let the door hit you on the way out." Colson waved impatiently toward the door behind Albert.

"But sir, I have been doing a lot of research, and, well, crunching the numbers, and—"

"What? What is it?" Colson's brows furrowed. Albert could almost see his nostrils flaring.

"And, well, sir, we, as a company, have no choice but to take the deal that Mr. Johnson was mentioning yesterday."

"Before I ask you politely one last time to leave before I get out of this seat and kick you right in the ass and make you, I'm going to say it very carefully. I am not doing that deal. End of fucking story."

"Sir, please, hear me out for just a second. You built this company from the ground up, right?"

"Yes, of course." Colson leaned forward in his chair and put his elbows on the table. "And don't let those idiots tell you any different!"

"Yes, sir, I didn't believe that for a moment. What I am saying is that if we don't do this deal—"

"We aren't!"

"Sir, please, just a second is all I ask. If we don't do this deal, regardless of what happens to me, Genovas will have no choice but to shut down. There is no other path for financial viability."

"I gave you your second, Mr. Murata. Time's up. Don't make me call security to get you the hell out of here."

"Sir, I went over the proposal after the meeting last night. I asked Mr. Johnson to send it to me."

"That proposal was supposed to be fucking confidential. After I'm done with you, that fat fuck is next!"

"Sir, the deal would make us number one in the market for gene editing. You built this company because of the work you did with supplantation, and this is an opportunity to do that again. Sir, it would put Genovas back on the map."

"The deal isn't ethical. Plain and simple. It's not about the goddamn money."

"It's about your name, sir. And your legacy. The money allows you to build that even further. When the scientific community looks back in history, they'll see Genovas and James Colson at the forefront of a reborn industry that will change humanity forever." Albert had no idea how he was coming up with all of this, but he was on a complete roll and wasn't about to give up now. "You'll be immortalized, and also, the industry will gain such important knowledge. Who knows what we could accomplish if it goes right?"

Colson's face unfurled from its previous expression and relaxed. He sat back in his chair and sighed very audibly. "And you read the whole proposal? What it all entails?"

"Yes, sir. I know ethics are a concern. I felt the same way, to be honest. I really did consider not even bringing it up and just accepting my termination. But then I thought about all the possibilities. How the scientific community will respond. How technology will grow by leaps and bounds if this project is successful." Albert wasn't entirely sure he believed what he was saying, but he couldn't afford to lose his job, especially with the possibility of being blacklisted.

"There are human subjects, Mr. Murata. And they have no goddamn choice."

"I know, sir. It's a very difficult step to take. But if I may talk freely?"

"Fine." Mr. Colson gestured toward Albert with an open palm.

"The subjects, sir? They made their choice already."

"And how's that?" Mr. Colson folded his arms across his chest.

"Correcticorp, they're only enrolling prisoners with life sentences. Murder, rape, and worse. They made their choice when they committed those crimes."

"That's not true, Murata. If that were the case, I wouldn't be facing the fucking ethical dilemma that I am right now. The deal allows them to enroll any prisoner they see fit."

"That's not what it said when I read it last night, sir."

"Then you read an old fucking copy. They won't do it unless we consent to them enrolling anyone in the whole goddamn system. Something about sample size and randomized crap."

Albert took a deep breath. He felt a wave of anxiety hit him alongside a pang of guilt. This was just wrong. He couldn't persuade Colson to take a deal like that. To destroy people's lives. To potentially kill them. But he had no choice. He had himself to look out for and his family back home. What truly mattered, anyway? Some criminals or his wife and two kids? He convinced himself that it was an easy choice, but it was the hardest one he ever made. "Mr. Colson, sir, it's still the only thing that will save this company. And cement your legacy. They're criminals, sir, and they will help further both your name and the entire field of gene supplantation."

"God fucking damnit," Mr. Colson said and slammed his fist on the table. "We don't have a choice, do we, Murata?"

"No, sir."

"Fine. We will do the deal. I'm going to call Johnson and get the ball rolling. God help us. And Murata?"

"Yes, sir?"

"You're one cold-hearted bastard. Take the rest of the day off. You earned it."

CHAPTER 13
POWER HOUR

"Available on all streaming providers in Illinois and the surrounding areas, this is *Windy City News*, and I'm Jeff Washburn. We have new insight on the Wrigley Field nightmare as well as an exclusive expert interview, so stay tuned after the news brief! Viewer and listener discretion is advised.

"Staff and tourists came upon a horrific sight just after nine a.m. today at Wrigley Field, the famous former baseball stadium and historical landmark in Chicago. A statue of body parts was created to look like a scarecrow of sorts and was placed right behind the pitcher's mound. We have learned from sources at the Chicago Police Department that they have pieced together a general idea of who may have committed such a heinous act.

"According to our sources, lab analysis revealed that the victim has been identified as Autumn Chandler, age twenty-eight. Each body part was put through genetic testing, and they all belong to the same victim, putting to rest the rampant theories that each part was from a different person. Furthermore, upon chemical analysis, a substance known as BTX, or batrachotoxin, was found on the hands, arms, shoulders, and genital regions of the victim. BTX is a toxin that is secreted by the skin glands of a poison dart frog. It irreversibly blocks the transmission of nerve signals from muscles, first causing paralysis and then finally death by cardiac arrest.

"According to our sources, this is not the result of someone placing the toxin on the victim but is the result of someone who was genetically supplanted with the genes of a poison dart frog. The assailant then proceeded to secrete the toxin onto the skin of the victim, paralyzing her. The investigation also revealed that the assailant sexually assaulted the victim while she was in this state. She died during or shortly thereafter.

"Unfortunately, police were not able to obtain any DNA from the assailant, as it looks like a cleansing chemical was used to wipe away the evidence. No HUDPhone was recovered from the scene, and privacy laws prevent any storage of personal data on both the HUDPhone cloud and taxi networks. Police have no further leads at this time, but they are urging the public to call in with any tips or information they may have about the assailant or victim that could lead to the apprehension of this horrible individual."

"Now, I want to throw it over to Speedy Powers, who is on set right now for a special breaking news edition of his afternoon talk show, *The Power Hour*."

"Thank you very much, Jeff! As you all know, I'm Speedy Powers, and I'm coming right at you, Chicago, with a special edition of *The Power Hour*. I have a very special guest here with me today. He is the head of genetic research at the University of Chicago, Dr. Matthew Gabel. Welcome, Dr. Gabel; thanks for coming to us on such short notice to join *The Power Hour*."

"Absolutely, Speedy; thanks for having me."

"Now, Dr. Gabel, did I get your position correct?"

"Yes, well, it's a joint research department, or team, really, with the University of Chicago and Barack Obama Memorial Hospital."

"And you have some history with the whole gene supplantation thing, don't you?"

"Yes."

"Can you tell us a bit more about that?"

"Sure. I was a medical student at Harvard University from 2044 to 2047, and I had the opportunity to work as a research assistant for Dr. Needleman."

"*The* Dr. Needleman? As in, going under the needle?"

"Yes, Dr. Larry Needleman. From him, I learned a great deal about the ins and outs of supplantation. It was an extremely exciting time, especially when we were able to transition our research to the public market. Unfortunately, there was no indication that there would be those horrible consequences we discovered later."

"You mean the birth defects, I assume?"

"Yes. It was a real shame because supplantation was beginning to open all sorts of new avenues for scientific progress. If that didn't happen, I think we really could have helped a lot of people."

"Got it. And I totally agree. Before we go into supplantation in more detail, I'd like to switch gears for a bit if that's okay."

"Of course."

"Great. Dr. Gabel, can you give my audience some of your insights on the Wrigley case as an expert in the field? What do you think about what the police investigation turned up?"

"I haven't had the chance to review their specific findings, of course, but based on their information, it does indeed look like the suspect is likely supplanted with genes from a dart frog or related species. The batrachotoxin residue is strong evidence of that."

"Wow, that is some crazy stuff, doctor. We have a sort of killer frog on the loose, it seems."

"It does seem that way, yes. Well, a person with the supplanted genes of a dart frog, at least."

"Okay. Crazy. A killer frog. Very crazy. What else can you tell us about this guy? Supplanting genes from an animal like that is surely illegal and always has been, right?"

"Well, as you probably remember, when supplantation was available to the public back in '47 and '48, there was a truly short list of approved gene donors, or species, that was allowed. Nothing that could harm another person for one. Nothing that allowed for any sort of inhuman appearance either. Basically, it was limited to supplantation that improved performance or quality of life. One of the classic examples was supplanting hawk genes for improved vision. Helped a lot of people get rid of their glasses."

"Great for golfing, too, I'm sure. How would someone get their hands on the genes of a poison dart frog, then, for example? It was never approved even back then."

"Well, that's a good question. I'm not here to get too political or anything, but there is undoubtedly a huge illegal black market for supplantation. And there, I would say there is little to no limit as to what sorts of genes would be available to someone."

"I couldn't agree with you more. Whether our representatives want to acknowledge it or not, it's a big problem and only getting worse. They would get flagged by gene sensors, though, wouldn't they? The people who use black-market supplantation?"

"Yes, the customary gene sensors that you see everywhere pick up on any genetic code that is not human nor on the approved list from '47 and '48."

"So, this killer frog. He would be flagged if he tried to get into any place that had one?"

"I would have to assume so, yes."

"All right, Dr. Gabel, I don't want to keep you for too much longer, but I'd like to talk a little more about the nitty-gritty of supplantation. What can you tell us about it in general? Those of us who are older than say thirty or forty remember the big craze back then, but we laymen don't know much besides the terrible things that happened to those babies."

"Well, to put it simply, it's the transfer of a small amount of genetic code from an animal or other organism into the genome of a living man or woman. Now, it must be done very carefully, or things can quickly go wrong."

"How so?"

"We found that, as a rule, supplantation has to be limited to a single organism and a single genetic trait. I'll give you an example to make that a bit clearer. I mentioned that popular hawk vision supplantation that people got when it was approved. If we tried to add extra genetic code from a hawk, for God knows what, let's say someone wanted talons, it caused a chain reaction of DNA instability. Think rapidly growing cancer or cell death. Luckily, we tested all of this in animals before we conducted the human trials."

"Wow. And what if you, say, wanted the vision from hawks *and,* well, let's use the killer frog example, skin that secretes a toxin?"

"Same result. We tested for that as well. Basically, if you insert too much foreign genetic code into the human genome, it becomes wildly unstable. And that goes for multiple traits from the same organism or one trait from multiple organisms. It just won't work."

"So, you're saying, this killer frog, it's safe to say he doesn't have any other superpowers, for lack of a better word?"

"Correct."

"All right, Dr. Gabel. I want to thank you for joining us on this special edition of *The Power Hour*, especially on such short notice."

"You're welcome, Speedy. Thanks for having me. It's an honor to be here and to share my knowledge with your audience."

"We all learned a lot today. And hopefully we're able to track down this killer frog and put him to justice. Brutal, swift justice. Thanks everyone for watching. I'm Speedy Powers. And this was *The Power Hour*."

CHAPTER 14
THE FUSE

Mik finished his gigantic chicken Caesar salad. He told himself that he had to eat some veggies and some meat that wasn't red. Or pork, which he thought he heard somewhere, was basically red meat that was disguised as white meat. Existing on steak and beer was going to rear its ugly head on him someday. He always went out for lunch alone. Ollie's and his lunch breaks were staggered in case something happened at the shop. He threw out his dirty paper and plastic and walked back to work. Ollie was outside unloading a truck. Friday deliveries were always a pain in the ass because they had to hold them over for the whole weekend.

"I'm back!" Mik shouted and waved.

"About fucking time," Ollie responded. "I'm starving."

"I came back five minutes early just for you, asshole."

"Sure, you did. I bet the guy in the toilet stall just didn't show up for your afternoon delight."

"These jokes are getting a little old. Just saying."

"Not as old as you. But, anyway, speaking of old, Filip's here."

Mik was taken aback a little. "Filip's here? At the shop?" Filip had been showing up less and less over the past couple of years, and it had been at least a few months since the last time he had.

"I don't believe I stuttered. Yes, he's inside. And he's looking for you."

"You know what, Ollie? I just realized you're a lot less funny when I'm sober."

"Then drink up, asshole. Also, you'd better get in there before he dies of old age, and you need to call the coroner."

"Prick. Go to lunch."

"You don't need to tell me twice. Later, *son*." Ollie latched the back of the truck and headed out down the street. Mik shook his head and sighed. Ollie could be downright intolerable.

Mik headed inside to see if Filip was actually there. He believed Ollie, but only as much as you could believe someone who was either sarcastic or joking most of the time. He pulled open the thin screen door that led into the back of the shop, and there he was. Mik could smell him as soon as he walked in. He always smelled like almonds. Filip was sitting on a high stool and chopping away at a slab of beef. Mik could tell he still had that precision from back when he hired him and started the apprenticeship, but it was taking him multiple swings to cut each piece. He looked as old as Mik could remember and maybe even older. Maybe not older, but weaker and thinner. Filip looked up, but not before he finished the piece he was already working on.

"Mikolaj." He always used his full first name, which added weight to everything he said.

"Hey, Filip. What's going on? Ollie said you were here, but I didn't believe him."

Filip grunted and placed the cleaver gently down on the block. "What do you mean you didn't believe him? Is he no longer trustworthy?"

The seriousness on his face made Mik burst out laughing. "No, Filip." He kept laughing. "It's just that he jokes around about every-thing, so it's hard to know when to take him seriously."

Filip kept a perfectly stone face. He clearly wasn't nearly as amused. "He jokes a lot, I know this. But can you trust him?"

"Of course." Mik was no longer laughing, but he still had a huge grin on his face.

"I am serious, Mikolaj. Can you trust him?"

"Yes, Filip. I can trust him." The grin faded. This wasn't as funny as it was at the beginning.

"Good." Filip slowly rose from the stool and started walking over to where Mik was.

Mik put his arm out as a signal to stop and walked over to the butcher's block. Filip sat back down. "What's this about, Filip? Why do you keep asking me if I trust Ollie?"

"I know he's your friend, Mikolaj. But he doesn't know about your supplantation, does he?" Filip said this more as a statement than as a question.

"No, but—"

"Keep it that way," Filip interrupted. "There are things that are happening, whether we want them to or not, and it is better for him not to know. At least for now."

Mik's eyebrows scrunched in confusion. "What do you mean things are happening? Are you all right?"

"Yes, yes, I'm fine. It doesn't matter yet what is happening, but it's important that you are careful."

"Okay, Filip. No idea what you're talking about. You sure you're okay? You showed up today after how many months and keep asking if I can trust Ollie. It's just a little strange, is all."

Filip sighed and coughed, then grabbed a tissue to dab his mouth. "Listen to me for a minute, will you?"

"Okay, sure. Sorry, Filip."

"Good. You must be careful. I say this because I heard about what happened last night."

"How did you—"

"Listen to me. I know what happened. I know they took you to the station and you went through the gene sensor." Filip looked deep into Mik's eyes, and it uneased him.

"I have no idea how you know that, but yeah, I went to the station and it was all good. The kid even thanked me for my service." Mik smiled again, attempting to defuse a bit of the tension that was now hanging in the room.

Filip finally broke his intense eye contact. "You *are* aware of the news today, yes?"

"About that fucking scarecrow at Wrigley Field?" Mik winced when he said that because he knew Filip was never a fan of profanity.

"Yes."

"What about it? I know the killer is some supplanted dude, but what does that have to do with me?"

"Things are happening, Mikolaj. The simple fact that the killer is supplanted puts you in danger."

Mik was just not grasping this. "Why? They're not going to accuse me of the crime. That's crazy. A quick test will show them that I have viper genes, not some weird poison frog thing."

"Because." Filip coughed again into his tissue. "Because they will use this as a rallying cry. All those people who want to go around hurting or killing supplanted people? They *were* considered crazy. They were disenfranchised. But not anymore. All they needed—" Filip paused to take a few deep breaths. He got up and walked over to the sink to pour a glass of water.

"All they needed was what? Filip, you're starting to freak me out here."

Filip took a few short sips and placed the glass down. "All they needed was something like this. A shining example of why they should target supplanted people. A gruesome, high-profile murder of a regular person committed *by* a supplanted person *with* their supplanted genetic trait for all the world to see. All those lunatics? They have evidence now. Cold, hard evidence. And politicians, government officials, law enforcement. Many of them have waited a very long time for something like this. A moment they could use to incite all those people to action. A moment to strike with their ideas and plans and laws that seemed so far-fetched until today. You can't see it now, but things are happening. Things are in motion. The fuse is lit. You have to be very careful, Mikolaj. The fuse is lit. And the explosion will consume us all."

CHAPTER 15
PACKING UP

Zen was back at her parents' place. The police had come and picked up Aiden yesterday, and he was being held overnight for processing. As soon as the police took her statement and left, she headed back to the condo in Oasis District. She told her parents she was coming in but didn't give them a reason. Her parents didn't press her nearly as much as she thought they would. Her mother was always good at reading her emotions, even over the phone, and could sense she didn't want to say anything further.

When Zen arrived, her bed was freshly made with new sheets, so she took a shower, careful not to press too hard on the bruised area of her shoulder, got dressed in some old pajamas, and quickly fell asleep. She ended up sleeping surprisingly deeply after such a crazy day. The mental toll must have exhausted her enough. That and the feel of clean sheets after a shower.

When she woke up, she walked downstairs. Breakfast was all ready for her on the dining room table, even though it was already early afternoon. Her parents were sitting on the living room floor, organizing clothes and books and stacking boxes. She rubbed the sleep from her eyes.

"What are you guys doing?" she asked with a yawn.

"What does it look like, dear? We're packing up our things. We have to be out of here soon." Her mother, Ada, smiled. She didn't press her on it last night, but with a good night's sleep, maybe she could get some answers. "What happened yesterday?"

Zen sighed. She knew this conversation had to happen sooner or later. "I went home after work to tell Aiden about the doctor visit." She paused, allowing her mother to follow up.

"How did he take it?"

"Actually, he took it really well. Said he understood and that we could try other options or whatever."

Ada squinted inquisitively. "Clearly that's not all that happened, or you wouldn't look so distraught. Tell me."

"I told him that I was done. That I wanted to break up, that I wanted to leave him. I didn't say divorce but—" Zen looked down at her feet.

"What happened?" Ada got up from her sitting position and walked over to Zen. She placed her hand on her shoulder to comfort her, but it made her wince instead. "What's wrong? Did I hurt you?"

"No, Mom."

"But *he* did, didn't he?" Ada's voice increased in volume. "Let me see. What did he do to you?"

"Nothing, Mom. I got out."

"Show me." Ada wasn't going to budge on this whatsoever.

Zen pulled down the neck of her shirt and showed her mother the red and purple bruise on the outside of her shoulder. "I told him I was done, and he got all mad."

"And he hit you?" Ada's face was tensed up. Zen's father, George, was still sitting on the floor but was watching and listening intently.

"He tried to. I turned before he could really hit me. He kind of just ended up punching my shoulder. Not a big deal."

"Not a big deal? Zen, this is as big a deal as it gets!" Ada could see that Zen knew how big a deal it was, but she was just trying to get past it. "What happened after?"

"Nothing really. I called the cops, and they came. They took Aiden to the station or jail or wherever they take someone. Took my statement. That's about it."

"What did you say—" Ada could see that Zen wanted the conversation to end. "Never mind. I'm sorry he did that to you. You know you're safe here with us."

"I know, Mom."

"Can we do anything for you?" Ada now looked more concerned than angry at this point.

"No, thanks, Mom. I'm okay. You guys need any help?"

"I don't want to make you do anything. You've been through enough."

"No, it's okay. I'm okay. Let's pack some stuff up." Helping her parents pack up for the move for a few hours would serve as a good distraction from everything else. She was also happy to help, considering the circumstances with the condo. She took a flattened cardboard box and reformed it, taping all the edges and openings.

"That one's gonna be for everything in my office desk," Ada said, pointing at the box. She knew the conversation about Aiden was over and done with and was almost as happy as Zen to change the subject. "Would you mind taking the stuff out of the drawers when you're done with that?"

"Yeah, sure, Mom. When are the movers coming?"

"Movers?" Ada laughed. "Honey, I rented our own moving van. We are doing it ourselves. It's coming tomorrow." George grunted in affirmation.

Zen had an immediate reaction of disappointment at having to do all that work, but then softened up. "Tomorrow? What do you mean? You already have a lease?"

"Don't think we were just wallowing in our predicament, dear. As soon as you left for work yesterday, we pounded the proverbial pavement online, and we found quite a decent place last night. Not too expensive either."

"Where?"

"Tem Tem District."

"Mom, you can't move there. That place is a total mess." Zen wanted to say something like *total fucking shithole*, but her parents wouldn't have approved. "No infrastructure, no maintenance—"

"Listen to me, Zen." Ada stopped packing for a moment and sat down on the living room rug. "A place is what you make it. I know you grew up in a rough area. So did we. Then, after a lot of hard work, we got out, and we found this place. But we've always remained a family throughout."

"But Mom—"

"Shush for a minute." Ada looked frustrated. George grunted, which clearly meant *listen to your mother*. "Tem Tem District is not a bad a place as you think. We're not renting again. We bought a house."

"A house?" Zen was surprised. She had thought Tem Tem District was just run-down apartments and tenements.

"Yes, for the first time in our lives, we have a place we can truly call home. Sure, it's not Oasis District, but we don't have to rent out the back of a condo from a rich white man anymore. We own it. It's ours."

Zen couldn't think of anything to say, so she just smiled. Maybe it really wouldn't be so bad. At least they wouldn't be at the whim of a landlord, worrying about being kicked out.

"We also have some money saved," Ada continued. "We can fix it up to our liking. Even keep some of the luxuries we got used to here. I convinced your father that we need a walk-in closet."

Zen grunted her approval, a lot more pleasant sounding than her father. "Okay, Mom, fair enough. You sold me. I'm really happy for you."

Ada's excitement quickly converted to seriousness. "You're coming to live with us."

Zen tensed her neck back in confusion. "What do you mean? I have a place already."

"You're not going back there. Not with Aiden. Hell no. Not again. This is enough." Ada shook her head vigorously. George grunted in anger.

Zen knew her mother had a point. Aiden's name was on the deed since it was his house first, and when he got out of jail, he had every right to stay there. But that didn't mean she should just give up the place to him. What kind of justice would that be? "Mom, I can't just not go back. All my stuff is there. It's my house, too. I don't care if he technically owns it. I'm the one who made it a home!" She was riling herself up.

"Call someone tomorrow to get all of your things then. I'm sure there are plenty of moving companies open on Saturdays."

"If you don't need a moving company, neither do I."

"Don't be ridiculous, Zen. This is completely different."

"Is it really, though, Mom?" Zen slumped her shoulders. "We're both being kicked out, just in different ways. I'll go there and pack everything up tomorrow."

"After helping us pack all day today? You're crazy."

"I'm young and spry, Mom. I can do it two days in a row. Also, I don't have nearly as much stuff as you do. Only clothes, my computer, and a few other things. It won't take me more than a couple of hours. I'll help you load up tomorrow and then head over."

"Suit yourself, dear." Ada shook her head disapprovingly. "I bet when you're done here, that's the last thing you're going to want to do."

CHAPTER 16
GROCERIES

"The usual?" Ollie asked as he locked up the back door to the butcher's shop. It had been a long day, as most Fridays were with weekend deliveries and weekend cuts. The sun had already nearly set, and the air was cool.

"Nah, man," Mik responded with a slight head shake. "I'm not feeling it. I have to stock up on groceries for next week anyway."

Ollie looked visibly upset, which Mik found both pathetic and comical. "What the hell do you mean you're not feeling it?"

Friday night was the night, well, one of the two nights, where they went all-out at the bar without worrying about having to wake up early. They hadn't missed tying one on at Old Tom's on a Friday in years. "Dude, we got escorted to a police station—sorry, public safety station—just last night. I don't think we want a repeat of that just yet."

Ollie clearly wasn't buying it, with his rolling eyes and pursed lips. "A barfight never stopped you from going back before. Plus, it wasn't the first time we've been thrown in the back of a cruiser."

"Yeah, maybe I'm just growing up a little." Mik immediately regretted saying that when he realized how insulting it would seem. "Sorry. Listen, Filip showing up yesterday kind of took me out of the mood."

Ollie's expression remained skeptical. "I know he's not much to look at, but how did seeing Filip take you out of the mood?"

"We had a talk. A long talk. You know how Filip is. He just totally took the wind out of my sails, to be honest." Mik foolishly hoped the line of questioning would end there.

"Yeah, man, he is definitely annoying and a downer. But I would think he would drive you to drink if nothing else. Don't you want to drown him with a few bottles of ice-cold refreshments?"

Mik sighed, knowing he wasn't getting out of this easily. "Look, he said some things that, I don't know—" He paused for a moment. "I just need a night to think about everything."

"What the hell are you talking about?" Ollie looked bewildered but amused. "What the hell did he say to you?"

"Listen, Ollie; he said a few things that really got me thinking. Serious stuff. And I just need a night to give it some thought."

"Why can't you tell me?"

"I will. I just can't yet. Trust me, okay?"

Ollie was about to continue pushing for an answer and caught himself. "Fine, all right."

Mik sighed again, half relieved, half frustrated. "Listen, we'll make up for it tomorrow night. We'll go twice as hard. C'mon, I'm serious. Just need tonight to think, okay?"

Ollie actually looked concerned. "It's okay. Really, it is. I know I fuck around a lot, but I'm serious. I'm not gonna press you on this, but if you want to talk, I'm here, seriously."

Mik nodded. "Thanks, Ollie. I appreciate that."

Ollie smiled. "No problem. But you owe me tomorrow. I'll be at Old Tom's if you change your mind. Pussy." He winked at Mik and walked down the street.

Mik headed down the street in the opposite direction. The local supermarket was only a couple of blocks from the shop. When he arrived, he pushed the doors open. They were the old-style automatic doors from many years ago, but once they had malfunctioned who knows when, no one bothered to repair them. The store was run down like most of Tem Tem District, with flickering fluorescent lights, rusting metal shelves, and a floor, once linoleum, that was so full of cracks it looked like a parched desert.

Its produce, however, was very much the counterpoint to its appearance. Supplied by local urban gardeners and farmers, the fruits and vegetables were always fresh and pesticide-free. The basic proteins were supplied by the very butcher shop where Mik worked, along with urban poultry farms in the area. There was nothing to be found for seafood, as the government usually allocated those products to the districts that could sell at a higher price and volume. Everything here, outside the shelf-stable goods, was grown or sold by the locals of Tem Tem District. Mik was proud of that. Despite its many flaws, the area had some of the most ingenious and generous people.

Mik filled up his cart, which only had three wheels, with fruits and vegetables, along with pasta and rice. He was looking forward to cooking up a Bolognese and some jambalaya over the weekend since he had brought home some ground beef and specially made andouille sausage from the butcher shop.

As he was about to wheel the cart down one of the middle aisles to pick up some seasoning, something caught the corner of his eye. A shot of fright drove through him as he turned to look toward the back corner of the store. There was a man in a long olive-green coat, awash in the fluorescent glow of the refrigerators, looking back at him. The light accentuated the sun damage on his face. He held a plastic gallon jug of milk in his left hand, but he didn't move. He just stood there, motionless, staring back at Mik.

Mik couldn't remember the last time he had been so suddenly unsettled to the core. Sure, he had gone through some truly terrifying moments in his life, but nothing unnerved him in quite the same way as this. Mik looked back to his cart and down the spice aisle. He shook his head and exhaled deeply. He walked down the aisle, the cart squeaking all the way, and almost laughed to himself. Tem Tem District had its excellent people, but it also drew the crazies. A place with no infrastructure lent itself well to bringing in extremely mentally ill people who had no one to help them.

He approached the front of the store and looked around in case the man was still staring at him. Nothing. He used his pit organ, courtesy of the military supplantation, and found the heat signature of the man. Still over by the fridge. *Probably trying to decide between whole and 2%,* Mik thought to himself, amused.

"Hey, Corinne." He waved at the woman behind the register, who had been there since he could remember.

"Hey, Mik. Let's see. What are you cooking up this weekend?" Corinne took a cursory glance at the contents of his cart.

"Gonna try some jambalaya, actually. We just made some andouille sausage this week, so I think it'll be fun to try. No shrimp, but what can you do."

"Let me know how it goes. If you're successful, maybe I'll stop by and pick up some of that sausage and give it a go myself." She rang up his purchases as she spoke.

Mik laughed. "Will do. How much do I owe you?"

Corinne laughed back. "I'm not even done ringing you up. So impatient. Gotta be somewhere? A date perhaps?"

"Oh, it's nothing. Sorry, take your time." Mik smiled, and although the man was still over by the fridge, he had the urge to leave the store as fast as possible.

When Corinne finished, Mik placed his hand on the palm pad and selected the payment. Not every place in the area had palm pads since some just used cash, but Corinne had insisted on them bringing one in. It was perhaps the only evidence of modern technology in the whole place. They bagged up the groceries together.

"Thanks, Corinne. Have a good night!"

"You too, Mik. Enjoy your jambalaya!"

Mik held a heavy doubled-up grocery bag with each hand as he left the store. The cool of the air greeted him as he turned down the street to head back home. He walked down the sidewalk and instinctually looked back into the supermarket. There, at the window, was the man, holding the milk jug in his left hand, staring at Mik with unblinking eyes.

Mik squeezed his fingers tightly around the handles of the bags and started walking more quickly. This was freaky as hell. *Should've just gone to the bar with Ollie*, he thought. After about two blocks, he turned around. The area was dark aside from the supermarket's white glow. But he was there. Outside. On the corner past the market. The heat signature was clear as day. Mik could tell he was facing him, still holding the milk jug because his left hand was balled up.

Fuck this. Mik broke into a jog, constantly resetting his grip on the bags. Part of his mind flashed with danger, and the other, more rational part quietly told him he was just dealing with one of the crazies in the neighborhood and *don't drop all the groceries you just bought.* He took a detour down an alleyway and cut through a few side streets. Despite the cool air, his hands were slick with sweat, and his forearms and shoulders ached with the strain.

He stopped a block away from his apartment. He had gone a completely roundabout way, but it was worth it, just in case. Just in case. He scanned the area. He picked up the heat signatures of a few people sitting on a porch outside a little way down the road. Probably some kids having a late-night beer where their parents couldn't see. Nothing else, though. No man with his left hand balled, holding a gallon of milk and staring.

Mik walked up to his front door. He looked around one last time, just in case. He put the key in and stepped inside. He dropped the bags on the floor and locked the door behind him. He placed his hands on his knees, bent down, and breathed deeply a few times. He wasn't sure whether the physical or mental relief was better, but he was thankful for both. He grabbed a beer from the old fridge in the kitchen and sat down on the couch. He took a swig and closed his eyes.

CHAPTER 17
MANTICORE

JULY 25, 2071

Albert woke up customarily early on Saturday morning, rubbing the night particles out of his eyes. He was immediately greeted with a wave of guilt that made his stomach turn. He couldn't believe he convinced the CEO of Genovas to get involved in such a horrible, unethical mess. His wife was still asleep in bed, so he made sure to be extra quiet. He washed his face, put his glasses on, and went into the kitchen. He poured himself a glass of water and swallowed the various pills of his anti-anxiety medication. He took his HUDPhone out of sleep mode with a voice command and noticed a voice message waiting for him from Mr. Colson.

"Mr. Murata," the gruff voice said, not exactly the sound Albert wanted to hear after waking up. "I trust that you enjoyed your little vacation yesterday. Unfortunately, my generosity has limits, and I need you in my office by noon. We're moving fast on the contract, and I want you to be here as my right-hand man as we iron out the details with our new partners. And Murata? Don't be late."

Albert closed his eyes, suddenly wishing he could return to his nice, warm, comfortable bed. "Damnit," he said under his breath. He brushed his teeth and got dressed in the only unworn suit he had left. He was planning to do laundry on Sunday, so he didn't think it would become a concern. He called a cab and headed to the Genovas building.

On the sixth floor, he stopped in front of the secretary, who took a quick glance at Albert's glasses and gave him a thumbs up. She waved him on and mouthed *good luck*. He had gone through some intense meetings up here, and this was the first time she had done that. That couldn't be good.

When he opened the thick wooden doors, Colson was already looking directly at him. Next to him to his left was a man with round spectacles and jet-black hair. Three seats down to his right was a stern-looking man dressed in military full dress, complete with countless medals and ribbons on the chest. Albert wondered what the hell a big-shot military guy was doing here, but it didn't take long to draw some potential conclusions. Likely this is where most or all the funding was coming from, and likely who was going to benefit in the end. At the two heads of the table were a middle-aged woman in a navy-blue suit and none other than the governor of Illinois, Bill Peters.

Albert was immediately taken aback by the formality and celebrity of the group before him. He could already feel sweat forming on his forehead, threatening to drip down his nose along the frames of his glasses. He had expected another one-on-one, or at worst, a meeting with some of the higher-ups at Genovas. Nothing like this, though.

"Mr. Murata, thank you for joining us," Colson said. "Everyone, this is Albert Murata, deputy CFO of Genovas, and the man who helped convince me that we should go ahead with this opportunity. Not only is he great at numbers, but he speaks Japanese and is a pretty decent little lawyer when it comes down to it." He seemed proud despite the condescension, which gave Albert a jolt of confidence.

Albert almost stuttered but caught himself. "Nice to meet you, everyone. Thank you, Mr. Colson. Glad I could be of help."

The man with round spectacles and jet-black hair nodded. "I admire your tenacity, Mr. Murata, and I'm glad you were enlightened enough to see the merits of this research."

The man in the military uniform stood up, almost unnaturally straight. "Mr. Murata, pleasure, sir," he said in a deep voice that seemed out of place even on a military man. "I'm General Terrence Fay, United States Army. I appreciate what you've done here. We have been waiting a long time for the chance to do this sort of research. It could truly help defend this great nation of ours in the future, allowing us to allocate resources elsewhere. Where they're truly needed."

Albert was about to salute in response but quickly realized how foolish that would look and nodded instead. "Pleasure's all mine, General."

"Hello, Mr. Murata," the woman in the suit said, still sitting. "There's not much to say that hasn't already been said, but I'm glad this is moving forward. The funding we're going to receive from the state and federal governments will allow us to tackle the prison overcrowding issue that is so pervasive here by building more modern and secure facilities throughout Illinois. Oh, and I nearly forgot. I'm Jane Witham, president and CEO of Correcticorp. I'm sure you're already aware, but we run nearly the entire state prison system. Thanks for helping this happen, Mr. Murata."

"I'm Bill Peters," the man at the other end of the table said.

"I know," Albert said, totally starstruck. "I know who you are. An honor to meet you, sir."

The governor huffed a quick laugh. "Likewise, Mr. Murata."

Albert felt warm inside. Being appreciated and thanked by all these important people started to outweigh his pervasive feelings of guilt and apprehension. He was beaming from ear to ear as he sat down opposite Mr. Colson. "Thank you, everyone, for your kind words," he said. "I was just trying to do my part for the company and, well, for scientific progress."

"That's the key," the man with round spectacles said. "Scientific progress, indeed." Albert thought that if he had a drink in his hand, he would have toasted to it.

"This is Dr. Isaac Cross," Governor Peters said. "An old friend of mine and a scientist at the forefront of genetic research. He will be running the project with the help of Genovas."

"Let's get down to business, shall we?" Colson said, clearly attempting to appear friendly despite his constant demeanor. "With the help of General Fay, Ms. Witham, and Dr. Cross, we've put together a plan of action that goes over the details of the research project. Dr. Cross, do you have the documents? I know you wanted to add the specifics of the research protocol before it was finished."

Dr. Cross rummaged in his briefcase and pulled out a stack of papers—a rarity these days.

Mr. Colson spoke as Dr. Cross placed the stack of documents on the table next to him. "We've printed these out only for those in this room today. After the meeting, we will shred them. It goes over—what was it, Dr. Cross, samples or something?"

"Yes," Dr. Cross responded. "With Ms. Witham's assistance, we've determined how we will enroll our study participants, making sure our sample sizes are capable of rendering potentially significant results. I don't want to bore the group here with scientific jargon, but in short, the documents go over the study protocol and methods. We will be using the diversity of the prison population to our advantage."

As Albert's appreciative high started wearing off, he felt more and more of the guilt come back. What in God's name did he do, convincing Mr. Colson to sign up Genovas to perform unethical and perhaps extremely harmful experiments on a population that couldn't consent to it? Was this job really worth it? Couldn't he have found another way to either save the company or bring in income for his family? Condemning people who were already being punished, already serving their time. This can't be the way to do it. Not even for scientific progress or prison overpopulation or military funding or future benefits to society or whatever the hell else. It was just goddamn wrong. He felt nauseous and dizzy.

"I'd like to go into just a few details if that's all right?" Dr. Cross asked, scanning the room. After a few affirmative nods, he continued. "The plan is to split our subjects into three, more or less, equal-sized and represented groups. By that, I mean race, age, gender, health status, that sort of thing. Helps weed out confounding variables. There will be a control group of those prisoners who receive only a single trait of supplanted genetic code. This has already been proven safe and effective, of course, with all the past research. The other two groups, using some new processes that I've developed over the last few years or so, will be supplanted with multiple traits.

I must say, I am immensely proud of the inroads I've made in this area. I'm confident that with the resources and manpower provided by Genovas, we will have an excellent chance at success."

Albert half expected the others in the room to be shocked by this, considering all past experiments using multiple supplanted traits had ended in the subjects' deaths. However, everyone was clearly already on the same page. Governor Peters smiled.

"Glad to hear it," Ms. Witham said.

"Excellent," General Fay echoed.

It suddenly dawned on Albert as to why the military was so actively involved.

"If I may continue, those two groups I just mentioned," Dr. Cross said. "They will consist of a group receiving two traits from the same organism and a group receiving one trait from two different organisms. Does everyone understand what I mean by that?" He was met with nods. "If I may, Mr. Colson, I'd like to hand the documents around the room so people can read them and ask any questions they might have."

"Absolutely, Dr. Cross," Colson answered. "Please do. Thanks for doing your best at putting that into words we could all understand." Albert was stunned and reluctantly impressed with how Mr. Colson changed his entire vocabulary for this meeting. A very stark difference between this and how he talked to his staff in other situations.

Dr. Cross handed the stapled packets around the room. Albert received his last. At the top of the front page, there was the notation STRICTLY CONFIDENTIAL, and underneath was a list of the organizations involved in the study: State of Illinois, United States Army, Correcticorp, and Genovas. Below the list, in big, bold letters, were two words. Two words that sickened Albert to the core with trepidation: PROJECT MANTICORE.

CHAPTER 18
I'M HAPPY YOU'RE HERE

Zen and her father, George, shuffled down the front walkway, each of them holding the opposite underside of an old wooden dresser. "You go first," Zen said. "I can carry more weight."

George grunted, clearly disagreeing about that weight statement, but nevertheless, he started backing up the shallow ramp of the moving truck. Zen followed, and they placed the dresser gently down on the floor of the truck bed.

"Is that everything?" Zen asked. She was sweating through her shirt, and her lower back ached. It was much hotter out today than anticipated. The weather guys still always got it wrong. Perhaps she was a bit too bold about helping her parents move and then going back to her place to get her things, but she had her plan, and she was going to stick with it.

"Just some little things, dear," her mother, Ada, responded. "Go get some water and rest. Your father and I can finish up here. Two of his work friends are meeting us at our new place and can help us unload. Are you sure you still want to go to Hinsdale today? Why don't you come with us and take a shower and have some dinner? We can set up your bed for you first thing."

"Thanks, Mom, but I want to get this over with," Zen said. "Like I said, it shouldn't take me too long, and I can meet you there later today or tonight. Go on without me. I'll grab some food somewhere, and I'll meet you at your new place."

"If you say so, dear. You have the address, right?"

"Of course. It's in my phone."

"Okay, call us if you need anything or you change your mind and want to come over earlier. Thanks for your help today."

"Will do. No problem."

"Love you, dear," Ada said, then turned to George and yelled, "George! Do you have the key to the truck?"

George grunted an annoyed *yes* and dangled the key ring dramatically from his fingers.

Zen laughed. "Love you too, Mom. See you later." She called a cab and headed to her house in Hinsdale.

When she arrived and went to get out, she felt the back of her shirt stick to the faux leather seat of the taxi. So gross. She paid the driver and walked up to the house. It felt decidedly less inviting today than it had in the past, knowing she was there just to get her things and never come back. She put her hand in her pocket to get the key, pulled it out, and instinctively tried the doorknob before putting it in. The knob turned without resistance, and the door opened. She immediately was greeted by momentary panic, but then remembered that the last time she was here, she was calling the police from the middle of the cul-de-sac and never went back to lock it. She breathed a sigh of relief.

She walked upstairs to her bedroom. Everything was so neat and tidy. Her work clothes hung color-coded in her closet, and her shoes lined the floor organized by style. In the closet rested two large suitcases, used for countless past vacations with Aiden during the good times, to Scotland, Costa Rica, and her favorite, the Galapagos Islands, where she got to take pictures with one of the last living giant tortoises. She shook her head, wheeled the suitcase out onto the bedroom floor, and opened it. It still had a little sand in it from whatever tropical beach trip and still smelled like sunscreen and happiness.

She grabbed some clothes from the closet and sat down on the rug in front of the suitcase. She packed her pants in first and was beginning to line it with her shirts and blouses when she heard a door open and close downstairs. She stood up and walked out of her room to the railed balcony. She didn't see anyone, but she called out, "Hello?" and waited for an answer. There was none. She waited for another minute or so and went back into her room to continue packing. Maybe she imagined it. She finished putting her shirts in the suitcase when she heard it again. A door opened and closed shut, this time louder and unmistakable.

She walked out of her room again, and there he was, just inside the front door in the foyer. Aiden. He was looking directly up at her and holding some of his belongings in a clear plastic bag. "What are you doing here?" she asked, surprised and afraid but not wanting to show it.

"I'm home, baby."

She cringed at his use of that word. "What do you mean you're home? Weren't you being held in jail or something?"

"I was in a holding cell, yeah, but at the station. I went to a quick hearing yesterday, and they set my bail. I was able to reach my parents, and they wired the money. So, I'm free."

"You're free until you go to court again, right? Isn't there something about you not being near me because of all this?" She was doing her best to suggest he leave without just coming out and saying it.

Aiden seemed oblivious to it. "Yeah, you're right, there is. I didn't think you'd be here, though."

"And why wouldn't I be here? It's my house, and I live here."

"Technically, it's my house, but it's okay, baby. I'm happy you're here."

Zen couldn't contain it any longer. "Get the fuck out of here, Aiden," she said loudly from the balcony. "Let me pack my things and kindly fuck off until I'm done so I never have to see you again unless it's mandated by a goddamn judge."

"Look—"

"And you're right, Aiden," she continued. "It is technically your house, and you can fucking keep it. Now leave me the hell alone so I can finish up here and leave."

"Fine," Aiden said. "I'll leave you alone." He slinked off into the kitchen and out of her sight.

She stood at the edge of the balcony with her hands on the railing for a couple of minutes until she noticed just how slick her palms were. She tried to pass it off as a delayed effect from helping her parents move, but she knew it was from fear. After a little while, she went back to packing up her suitcases, hoping against all hope that Aiden would just wise up and leave the place until she was all done and out of there forever.

She zipped up the first suitcase after she filled it to the point of popping open and started on the second one with shoes, socks, underwear, and knickknacks. She was trying to stuff a desktop figurine into a pair of her boots when her vision blacked out for a second and came back hazy. She looked at her hands and the pair of boots again when the pain hit. Along with another punch to the side of her head. She felt her legs, which were kneeling, go limp, and she sprawled out on the rug with her head resting in the suitcase. She tasted blood in her mouth and her eyes fixated on a string of pink saliva that was attached to a high-heeled shoe.

She moaned and tried to turn over, her hands going up to the sides of her head to prevent further damage. Her vision went in and out in blurry waves, and her head swam in dizzying darkness like after a night of heavy drinking. She managed to turn onto her back, and she saw Aiden standing above her, his face twisted with rage, just before she felt a sharp, sudden pain in her ribs. She didn't see the kick but saw Aiden's leg retreat to its straight position. She croaked out meekly and gasped for air, each breath a dagger in her side.

Aiden was yelling, but she was having trouble making it out. In her semi-conscious mind, she thought she might have a busted eardrum. "You fucking bitch—" she heard. "My fucking house—" she heard a moment later. "And I loved you—" she heard after that. The release of unconsciousness threatened to bring her underwater, but she fought with all her being to stay above. *If I pass out*, she thought, *he might fucking kill me. I might die. Like this.*

She slowly reached into her pants pocket, hoping Aiden wouldn't notice. She grabbed her phone with all the strength and desperation she had, trying to press the correct buttons to send out an emergency call. Aiden stopped yelling. He clearly noticed. "You bitch, you're not getting out like this again!" He grabbed her arm, the one that was holding the phone, and pulled it hard. She heard the sickening pop of her dislocated shoulder and felt the dull, searing pain, but still, she held the phone. Like it was the only thing that mattered in the whole world. Aiden started prying her fingers off, one by one. She felt a bone in her pinky finger snap, and the pain that followed joined all the others in its hell, but her thumb found the emergency button, and she pressed it. The call went through. And Aiden saw that it did. She bared her red-stained teeth right at the fucking bastard. She saw the fist, and she succumbed to the darkness.

CHAPTER 19
FAVORITE SHIRT

Mik saw the text message notification on his HUDPhone display from Ollie. *Meet me at Old Tom's 20 mins don't puss out.* Mik smiled despite himself and started getting dressed. The whole thing at the grocery store last night felt more like a fading bad dream than anything else, and he was convinced it was all in his head. He buttoned up one of his favorite shirts, a flashy, colorful one with natural fibers that had been a gift from an ex-fling a few years back. That relationship was a disaster, but it was almost worth it for the shirt. He called the cab and headed to Old Tom's, using the touchscreen in the back as a makeshift camera mirror to make sure his hair looked good. He didn't know why, but he felt a little surge of hope at maybe meeting someone tonight and wanted to look his best.

He walked into the bar and saw Ollie. He was leaning on a barstool and patting the one next to him. The music was pumping loud, so Mik had to nearly yell. "How'd you get seats at the bar this late?"

"They heard about the ass-kicking you laid down on Thursday, and they ran away scared shitless," Ollie responded. "Who the hell am I kidding? You punch like a girl. This older couple was just getting up when I walked in. They obviously didn't like when the boys cranked up the tunes." The bartenders at Old Tom's liked to increase the music volume when dinner hour passed into drinking hour, especially on weekends.

"You've been lucky enough to not be punched by me," Mik said. "God knows you've deserved it a time or a hundred."

Ollie seemed entirely unimpressed. "Sure, buddy. Anyway, I'm holding you to your word. Double it up tonight. Speaking of—" He waved down the grizzled old bartender, Eli. "Two shots of your finest bottom-shelf whiskey. And make 'em doubles."

"Fair enough," Mik said. "I'm a man of my word." The two men slammed their doubles, grimacing all the way down and for a good ten seconds after. "Oh man," he said, his face a picture of disgust. "That is some really good, really bad stuff. How about we go at least to the middle shelf for the next one. And you know what, fuck it, I got the next round." He waved Eli over. "Two more shots for me and my friend, please. Some of the good stuff."

"Listen, guys," Eli said. "I know you weren't at fault. I mean, I saw the whole thing, but maybe just be careful tonight, huh? Go a little easy for Old Tom's sake?"

"Sorry, man. I promised Ollie here I would go all out tonight since I—" He cleared his throat extra loud. "Bailed on the poor boy yesterday. I hope that's all right."

"Sure thing, Mik. I don't want to put any restrictions on two of my best customers, but just, you know, be careful."

"We'll take your wise words under advisement," Ollie piped in. "But for now, two doubles on the double, my good man."

Eli poured two generous doubles of surprisingly good whiskey and put them down on the bar. "This one's on the house, gentlemen. I didn't mean to be a wet blanket or anything. You guys earned it."

"No harm done," Ollie said. "How about you pour yourself one, too? It's on Mik here."

Mik shook his head and laughed. "Absolutely."

The three of them clinked glasses and pounded the whiskey together. Mik noticed that he winced considerably less on that one. "Yeah, that had way less burn than the first round. What'd you give us anyway?"

"The secret stash," Eli answered with a wink. Mik laughed. "Say, Mik, that girl has been eyeing you up and down ever since you got in here."

"What do you mean? What girl?"

Eli gestured with his empty glass toward one of the tables near the corner of the room. The woman was looking attentively in their direction. When Mik turned to face her, she smiled coyly.

"Oh, that's bullshit," Ollie said. "She's clearly looking at me. You guys must have some pretty terrible eyesight."

"No, Ollie, she's definitely looking at Mik," Eli said.

Mik nodded and smiled at the woman. She was very pretty, almost elf-like, with what he guessed were green eyes, although the lighting in the bar could screw with you a little. She smiled back, a little wider.

Ollie looked at her and back at Mik and again once more. "Okay, you bastard. She's looking at you. For once in your poor miserable life, the girl likes you instead of me. Well, aren't you gonna do something about it? Now's your chance to lose your innocence, my man." He poked Mik on the shoulder.

Mik was staring, entranced by the woman, and the poke from Ollie broke him out of it a little. He turned to Ollie. "What do I say to her, dude?" He was always nervous talking to girls, ever since middle school, and he was only two (or four) drinks in, a far cry from uncaring drunkenness.

"I don't know. But I know it's gotta be something," Ollie said. "If you say nothing, you'll be back at your apartment dingling your dangle, and I've had enough of you not even making a move. Just go over there. It doesn't even matter what you say, just say *something!*"

"I need at least one more drink," Mik said. He still felt nervous. The buzz had hit him, but it hadn't calmed down the anxiety, only made it more generalized.

"You don't need another drink to talk to her, but I sure as hell need one to keep talking to you about this," Ollie said as he flagged down Eli one more time. "Two more doubles. Mik here needs his liquid courage. The good stuff."

Mik and Ollie pounded back another one. "Okay there, champ," Ollie said. "I think your battery is charged. Now go!"

Mik felt a warm surge of comfort wash over him. There was still that little twinge of anxiety around the corners, but it was dulled enough for him to make a move. He took a deep breath and smiled. "All right, well, here goes nothing." He stood up and started walking over to the woman, moving with the carefree lightness of the alcohol with each step. She was still looking at him and smiling.

"Hi," he said to her, glad his voice sounded confident and stutter-free.

"Hello," said the woman. Her voice had a singsong quality that made Mik's heart leap with infatuation.

He smiled back, almost dumbfounded, but then rediscovered his voice. "I'm Mik."

"I—" She paused for a barely noticeable split second. "Nice to meet you, Mik. I'm Stella."

"So, what brings you here?" Mik hated himself for asking one of the most generic questions in the book.

Stella smiled, perhaps picking up on that. "I'm in town for a conference, actually."

"And you're here? In this dump? What kind of company sets you up in a place like Tem Tem District?"

She laughed a melodic giggle that raised pleasant goosebumps on Mik's skin. "Well, it just so happens the conference is at Tem Tem headquarters. Don't worry, though. They put me up in a company suite right next to it."

"So, you don't even need to travel anywhere? That is a pretty good deal. That begs the question, though, why'd you come to Old Tom's? We're like a mile or two from where you're staying. Plus, it's a total dive."

"Who said I don't absolutely love dive bars?" Stella asked wryly. "It's not every day you see wooden doors and original neon signs. Not to mention the stale beer."

"Fair enough, you got me there," Mik said, smiling widely.

"You have a really nice smile."

Mik blushed beet red. "Umm—" he responded. "Thanks. So do you." *Damnit, Mik, that was weak.* "I mean, you're beautiful. Your eyes are like this amazing emerald—"

Stella laughed. "Thanks, Mik." Clearly, she could tell how uncomfortable he was with this type of conversation. "You're not so bad yourself. Hey, why don't you get us a couple of drinks while I go freshen up a little?"

"Sure, is there anything in particular that you want?"

"Surprise me." She winked at him and headed over toward the restrooms.

Mik headed back up to the bar, where Ollie sat, talking to a couple of other patrons. His seat had already been snatched up by someone else. "Hey, Ollie."

Ollie turned to him. "What the hell are you doing over here?" He looked back over to the table, now empty. "Did you scare her off? What happened?"

"No, no, I didn't scare her off. She's freshening up or whatever. Asked me to get us a round of drinks." He waved Eli over.

"Nicely done," Ollie said as he patted Mik on the back. "Keep it up, will you? I don't want to see you going home alone tonight. For once."

"Yeah, yeah," Mik said. He turned to Eli. "Two more of that good stuff you gave us earlier, please. If this girl likes whiskey, then she might be fucking perfect." Eli laughed richly, poured two generous glasses, and handed them to Mik. "Thanks, man," Mik said. "Can I pay on the way out?"

"Sure thing," Eli responded. "If you're busy then, you can get me next time."

Mik nodded and carried the two filled glasses back over to the table where Stella had returned and sat waiting. "I hope you like whiskey," he said as he placed one in front of her.

"It's just about the only thing I drink," she said. "Give me a good barrel-strength bourbon any day, and you've stolen my heart."

"Well, I don't know exactly what this is, but Eli, the bartender over there, recommended it."

Stella took a small initial sip. "Bourbon for sure. I can taste that caramel and cinnamon. Yeah, you've done well here, Mik. It's good stuff."

"Glad I could be of service." Mik kicked himself for a lame line like that.

Stella raised her glass, and Mik met it with his. They drank the rest of the whiskey down in one go. "I think you could be of service, all right." She leaned over the table and gently pulled on his shirt collar.

Mik had an immediate gut reaction of trying to protect his favorite shirt, but when she leaned in for a long, passionate kiss, that concern instantly melted away. He returned the kiss with almost desperate enthusiasm. Their tongues intertwined and looped around a few times. Stella finally broke the kiss, but her face remained within six inches of Mik's. "Come here," she said. She pulled on his collar again, harder, but he had stopped caring about his shirt.

Mik got up, and her hand moved from his shirt collar to his wrist. Stella led him away from the table toward the restrooms. He followed in a daze. When they got to the men's room, she knocked playfully on the door and waited for an answer. A few seconds later, she pushed it open and walked in. He followed. She pulled open a door to the nearest of three stalls and kicked down the toilet lid. She let go of his hand and turned around. She once again grabbed hold of his shirt collar and pulled it as she sat down on the lid.

As Mik let her bring him down to kiss her again, he noticed legs in the farthest stall. He almost laughed, but he was muffled by the kiss. When their lips separated again for a moment, he laughed and said, "I thought you knocked." She smiled. They kissed again, deeply and passionately. She started unbuttoning her shirt, revealing just the very top of her bra.

When their lips separated, Mik looked over to the far stall. As he was about to be pulled down again for another kiss, he noticed that the pants on those legs weren't bunched above the shoes. They were on. Fully. Someone was just standing there in the stall. He had been so distracted that he hadn't even thought about using his infrared vision. As his pit organ worked, he saw a man standing there still as a statue, looking directly toward him. All Mik's lust and happiness and drunkenness faded in a flash, replaced by knives of fear. He looked back at Stella, who didn't give any indication that she noticed anything. She gave the faintest look of impatience and pulled harder on his collar. This time, he resisted. She kept pulling, and he jumped back, sending two of his shirt buttons flying to the floor. He turned and pushed open the stall door. He opened the men's room door and ran. "Where are you going?" he heard her shout after him.

"What the hell are you doing?" Ollie yelled across the loud room. "What the hell happened in there?" Clearly, he had been watching their whole interaction with a vested interest.

Mik ran out of Old Tom's into the street, leaving Ollie and Eli to look at each other in confusion. He ran down the street, darted into an alleyway, and ran down random streets until he doubled over in exhaustion. He walked the rest of the way home, wondering if he was finally losing the rest of his marbles.

CHAPTER 20
BRUNCH

JULY 26, 2071

The Equarian Hotel was simply beautiful. Nestled in the heart of the business area of Oasis District, it was where the wealthy and those wanting to appear wealthy stayed when in town. It was shaped like a great pyramid but with slightly concave sides. This was done not only for the architectural merit but to enhance the exclusivity of the rooms on the top floors. There was one single penthouse suite, usually reserved for visiting dignitaries and the like. The entire building was equipped with two-way windows, so guests and patrons could see out to the city perfectly fine, but those looking at the hotel from the outside would be met with dazzling video and light displays, a mirrored sheen, or any combination of colors, depending on the season, holiday, or event. Beyond all that, perhaps the most impressive thing about the hotel was their Sunday brunch. It was legendary.

Sarah excitedly pulled on her father's hand after they had passed through the retina scanner and gene sensor at the massive front entrance. Her mother followed behind, clearly in much less of a rush. "Dad, this is supposed to be like the best brunch in existence," Sarah said. "C'mon, I'm starving."

Her dad nodded. He was hungry himself but lacked her unbridled enthusiasm. He had already looked at the menu online. With those prices, it had better damn well be the best brunch any human has ever consumed. "All right, all right. Our reservations aren't for another ten minutes, anyway."

Sarah and her parents were in town because she had been accepted to the University of Chicago for her freshman year, along with several other schools, and she was still hemming and hawing about going there. Although it was the most prestigious university she got into, it was far from their home in Ohio, and she was worried about being away from her family for the first time. The campus visit was scheduled for tomorrow, and despite her apprehension about moving to a new place, she was excited at the prospect of living in a big city. She had spent the last two weeks researching fun things to do in the area, and the brunch at the Equarian Hotel would be perfect timing.

Sarah pulled her dad all the way to the host stand. Her dad, with a reluctant smile, said, "Hi, we have reservations at eleven. I know we're a bit early."

"No problem at all. What's the name?" the host asked.

"McAllister, for three."

"The table's all set, actually. I can take you there now!"

They followed the host to their table, near the middle of a large, opulent hall. In the very center was a beautiful display of seafood. Smoked salmon. Lobster tails. Raw oysters on the half shell. All kept fresh by a pearlescent liquid cooling system underneath. Sarah smiled. "You guys are gonna love it here," she said to her parents.

"How do you know that?" her mother asked.

"I just know," Sarah responded. "I mean, look at that." She pointed to the seafood display.

"You have to admit it does look pretty good," her dad said to her mom.

"OK, I need to run to the bathroom," Sarah said. "Can you order me a mimosa to start?"

"Very funny," her dad said. "I'll order you a mimosa without the champagne."

"Fine. OK, I'll be back in a bit." Sarah looked around the giant hall for any signs of a restroom. Seeing none, she walked toward where the bar and kitchen were. She asked the woman behind the bar, who was busy making at least five cocktails all at once. She pointed toward the back, past the kitchen, and gestured with an apologetic shrug that she couldn't be of more help.

Sarah walked past the kitchen until she found a busboy fixing the embroidered cloth on one of the back tables. "Excuse me," she said. "I was wondering if you knew where—"

The busboy turned around and stood up, much taller than he looked when he was fixing the tablecloth. She immediately forgot what she was going to ask. He was one of the most attractive men she had ever laid eyes on. High cheekbones, chiseled jawline, and the most incredible piercing blue eyes that looked almost like colored contact lenses. He smiled at her with perfectly white teeth. *If this is any indication of what the men look like in Chicago*, she thought, *I might just have to go to school here.* "How can I help you?" he asked with a voice like crushed velvet.

"I uhh—" she stammered. "I was wondering if you knew where the restrooms were."

"Just around those tables to your right." He pointed toward the back of the room past the kitchen. "Anything else I can help with?"

"No, no, thank you," she said as she hurriedly walked toward the restrooms to avoid any future blushing. She went to the bathroom and washed her hands. She couldn't help thinking about that busboy, but those thoughts were gradually being replaced by hunger and how amazing the brunch would be. She left the restroom and walked back to the table where her parents sat, constantly scanning the room for signs of him.

"What took you so long?" her dad asked half-jokingly.

"I had to ask two people where the bathroom was. Place is a maze. Anyway, I'm starving. Can we just go get food now?"

"Well, yes, Sarah, we were waiting for *you*. I ordered you a glass of Diet Coke, by the way."

"Oh, thanks." She didn't really want a Diet Coke but didn't want to appear ungrateful. There were juice dispensers near the food displays anyway. She got up and went over to grab some food. She noticed that they even had caviar tins lined between the oysters and various spreads. She never had it before and didn't really want to try it, but it was fancy either way. She filled her plate with oysters, smoked salmon, lightly toasted bread, and cream cheese and headed back to the table. On the way, she noticed the busboy again. He was wheeling a cart and looking at her. Her face flushed, and she felt hot all over. She couldn't help but smile at him, and he reciprocated with his own.

She placed the plate down and looked back over to him. He was gone. She immediately felt disappointed. She slurped down an oyster, and the disappointment vanished. Her parents joined her at the table, and they ate the rest of their meal in delighted silence.

Sarah felt very stuffed. She had gotten new plates of food at least three or four times, making sure to try a little bit of everything. "That was so good," she said.

"Yes, very tasty," her mom said. "I couldn't eat another bite." Sarah rolled her eyes. Her mom ate like a bird, pecking away at just a single plate of food. She was like that everywhere.

"So good," her dad said, letting out a burp as quiet as he could make it. He had wolfed down at least five plates, piling up his food into grotesque sculptures of random ingredients. "I'm gonna flag down our waiter. If you need to pee before we leave, you should go do it now."

Sarah didn't really need to go, but the prospect of running into the busboy again was worth going to the restroom one last time. "OK, I'll be back in a second." She slowly walked in the direction of the restrooms, her head on a swivel, looking for him. She was let down when she arrived at the restroom and didn't see him. She ended up having to go pretty bad after all, so either way, it was worth the trip. She washed her hands, fixed up her hair a little, and left to go back to the table. There he was, standing in the hallway, wiping his hands on his apron. He must have just gotten out as well. Perfect timing.

She walked over to him and smiled. "Hi," she said, trying to appear cute and demure.

"Hi," he responded with his silky baritone. "I might be a bit too old for you, but I was wondering if you'd like to go out sometime."

Her head was filled with excitement, but she was also trying to determine just how old he was. His face had no wrinkles. Perfect skin, but tight around his cheekbones and jawline. His age was shockingly difficult to ascertain. "I'd love to," she responded. She found herself not caring about his age whatsoever. "I'm Sarah, by the way."

He reached out his hand, and she grabbed it with her own. He held it tightly for what seemed like an awfully long time. "Nice to meet you, Sarah."

CHAPTER 21
THE LAND OF THE LIVING

It was difficult to wake up fully. It felt like weights were pressing down on her eyelids and her limbs felt lead-heavy, like she was being chased in a nightmare. When her eyes finally opened, it was to shadowless white light. Blurred forms shifted in her vision, silhouettes against a blank canvas. She strained her eyes to focus and her fingers to work into a fist. After a few minutes, the figures began to take shape. Her mother and father were at the end of the bed, and doctors and nurses walked behind them.

"You're finally awake!" Ada Thomas said with overt excitement. George Thomas grumbled in happy agreement. Zen looked around the room, still feeling extremely groggy, but she was clearly alive. She could feel the pain in her face and her ribs, but it was dull and seemed far away. *Great drugs*, she thought. As full consciousness slowly came back to her, she gingerly sat up straighter in the hospital bed. The diffused photon lighting that they had installed in modern hospital rooms was always difficult to get acclimated to. It was a relatively new technology that removed areas of shadows, so healthcare workers could always have a good view of whatever they needed to work on. The downside was that it felt so surreal, so unnatural, not to have a light source with corresponding darkness.

"Mom—" Zen said, her voice sounding like sandpaper. She hadn't noticed it before, but her thirst was now overwhelming. "Some water, please. Can you—"

"Sure thing, dear." Ada quickly poured water from a pitcher near the side of the bed into a plastic cup and handed it to her. Zen took it and greedily chugged it down. The first sip hurt, but the relief outweighed the pain of her sore throat.

"You're up," said a woman wearing a white lab coat. "How are we feeling?"

"I'm all right, I guess," Zen answered as she slowly turned her head left and right to loosen up her neck.

"Oh, we haven't met yet. I'm Dr. Laura Wentz. You can call me Laura or Dr. L. Whichever you prefer."

"Oh, umm, nice to meet you."

Dr. Wentz smiled warmly. "Glad you're back to the land of the living." Perhaps realizing that wasn't the best joke for the moment, she continued. "We had to give you a general anesthetic. We fixed you up, though. You were a little worse for wear."

Zen attempted a weak smile of her own. "Thanks." Her throat still hurt, and so did her cheeks, and she wanted to keep her speech to as few words as possible.

"You're already looking much better. With the help of some quick intervention and some pretty cool new laser surgery tools we have here at the hospital, you'll look almost as good as new in no time."

"Almost?" Zen closed her eyes. Her head was starting to pound.

"Yes, there will be a bit of scarring, but nothing too noticeable," Dr. Wentz said. She noticed Zen's eyes were closed. "Headache?"

Zen nodded her head but kept her eyes closed.

"Ah yes. You might still have a low-grade concussion. It could also just be a side effect of the anesthetic wearing off. We did some scans, though. Nothing serious up in that noggin. Do you remember what happened? Why you're here?"

Zen nodded again. She breathed deeply, trying to calm down the headache. She didn't want to do any more talking. "My—Aiden attacked me."

"He called the ambulance. Must have been right after he did that. They were able to get you here quickly, so you didn't experience any other tissue damage due to internal bleeding or inflammation."

How nice of him, Zen thought. "Where—" Every word hurt her throat and made her head pound even worse.

"He's in jail, dear," her mom said. "Police came too. They brought him in. He's not getting out now. Not after what he did. The judge denied bail after yesterday. Called him a major risk to your safety or something like that."

"Let me give you something for that headache," Dr. Wentz said. She filled a needle with a slightly orange liquid and injected it into her IV along with the fluids she was already receiving. Within seconds, Zen felt the headache lift away deliciously. "When you're feeling up to it, your parents can drive you home."

"Yes, dear," Ada said. "Want some more water? You can stay here as long as you like. When you're ready, your father and I will bring you back home. To our place."

Dr. Wentz nodded. "Take your time. No need to rush."

"I'm already feeling better," Zen said, her headache no longer preventing her from speaking. "I'm ready. I just want to go home."

"Are you sure, dear?" Ada asked.

"Yes."

"Okay then!" Dr. Wentz said. "Let's get you going." She removed the IVs from Zen's arm and applied small bandages. She and George helped Zen out of bed and into a pair of crutches. "Take care, Zen. Great meeting you. And be careful!"

Zen nodded and attempted a smile as she adjusted the crutches. She felt surprisingly strong on her feet. She let the crutches help her walk, but she felt like she didn't need them. Ada and George walked on either side of her in case she lost her balance on the way out. They exited through the automatic front doors of the hospital. The fresh air was sweet. It didn't matter what fancy filtering systems they installed. Hospitals always smelled like hospitals. Zen and Ada waited out there while George brought the car around. It was a nice perk every now and then that her parents could drive their own cars.

Ada let Zen have the front seat for the extra room. Zen slowly extended her legs out, giving them a little stretch. It felt good to sit down. Although her headache was gone, she was still a bit woozy.

She was starting to doze off when she felt a buzzing on her left hip. Her mom had placed her purse next to her on the front seat. She shook some of the cobwebs out of her head and reached into her purse to get the buzzing phone. COOK COUNTY CORRECTIONAL was on the screen. *You've got to be fucking kidding me,* she thought. She closed her eyes in disbelief.

"Who is it, dear?" Ada asked.

"I don't know," Zen responded. "I think—I think it might be Aiden."

"What?" Ada lurched forward from the back seat, her face plastered with shock. "What do you mean it's Aiden?"

"I think it's the jail. I have to answer it." Zen accepted the call and put the phone to her ear. "Hello?"

"Don't answer—" Ada said, then realized it was too late. She lowered her voice and shook her head. "You shouldn't have answered."

"Why are you calling me? What do you want?" Zen yelled into the phone.

"Zen. Listen to me for a second. I have to tell you something." Aiden's tinny voice on the other end of the line seemed desperate.

"I've already listened to you plenty. All your promises. All your apologies. I'm done."

"No. Zen, please, listen. I don't have much time. They might hear me."

"What the hell are you talking about? I'm hanging up. Goodbye, Aiden."

"Please, *please!* Zen!"

"*What?*"

"Please just listen. There's something going on here. There were a couple of people who came in. All dressed up in suits."

"So? Aiden, I'm done. Bye."

"Zen, please! They came in, and I overheard some of their conversations. They were talking all kinds of crazy shit. Enrolling prisoners in a gene supplantation study. Using prisoners as test subjects!"

"What? What the hell does that have to do with me? You're out of your damn mind. Call a fucking lawyer or something."

"The company that's doing it. It's called Genovas. Didn't you work with them for Guardian Hill?"

"Yeah. Can't believe you even remember that. So what?"

"Zen, please. Yes, I remember. You *need* to find out what you can about this. They're starting this week. *Please!*"

Zen sighed and closed her eyes. Somehow her headache had come roaring back. "Goodbye, Aiden."

"Zen, please—"

She ended the call and put the phone back in her purse. She kept her eyes closed for the rest of the ride home.

CHAPTER 22
GUT FEELING

Albert felt like absolute garbage. The high of the praise from the meeting yesterday had worn off, and the guilt and its accompanying nausea had come roaring back with a vengeance. He sat at the dinner table, picking at his food. His wife had cooked a wonderful meal of pot roast with roasted root vegetables, and normally he would have already finished his portion and gone for seconds. He could never get used to that lab-grown crap that everyone was pushing. Tonight, most of the food was still on his plate, getting cold. He smiled weakly at his wife and kids. "I'm sorry," he said. "I'll cover my plate and put the rest of the food in the fridge. I'm just not hungry tonight. My stomach has been acting up."

"Are you sure?" his wife asked. "You can tell me if I overcooked the roast."

"No, it was perfect as always. Just having a few issues. I'll be back in a bit. I'm going upstairs to take something for it." It was true that his stomach was upset, but he wasn't going upstairs to take a pill. He was going to make a phone call.

He sat on the edge of his bed with his HUDPhone, asking him if he wanted to call James Colson. *Dinner time on a Sunday night and you're going to call the big guy? To tell him what, that you're having second thoughts? After you convinced him to do all of this in the first place? Real smart, Albert. And you're going to leave a message at the office, so when you go into work tomorrow, you're going to get a nice don't let the door hit you where the lord split you?* Still, outweighing all of this was that single thought. That he had to stop this before it got going. No amount of praise, money, or security was worth living the rest of your life knowing you helped condemn other human beings to some horrible fate. Where was that single thought when he waltzed into Mr. Colson's office and performed the best sales pitch of his life? Pushed way down deep with the hope it wouldn't come back. And, well, it sure as hell came back. It came back worse than ever.

He put the call through, waiting for the voicemail to answer. "Colson here." Oh, shit.

"Uh, hi, umm, Mr. Colson?"

"Yes?" The impatience of the voice at the other end of the line was palpable.

"Mr. Colson, sorry to bother you, but—"

"Who the hell is this?"

"It's Albert, sir. Albert Murata."

"Ahh, Mr. Murata." Colson's voice immediately shifted to a happier tone. "To what do I owe the pleasure?"

"Well, sir, I was just calling to—"

"And you're quite welcome for making those introductions."

"Sir, I wasn't calling for that reason, but yes, I really do appreciate you bringing me in for that meeting."

"I see." Colson's voice reeked of disappointment. There was a long pause, and Albert almost started speaking again until Colson continued. "Then what is this about? What couldn't wait until the morning?"

Albert felt stupid. Whatever the nature and magnitude of his concern, of course, he could have waited until tomorrow. Then, a gut feeling swept over him that told him one thing very clearly. He absolutely could not let this go a single extra minute. Sweat was already starting to break out from his pores, and he would have to take another shower. "Sir, you can't go ahead with this," he finally said.

"Go ahead with what?" The impatience was starting to seep back in.

"The deal. The experiment. With Correcticorp. It's just not right." Albert's anxiety was making the words spew out rapidly.

"Are you fucking with me, Murata?" Colson's voice was so loud that Albert had to turn down the volume. "You couldn't stop extolling the benefits of the deal, and now, while I'm trying to relax on a fucking Sunday night with a fucking twenty-year-old single malt, you call me with your little misgivings?"

"Sir, please!" Albert nearly cried out. *There goes the sweat. Damnit.* "I was wrong to convince you to do it. I was thinking about my family and my job security and not about the human lives that are going to be put at risk. I was selfish."

Colson's voice suddenly got much quieter and more measured, and Albert had to turn the volume back up. "You weren't selfish, Murata. You had a moment of fucking clarity. Like you so eloquently said during your speech, it's about scientific progress. It's about the greater good. It's about legacy. And at the cost of some criminals? That's basically nothing."

The calmness of Colson's voice somehow gave Albert more courage to speak his mind. "With all due respect, sir, my moment of clarity is right now. I was wrong to say those things. We are wrong to accept this contract and start this experiment. We can't—"

"Let me stop you right there, Murata," Colson interrupted. "I'm going to speak to you in plain fucking English so you can understand. You fucked up big time with the investors. The only reason you weren't out on your ass the next day was what you said to me about signing that contract. I brought you in so you could be my right hand on this. I introduced you to—"

"Sir—" Albert just had to get his point across before it was too late.

"I'm talking. I went out on a limb because you made up for your investor bungle. I gave you a shot because, for once in your goddamn life, you said something smart. Now you call me on a fucking Sunday night to do your best at undoing the one decent thing you did. I'll tell you what, Murata. Don't bother coming in tomorrow. You're done. You're finished at Genovas. You'll say whatever comes into your head just to save your own ass. You lied to the investors, and then you lied to me. You have no fucking integrity, Murata. No fucking spine. And you'd better be sure I'm going to let everybody know."

The call-ending notification flashed on Albert's HUDPhone. He went into the bathroom, quickly flipped up the toilet lid, and threw up violently into the bowl.

CHAPTER 23
TWEEZERS

JULY 27, 2071

The annoyance of waking up this early on a Monday completely wiped away the rest of Mik's thoughts about the weekend. The events at the grocery store and the restroom at Old Tom's seemed like foolish daydreams in the wake of having to do all the prep work. Ollie would be just as bitter about it as he was, and misery sure does love company. He took a more scenic route to work today. That is to say, he went through the same route that he had on Saturday night, just in the opposite direction. Part of it was his curiosity to see just how far out of the way he went in his bout of fear, and the other part was that it would delay the inevitable slog of a long workday.

He turned onto the street that led to the back entrance of the shop. It wasn't quite an alleyway, but it was a narrow one-way that often had trucks parked half on the curb for loading and unloading at various businesses. There was a truck that was blocking his vision, but for a second, he thought that he saw Filip out back. Filip never ever showed up before noon, and with the surprising exception of last week, hardly showed up at all. Mik walked around the truck, and there he was. He couldn't believe it. Filip was standing at the screen door, looking into the shop. He didn't seem to have noticed that Mik was there. "Hey, Filip?" Mik said, half greeting, half question.

Filip spun around. His face looked shocked and drained of what little color it normally had. "Mikolaj!" If he could have yelled, this would have been it, but it came out like a gravelly croak.

"What's up? What is it?" Mik was suddenly worried. His mind raced back to the events of the weekend and his talk with Filip before that.

"Come here, quick!" Filip beckoned to him exaggeratedly. Mik wondered if his arm would fly out of its socket.

"What? What's going—"

"Come inside, now!" Filip held the door open and hurriedly beckoned him to enter.

"What—" Mik had already started walking toward the door.

"There's no time, Mikolaj!"

Mik jogged faster and went inside the shop. Filip followed and closed the screen door and the sheet metal door behind it with a slam.

"Can you tell me what the hell is going on, Filip?" Mik was already half out of breath with the combined surprise and jogging.

"We don't have time. We don't have time at all! Get over there by the sink!" Filip was breathing so heavily Mik could see his chest rise and fall underneath his cotton sweater.

"What's going on?" Mik asked louder. He knew better than to argue, especially with what had been going on, but he had to know what was happening. He walked over to the sink.

"Did you see anyone on your way here?" Filip pulled a nylon case from one of the steel drawers on the back wall.

"No, I umm, no I didn't. Except for like one guy who was unloading a truck down the street. Why?"

"Are you sure?" Filip rummaged through the case, momentarily glancing up at Mik.

"Yeah. What's going on? Seriously, Filip, tell me what's going on!"

"Because, Mikolaj, some men were here not ten minutes ago looking for you."

"Some men? Who were they?" Mik was suddenly thankful that he took such a random route to work.

"They weren't nice men if that's what you're asking." Filip held up a small shiny knife that looked almost like a surgeon's scalpel.

"What did they want?"

"You," Filip said, looking directly at Mik. He then looked back into the nylon case and found another shiny tool. "Ah, here we go." He held up a pair of tweezers.

"What's that?"

"A pair of tweezers; what does it look like?"

"Umm, okay. What did they want with me?"

"I didn't think to ask them. They had guns on their belts. Now, sit on that stool." Filip pointed to the nearest one next to the butcher's block.

Mik sat down, not entirely sure why. "Where are they now?"

"Most likely in your home, going through and destroying every-thing to find you. That would be my guess."

"Why? What the hell—"

"Because you weren't here. Now, rest your head on the block, left side down."

Mik didn't move. "Filip, tell me what the hell is happening!"

Filip sighed, exasperated. "I told you to be careful. Remember this? It was already too late. They're looking for you. Now, put your cheek right on that block!"

"What—"

"They came here. I told them you were out of town, but I seri-ously doubt they believed me. Now rest your head on that block, now, Mikolaj!" He brandished the little scalpel-like knife.

"Whoa, what the hell are you doing?" Mik sat up straight and was about to leap off the stool and run out of there.

"I have to take out your HUDPhone implant."

"What? Why?"

"Because, Mikolaj, it's only a matter of time before they find a way to hack into it and lock onto your location."

"How can—"

"Because these men are sent by people who have money and resources, and they will find a way. Now. Put your head on the block, or they will come back and find us here waiting for them like little rabbits frozen with fright in the middle of the street."

Mik slowly lowered his head to the butcher's block. He felt the cold wood on his cheek. He looked up at Filip, who was sterilizing the blade with a plasma lighter. "Okay." He resigned himself to what was going to happen.

"Now, hold very still, Mikolaj. This will hurt a little, but the knife is sharp, so it won't be too bad." The knife left Mik's vision. He felt a pinching sensation and then felt the warm blood flow down his face and the back of his neck. It was almost pleasant. "I've made the incision. I can see the device."

Mik grunted and unconsciously shifted his head. "I said don't move," Filip said. "I still have to remove the thing." Mik did his best to remain perfectly still. He felt the tweezers on his raw open wound. He gritted his teeth as pain shot from the area into his head. With every movement, a new flash of pain ripped through him. "There," Filip said with subdued excitement. "I have it. You're lucky these things don't go farther into the head." With that, Filip pulled out Mik's HUDPhone, caked with quickly drying blood.

Mik turned to look, but Filip held his head down with his left hand as he held the device aloft between the tweezers in his right. "Stay there," Filip said. "I need to bandage you up. What use is it of removing the implant if they can just follow a blood trail right to you?" He placed the HUDPhone down on the butcher's block. Then he grabbed some bandages and ointment from the first aid kit next to the sink and patched Mik up. "All better. You can sit up now."

Mik sat up, the blood rushing back to his head. He shook off the momentary dizziness. He felt the bandages over the fresh wound.

"Would you like to do the honors?" Filip held up a meat tenderizer.

"Why not?" Mik took the tool from Filip and smashed the HUDPhone into tiny pieces. He swept up the fragments with a broom and dustpan. Then Filip handed him some wet cloths to wipe the blood off his face and neck.

"How are you feeling?" Filip asked.

"Fine. Now what?" He looked at all the wipes that had turned red with his blood and threw them in the trash.

"Now? We leave."

"Where?" Mik was still in pain but didn't want to let on about it.

"Someplace safe. Let's go."

CHAPTER 24
TRANSFER

Zen wore massive sunglasses when she entered the Guardian Hill building just outside of metropolitan Chicago. She was usually on the road for work, but with everything going on with her parents and Aiden the past week, she had just been coming into the main headquarters when time and health allowed. It was just another nondescript building in an office park, and although her office had a big window, it had a depressing view of the parking lot.

The sunglasses covered the worst of the damage, but there were still a few visibly healing scars that ran across her cheek. She walked quickly, hoping not to get too much notice and, therefore, inevitable follow-up questions. She went into her office, closed the door behind her, and shut the blinds.

Guardian Hill had an extremely secure database of their clients. It was from so many data breaches, stolen bank accounts, identity thefts, and any number of crimes that had convinced Zen to use a regular phone instead of a HUDPhone implant. While her job as a legal executive never pertained to the data security sector, it was nevertheless a heavy influence on her distrust of technology. Her main task was jumping over the legal hurdles of random lawsuits, company communication, client security contracts, and other regulatory issues.

She should have been there to check up on her team since she had barely been in to work the last week, but she couldn't get what Aiden said out of her head. *Goddamn him,* she thought. *He beats the shit out of me, and I can't ignore him for one single day? A lunatic phone call from jail and I'm here at work just to look up the company that he was hallucinating about?*

She had worked closely with some of the staff at Genovas nearly five years ago when they were moving their headquarters from Philadelphia to Chicago. She made sure that the protocols and contracts were up to snuff at the building, along with helping provide security against research theft and tampering. But that was about it, and once they had their building all set up, Genovas had decided to go with internal security and ended the contract with Guardian Hill.

She logged in with the palm pad and her personal security code. She had to go way back to find the Genovas files, but there they were, date marked back to 2066. As she expected, the personnel files were encrypted. Once a contract was over, the company protected the client's private data against any further access. The encryption allowed for eventual reopening if a contract was renewed, but that required an electronic sign-off from the CEO of Guardian Hill and the person whose file it was.

Zen shook her head. She didn't even know why she was doing this. Some crazy experiment that Aiden was rambling on about? How would looking up the Genovas files even help with that? Nevertheless, she continued looking into it, knowing that she would be mad at herself for not totally following through, as irrational as that was. She found some files that were still unencrypted. Security guard schedules. Alarm system details. The usual safety regulations and protocols that every workplace had to put into effect by law. And a ton of the typical legalese she was so familiar with that was a part of every client file. Nothing about any experiments. Besides the fact that the contract was nearly five years old, it's not like Guardian Hill had anything to do with the specifics of their research.

She was about to turn the computer off when her conscience got the better of her again. Maybe she could transfer the Genovas files to another device or something. Who knows, she was already looking at this stuff because of her crazy, abusive husband, so why not go all out and bring the files home and try to make better sense of them? She understood this line of thinking made almost zero sense, but what if, on the tiny chance that he was telling the truth, she could help? She started scrolling through the options in the on-screen menus, but her lack of technological expertise was rearing its ugly head, and she had no idea how to go about transferring anything.

She had hoped to go into the office unnoticed and leave the same way, but if she wanted to follow through with this, she would have to get help from someone else. She grumbled to herself, sounding way too much like her father, and left the office. The receptionist, Julia, was standing at the front desk, a tall, black marble square that was supposed to give potential clients an impression of strength and security. Julia must have been sitting down when Zen entered, so they didn't see each other. The functionality of the desk was questionable.

"Hi, Mrs. Thomas!" Julia said, perky as ever.

"Hi, Julia."

"Are you all right?" Julia looked concerned. Zen's sunglasses clearly weren't fooling her.

"Yes, I'm fine, thank you. I've been taking a self-defense class, and my partner got a little too excited." *That was half true, at least,* Zen thought grimly.

"Oh, okay! I heard you were going through some personal stuff, so I was a little worried. Glad that you're okay." The concern vanished from Julia's face as quickly as it had arrived.

"I appreciate that, Julia. Say, I was wondering if you could help me out with something."

"Of course, Mrs. Thomas! What can I do for you?"

"Would you mind coming with me to my office? I need help transferring some files."

"Sure thing!" Julia said excitedly, but she didn't move.

"Now would be ideal." *Not the sharpest knife in the drawer.*

"Oh, of course!" Julia turned on the automatic answering service and followed Zen to her office.

Zen pulled another chair over to her desk and sat down. "I'm trying to figure out how to transfer these files to my phone or something so I can look at them at home. I haven't been in the office much, and it would be great if I could do it on my own time."

"Genovas?" Julia had an exaggerated look of surprise on her face. She was so damn animated all the time that it was almost like watching a marionette pulled by strings. "We don't have a contract with them anymore, Mrs. Thomas. See?" She pointed to the screen. "It was closed in 2066."

"I know, Julia. I was hoping to go over some old contracts that I used to work with. Make sure that I was following the correct steps when filing all the documentation." It was a reasonable excuse, although she wasn't sure that Julia needed much convincing.

"Oh, okay! Well, Mrs. Thomas, we aren't allowed to transfer files to personal devices like phones, but I could transfer them to a company tablet that you could bring home to work on. Would that be all right?"

Zen figured that would work. The screen would be bigger than her little phone anyway. "Sure, Julia. That would be great."

Julia left the room and came back with a tablet. With a few key presses and finger swipes, the files were transferred. She handed the tablet to Zen. "Here you go, Mrs. Thomas. It's all set. I just have to register the tablet out to you and markdown what's on it."

"Is that really necessary? It's just an old contract that I'm looking at."

"Yes, I'm sorry, Mrs. Thomas, but it's company policy."

Zen sighed but then quickly smiled, hoping to appear appreciative. "Okay, thanks for your help, Julia. I have to head home again to get some work done."

"Anytime, Mrs. Thomas! Have a great day!" Julia beamed ridiculously.

CHAPTER 25

DIVISION

Mik followed Filip down some side streets. He was somewhat impressed by Filip's speed, considering how slowly he generally moved. "Where are we going?" He was anxious and outright confused at the same time.

"I told you before, Mikolaj. A safe place."

"Where?"

"A place away from the prying eyes of men with guns. Now, be quiet, and follow me. I only have so much breath, and I need to use it for running." Running was a generous term, as it was more of a spastic half jog, but either way, the point was taken. Mik could tell they were running southeast toward downtown Chicago where Tem Tem District gave way to the government-controlled sector.

They arrived at a chain-link fence that surrounded an abandoned area of Tem Tem District close to where it bordered downtown. The buildings within were in total disrepair, and the streets and sidewalks were full of cracks where nature had sprung up in the absence of maintenance. Signs and notifications were attached to windows, but no one was there to read them. "Here!" Filip exclaimed as loudly as he could muster. He pointed to a hole in one of the fence corners about three feet tall and two feet wide. "Go in and help me through."

Mik crouched and entered, careful not to snag his clothes on the frayed edges, then helped Filip through. That seemed to take ages as Filip had quite the difficulty bending down and then straightening up again, complaining about every ache and pain along the way. Filip once again took the lead, walking down the crumbling street behind a few brick buildings.

"Here we are," Filip said breathlessly, doubled over in exhaustion. They had arrived at the entrance to an old subway station. A few stairs led downward from the sidewalk, but beyond that were stacks of concrete blocks preventing people from entering. A bent and rusty signpost stuck out from the sidewalk. On it was the word DIVISION in white letters on a heavily faded blue or gray background. The L had shut down just after corporate districting had begun. Funding from the city government was reallocated to the historical areas, and there was no longer the infrastructure needed to maintain public mass transportation.

"Here we are where?" Mik asked. "You mean the subway? I'm not sure if you remember, but it hasn't been in service for a while."

"Yes, the subway. Now would you do me a favor and start clearing a path for us?" Filip still had his hands on his knees but lifted one arm up to point at the concrete blocks.

"What? You want me to unstack those blocks so we can enter an abandoned subway station?"

"Yes, and once we're in, I want you to restack them behind us. Are you going to make an old, crippled man like me do it? Hurry up."

Mik rolled his eyes and sighed. As little sense as this made, the specter of danger was always present, and he didn't feel the need to argue further. He started at the top of the stack. *Goddamn, these are some heavy bastards*, he thought. *I thought I was in halfway decent shape.* He slowly moved the blocks back from the entrance up to sidewalk level so they could eventually go inside, and he could replace the blocks from the other direction. It was starting to rain lightly, which helped ward off some of the heat, but he was still sweating from the exertion. Filip stood watch, leaning against the wall of the closest building, occasionally signaling to Mik to speed things up. After what seemed like hours but was really only about fifteen minutes, Mik had opened a small pathway between the blocks that led downstairs. The dank, musty smell hit his nostrils as he peered into the darkness.

Filip left his makeshift watch post and followed Mik through the gap. Mik spent the next fifteen minutes restacking the blocks until the last sliver of daylight disappeared from where they stood.

Even after waiting a few moments to let their eyes adjust, it was still almost impossible to see anything. Filip pulled a tiny flashlight out of his pocket and illuminated the area in what was almost high-noon light. They walked down to the subway landing. On each side were the tracks that used to shuttle thousands of people to and from work every day and now lay empty and cavernous. There were a few benches in the center, the wood on them slowly taking to rot. The fluorescent lights were half-shattered, and the screens that once showed the arrival timings hung black and lifeless from the ceiling. Power had been shut off to this area for a very long time.

Filip walked ahead of Mik and slowly lowered himself down onto the track. "Come, follow me," he said, pointing the flashlight ahead into the tunnel. Mik followed carefully, every footstep amplified. About a hundred yards down, Filip stopped at a maintenance door. "We are here," he said and pointed the flashlight at it.

The door looked the same as a couple they had already passed. Mik examined the door and discovered a small black squiggly design on the very bottom. He crouched down to figure out what it was when it hit him. It was a helix. Filip knocked seven times on the door in what seemed like a random pattern, and a moment later, the door opened just an inch. He leaned into the small opening and whispered a few words that Mik couldn't hear.

The door opened all the way. Standing there was a muscular man with a geometric tattoo that covered his entire bald head. Behind him, Mik could see a fine mesh gate, and beyond, the dancing colors of neon lights. They would have been harsh on his eyes if it weren't for the flashlight that Filip had so recently used. The man looked at Mik with an acutely distrusting look but then nodded at Filip. He pulled open the gate and stepped aside. Filip went in first, but Mik stuck close behind him, not wanting to make any sudden movements in front of the man. He glanced at him quickly, and the man was staring at him. Yes, no sudden movements.

Mik took in the scene before him. It was a massive room that looked like it had been carved out of the dirt and rock below the city.

What had once been a maintenance closet had been transformed into what could only be described as an underground bazaar that stretched as far as he could see. The ceilings were about ten feet high and were supported by numerous steel and concrete beams and poles. There were shops and storefronts in every direction, made of corrugated sheet metal and plaster. Neon signs hung everywhere like a carnival, covering the room in a rainbow glow. Children ran after each other, laughing and screaming, and shop owners hawked their wares and bickered over prices.

"Where the hell are we, Filip?" Mik's eyes were wide with awe.

"Welcome to the Haven, Mikolaj."

CHAPTER 26
PENGUINS

Isabella was obsessed with penguins. Ever since her first-grade class went on a field trip to the aquarium in the spring, it was basically all she talked about. Ever since school had been out for the summer, she begged her parents every single day to go back. Her mom and dad were putting it off. It was more expensive and not to mention crowded on the weekends, and they both worked full-time. Today was the first day they could both get off from work, and when they told Isabella that they were taking her to the aquarium, she let out a bloodcurdling scream of joy.

On the cab ride there, it was a consistent stream of consciousness, mostly about penguins but about sharks, dolphins, and turtles as well. A deluge of information filtered through the lens of a manic six-year-old girl. Peppered in between the so-called facts was begging for a stuffed penguin to take home. Her first-grade teacher wouldn't allow children to get any toys on the field trip to make sure everyone felt equal, which really annoyed Isabella because her parents had given her a twenty-dollar bill to spend at the gift shop. The extra three-month wait only served to fuel her desire for it.

When they arrived, Isabella ran in ahead of her parents as soon as the front door was opened by someone else. "Hold on, Isabella," her mom said. "Stay with us."

"I wanna see the penguins!" Isabella responded. "Hurry up, Mommy!"

"We have to buy tickets first, honey. We'll head right to the penguins once we have them, okay?"

"Fiiiiiiine." Isabella huffed and puffed ridiculously.

"Um, two adults and one child, please," her mother said to the pimple-faced teenaged boy behind the ticket counter.

"Is your child under twelve, ma'am?" the boy asked.

"Uhh, yeah, she is." Isabella's mom pointed to her dancing around, presumably with an imaginary penguin.

"Okay, great. Would you like to add any exhibits or shows to your experience today?"

"Exhibits? Which ones aren't included with the ticket?"

"We have a special iguana exhibit today and a show about the vanishing Arctic circle and its marine life."

"Oh, no, thanks, that's okay. We're mostly just here for the penguins." She nodded in the direction of Isabella, although she wasn't sure the boy caught on to her meaning. She paid for the tickets, and the family cleared the gene sensors and entered the main area of the aquarium.

"Penguins, penguins, penguins," Isabella chanted like a mantra.

"Those are on the bottom level in the polar area," the boy said. "If you'd like, I can automatically upload the walking map to your HUDPhones."

"Sure, that would be great," Isabella's mom said. "Thanks."

"Penguins, penguins, penguins," Isabella repeated.

"Okay, honey, we're gonna go there right now."

Isabella ran ahead of her parents in the direction of the staircase leading to the penguin exhibit, her memory from the field trip undoubtedly kicking in.

"Don't run, Isabella," her dad said. "Stay with us. Be patient."

"I wanna see the penguins!" Isabella said. "Daddy, you'll love them. The little ones are all fluffy and cute."

"Can't wait," her dad said. Her mom picked up on the slightly sarcastic tone in his voice and looked at him. He winked back.

They headed two floors down to the exhibit, all the while Isabella circling them like a herding dog. Her parents wondered how she got so much energy to run up and down the steps like that. When they got to the edge of the exhibit, Isabella peered over the wall, which was about neck height for her, and screamed, short and painful to anyone within earshot, especially her parents.

"Oh my god. Oh my god. Oh my god. Mommy. Daddy. Looooook. There they are!" Isabella pointed to the many penguins that filled the area. Pointing wasn't exactly a requisite for finding them. The penguins waddled along the little manmade banks, dove off little pedestals into the water, and swam like darts. The smell was pungent, but Isabella didn't care at all. She was jumping up and down. "They are so *cuuuuuuuute*. Oh my god. Oh my god. Oh my god." She kept spinning around toward her parents, making sure they were also looking and excited about the whole thing. She saw her dad look in a different direction for a second and wasn't happy about that in the least. "Daddy, why aren't you looking at the penguins? Look, one just jumped into the water, and you missed it!" Her face went all pouty.

Her dad smiled back. "No, baby, I saw it. It was amazing." He and her mom looked at each other and smiled knowingly.

"I want a stuffed penguin now," Isabella said matter-of-factly. She had stopped dancing and was peering over the edge of the exhibit.

"Well, that was a little rude," her mom said. "We ask politely for things. What's the magic word?"

"Please."

"Please what?"

"Please, I want a stuffed penguin now."

Isabella's mom rolled her eyes, and her dad shrugged. "Close enough," he whispered to her.

"Okay, honey," her mom said. "You can have your stuffed penguin when we get to the gift shop."

"I want a penguin *now!*" Isabella folded her arms across her chest.

"You need to be patient, honey. We will get it for you when we are done with the rest of the exhibits on the way out."

"I want it *now!*" Isabella pouted. As if realizing this mode of action wasn't working, she added, "Please?"

"When we get to the gift shop. Now, don't be impatient. It's not a good quality for a young woman. There are lots more things to see here anyway. I'm sure you didn't want to come here for just the penguins, did you?"

"Well," Isabella said and paused. She seemed resigned to having to wait for the stuffed penguin. "I guess I like turtles and sharks too."

"Great!" her dad said. "Let's go see them." He pulled up the walking map on his HUDPhone. "It looks like the sharks are on the floor above us, so let's go there first."

"Fine," Isabella said coldly, apparently still harboring a bit of a grudge.

"I thought you liked sharks," her dad said.

"Hmm. I like sharks," Isabella said. "But I like penguins more."

"But you just saw—never mind, baby. Let's go."

They headed up to the reef exhibit. Through a massive window that had interactive touchscreens built into it, they could see all different species of sharks, jellyfish, and all sorts of marine creatures swimming in and around what looked like a real coral reef. A relatively large shark crossed their vision, and Isabella's dad pressed on the window with his fingertip. Some sort of scanning device inside told him that he was looking at a zebra shark.

"That's a zebra shark." Isabella's dad smiled and pointed at it. He pressed the window again as a smaller shark passed by. "And that's a dogfish."

"Zebra shark and dog shark?" Isabella giggled. "They have funny names."

"Come here, want to try?" her dad beckoned her over. "Just press on the window when you see something and you want to know what it is."

Isabella pressed on the screen, telling her that the little colorful fish was called a clownfish. "Eww, I hate clowns," she said.

"You're silly," her dad said. "That's just a name."

"Oh, what's that?" she asked excitedly. She pressed the screen again, telling her that the strange amorphous undulating creature was a moon jelly. "Moon jelly? That's pretty, but I liked that zebra shark the best," Isabella said. She seemed to suddenly go deep in thought. "I love sharks," she finally exclaimed.

"I thought you loved penguins," her mom said.

"I like penguins, but I like sharks more."

Her parents sighed at the same time.

Isabella walked to the far-right corner of the window and pressed on it again. It told her that it was a starfish. "Daddy, that's not a starfish. This thing is being stupid."

"What do you mean, baby?" her dad asked.

"Look, Daddy, that's not a starfish." She pointed between two large rocks underneath the coral.

He looked where she pointed. Isabella was right. That wasn't a starfish at all. It was long and flowing. He looked closer. For a second, it looked like a full head of hair. Then he realized that's exactly what it was. A head of long, blonde hair. And it was attached to the body of a young woman.

CHAPTER 27
SHOELACES

Zen decided that she wasn't even going to look at the Genovas files tonight. It was enough for one day to go into the office and deal with all that nonsense. She took a nice long shower at her parents' place to relax. She was going to stay there until all the legal proceedings with Aiden finished up. If he ended up going to prison, which she was kind of hoping for at this point, she could move back into the place in Hinsdale without having to deal with him. Her salary was good enough to keep up the mortgage payments, at least for the time being.

She was almost done drying herself off with a wonderfully soft towel when she heard her phone ring from the bedroom. It was right at that moment between letting it go to voicemail or rushing the drying process and picking up the call. She decided on the latter because she hated having to call people back. She quickly wrapped herself with the towel, scurried into the bedroom, and barely managed to get to the phone. COOK COUNTY CORRECTIONAL. *Are you kidding me,* she thought. *Not again! What sort of bullshit is Aiden going to tell me now?*

"Hello?"

"Mrs. Thomas?" It was a voice she didn't recognize.

"Umm, yes?" She fully expected the person to put Aiden on the phone.

"Hi, Mrs. Thomas. This is Rami Levenson." The name was familiar. Zen was racking her brain, trying to figure out where she knew it from. Before she could retrieve it from her memory, the person answered her internal question. "I'm your husband, Aiden's, lawyer. We briefly met a few years ago. I'm not sure if you remember."

"Oh, yes, of course," Zen answered, fully not remembering at all.

"I'm glad; yes, it was nice meeting you."

"Likewise." *Fake it till you make it,* Zen guessed.

"Well, I'm sorry to reconnect with you in such an unfortunate way, but I have some awful news. Ah, I should just get right to it. Again, I'm sorry." Rami sounded extremely nervous.

"What is it?" Zen asked, wondering what the hell he was going on about. Was Aiden already going to trial? Did he plea bargain? Is he out on bail? That would surely be awful news for her, but she doubted his lawyer would see it that way.

"Well, I'm sorry, but Aiden was found dead in his cell this morning."

"What?" Zen couldn't even separate the emotions from one another in her head. Was that relief? Sadness? Or just shock taking everything over in its loud numbness?

"Ah, yes, I'm sorry again to be the bearer of such bad news."

"What happened? Tell me what's—" Impatience was starting to creep in, despite everything. She needed answers right now.

"Ah, Mrs. Thomas. I am deeply sorry. I know you're upset. He was found, um, hanged in his cell. Suicide, apparently."

"What the hell are you talking about? How the hell did that happen?"

"Um, ah, shoelaces, I think."

"Not what was around his neck!" Anger ripped through her.

"Oh, yes, of course, I'm sorry," Rami said, clearly made even more uncomfortable by the outburst. "I'm not sure. I did ask, and they told me that they don't do twenty-four-seven surveillance on the cells. He must have, um, done, um, *it,* when there was no one around."

"Was there a note? Anything that might have given any indication why he did it?" She didn't know what she was hoping for, maybe an apology, or at least an admission. He was always so apologetic, even after smacking her around.

"Nothing, I'm sorry."

Zen felt like throwing up. *Maybe it was a good thing, you know, that he's gone. You don't have to testify. He won't show up and hurt you again. No more bullshit; you finally have freedom. But he was your husband, and you loved him once, and he loved you, despite that*

SHOELACES

little ol' violent streak. He didn't deserve to die. Maybe one or two ass-kickings, but not that. Why did he end it like that with no closure, no anything? No, no, no, that makes no sense at all. He didn't do it. Of course, he didn't. Not after that crazy call barely a day and a half ago. He wasn't crazy. Not about that, at least. When it came to losing his temper and beating the ever-loving shit out of you, sure, he was crazy, but not about other stuff. He was always even-keeled about everything else. He was telling the truth, wasn't he? He was onto something. Something big.

"Are you still there, Mrs. Thomas?" Rami sounded concerned.

Zen realized that with all the thoughts racing through her mind, she had forgotten to respond. "Yeah. Still here."

"Well, I have some more, um, bad news."

She closed her eyes. Her lips trembled. "More bad news? You mean on top of the news about my dead husband?" She almost laughed with the absurdity of it all.

"Uh, yes, about the suicide. I'm sorry."

"What about it?" Her voice had become almost monotone and mechanical.

"Well, as I'm sure you're aware, state law dictates that when a suicide is committed without going through the proper channels—"

"Fuck," Zen said involuntarily. She knew exactly where this was going. How could she forget?

"Sorry, Mrs. Thomas?"

"Continue, please."

"Ah, yes, of course, well as you know," Rami said, obviously wary of further interruptions. "When someone commits suicide in the state of Illinois without going through the proper channels, as in seeing a government-mandated psychiatrist until the suicide is approved, all the assets are forfeited to the state government or the corporate district owner, whoever controls the area of residence."

"You have got to be kidding me." Zen knew the law in and out, but she was convinced Aiden didn't do it. This was all a goddamn setup.

"I'm sorry, Mrs. Thomas," Rami said. "I know this is difficult. Trust me, I did not want to be the person to tell you all this, but it's my job. May I please continue?"

"Why not." She was barely listening. Something had to be done. All she could think about was what Aiden told her. Genovas, prisoners, experiments. Her heart was pumping with the urge to delve into the files on that tablet. Still, she had to keep up appearances on the phone call for the time being.

"Yes, as I was saying, since he didn't go through the proper steps, unfortunately, the house in, um, Hinsdale, must be forfeited to the government as it was in Aiden's name. And the joint bank accounts will be frozen until they can look into your personal contributions and withdrawals and create a new account for you. Anything that he put in goes, again, to the government. I'm very sorry, Mrs. Thomas."

"Yeah, I get it."

"Is there anything I can do, Mrs. Thomas?"

"No, not right now, thanks." Zen could use the lawyer's help later, so she didn't want to come off totally unappreciative. "Thanks for keeping me informed. Can I contact you later to figure things out?"

"Of course, Mrs. Thomas. I hope you have a good rest of your day."

"You, too." She hung up.

She now had no choice but to stay at her parents' place. Governments moved extremely quickly when they could take something from you, and just about the opposite when they had to give something back. She wasn't holding out much hope of the bank account being unfrozen anytime soon. At least this all made her next steps a lot simpler. In a weird, twisted way, she didn't have to worry about any post-mortem issues with Aiden. With the government taking the house and seizing the accounts, she had nothing to deal with personally, at least for right now. She had one thing to work on. What the hell was going on with Genovas and the prison experiments? She immediately pulled out the tablet and turned it on, ready to scour for clues.

CHAPTER 28

WINDY CITY NEWS

"Available on all streaming providers in Illinois and the surrounding areas, this is *Windy City News*, and I'm Jeff Washburn. Ladies and gentlemen of the great city of Chicago and the world at large, we have some late-breaking news. Viewer and listener discretion is advised. The body of a young woman was found earlier today at the Chicago Aquarium, allegedly another victim of whom you all know as the Killer Frog! A family was visiting the aquarium and, in a macabre discovery, found her lodged between two rocks in the wild reef exhibit. A team of police, complete with divers, recovered the body from the exhibit, and forensic scientists once again discovered trace amounts of BTX toxin on the corpse. We are still waiting on a confirmed identification of the victim, but—

"Hold on a second, ladies and gentlemen. Scratch that. I've just been notified that the victim has indeed been identified. Her name was Sarah McAllister, aged eighteen, from Sandusky, Ohio. Apparently, she was here to visit a college campus. Thoughts and prayers go out to her family and friends.

"Now, we have some late-breaking new information about this Killer Frog, so please pay attention. This audio is from a police interview with a friend of the first victim, Autumn Chandler, and *Windy City News* is the first outlet to have access to it."

"Please state your name for the record."

"Um, sure. My name is Madelyn O'Hara. Maddie for short."

"Thank you, Ms. O'Hara."

"You can call me Maddie if you want."

"All right. Maddie, what can you tell us about what happened with your friend, Autumn?"

"We were just out on the town. We were, um, celebrating 'cuz she got a promotion, so we decided to go out. Like for happy hour."

"I see. So, when did you encounter the suspect?"

"The suspect?"

"Yes. The person who kidnapped and killed Autumn."

"Oh, yeah, sorry, I'm kinda out of it, I guess."

"You don't seem very torn up about your friend."

"I mean, she's great. I mean, she was great, but we weren't like super close or anything."

"I see. So, when did you encounter him?"

"Okay, yeah. So we were doing like a bar crawl, I guess you could call it. And we ended up at, um, I'm blanking on the name. Something Bee. Super fancy bar downtown."

"The Hazy Bee Parlor?"

"Yeah! That's it. So, yeah, we were just drinking there. I mean, we had already hit up a few bars on the way. You know, celebrating and all. But this guy, he bought us drinks. The um, suspect."

"Then what happened?"

"Well, I feel horrible. So horrible. I was like, 'Autumn, this one's yours 'cuz you earned it.' I hate myself for that. I wish I was selfish and made it about me."

"It's not your fault. Can you tell us what happened then?"

"Well, he came over, and I left, you know, to give them some time to get to know each other. I, uh, never—I never saw her again, until the, uh, news. I feel so horrible."

"Can you describe the suspect? The man who bought you drinks?"

"I feel totally awful for saying this, but he was like, super, super hot."

Audible sigh "What do you mean by that?"

"Well, he had these, like, icy blue eyes. They were like nothing I've ever seen. And oh my god, his jawline. It was like, chiseled from, like, stone or something."

"I see. Is there anything else you can tell us about him?"

"I dunno. I mean, I would guess he's in his thirties or something, but it was like, hard to tell. Kinda tall. Dressed really well."

"What do you mean it was hard to tell? His age was difficult to discern?"

"Discern? Oh, um, yeah. I dunno; his skin was like, super smooth. No wrinkles. It was kinda weird, I guess, but I just assumed he used some good moisturizers or something. And definitely didn't smoke."

"Well, there you have it, ladies and gentlemen. Testimony about the Killer Frog directly from the horse's mouth. Well, the horse's friend's mouth. Scratch that. Anyway, you now have an idea of his appearance. If you see anyone who might match that description, please notify your local police office or corporate public safety—

"Hold on a minute, ladies and gentlemen. I'm just getting word that during this broadcast, a demonstration has started in downtown Chicago calling for justice for the victims of the Killer Frog and stricter laws against people with supplanted genes. I hear that so far, it has been mostly peaceful, but there was, only minutes ago, a skirmish between the demonstrators and members of a small pro-supplantation organization. One woman was hurt in the melee, but I'm told her injuries are non-life-threatening. We will be following up as more details come to light.

"Before we sign off for the night, I want to remind everyone to tune in tomorrow afternoon at four P.M. local Chicago time for *The Power Hour* with your favorite streaming show host, Speedy Powers. I'm told he has an incredibly special guest in store whom you don't want to miss. For everyone at *Windy City News*, I'm Jeff Washburn. Stay safe out there, Chicago."

CHAPTER 29
HAVEN

Mik and Filip walked through the marketplace. It was blaring loud with the yells of the shopkeepers and all the random noises from construction and the transport of wares. Despite all this, Mik found it somewhat comforting, almost like being in the middle of the loud music and conversation at Old Tom's. There were strong aromas of barbequing meat, gasoline, and sweat. It was strange, but it was pleasant and beautiful in its liveliness.

Beyond all the lights and the shops, there was something that stuck out to Mik visually more than anything else. He was passing by people who were *obviously* supplanted. He was aware that he wasn't the only person in the world with a supplantation, but he had never before noticed anyone with the outward appearance of it. The pit organ on his face was tiny and looked like a small freckle at a glance, but most supplantations were almost entirely in function, not form. That was not the case in the Haven. There were men and women completely covered in fur of all sorts of colors and patterns. There were people with horns, antlers, tusks. Giant ears, long noses, mouths filled with sharp teeth and fangs, and tails of all shapes and sizes.

"Who the hell are all these people, Filip?" Mik had been walking in stunned silence until now.

"Just that, Mikolaj. People," Filip said, matter-of-factly. "There are lots of distractions here. I want to make sure you're keeping up with me."

"I'm pretty sure I can keep up with you. You move like you're in pain."

"I am always in pain, Mikolaj, and you do nothing to alleviate it."

"Anyway, I was serious, Filip. Who are these people? Is everyone here supplanted like me? I noticed the little helix on the door."

"Not everyone. You saw the children running around, didn't you?"

"Yeah, you don't need to be condescending about it."

"I'm sorry, Mikolaj. It has been a very stressful day. My heart already has enough trouble as is."

"It's all right."

"To answer your question, no, not everyone here has supplanted genes, but all who do are welcome. This Haven is for those who believe in personal freedom above all else. There are a few people like you who were supplanted for other reasons, but most here did it of their own free will, knowing the consequences of their actions. It is only getting worse out there. They came for you, and they will be coming for everyone else soon enough."

"So, this is basically like a hideout or something?"

"Yes, but it's more than that, Mikolaj. It's a community. It has been around for quite a while now."

"Why haven't you shown me this place before, then?"

"Because your father wanted a normal life for you."

"My father?"

"Yes. You were coming home from the military, from combat, and he wanted you to have the chance to lead a life without fear, without hiding, so you could pursue your future on your own terms. If we had shown you this place years ago, I would think that your life would no longer be yours to choose. It's only in this time of desperation that I bring you here."

"I guess that ship has sailed, huh?"

"Until something is done, I would have to say so. But that does not mean forever."

"So, my dad was involved in all this?"

"To the extent that he could be, yes. Soon after he heard about your experiment in order to help pay for his treatment, he confided in me. I know this took a lot of trust. Supplanting had been banned for so long, and admitting that to someone could be dangerous. He wanted you to have a normal life; he really did. But I told him about this place which took a lot of trust in kind. We both had a lot at risk, but we trusted each other. He was a good man. He agreed to let me bring you here only in the circumstances that your life was in danger. He would often come here and help out when he had the energy. Mikolaj, he believed in this place as much as I did."

"Jesus. I don't even know what to say. I can't believe it. So, you've known about this place for how long?"

"A long time, Mikolaj. I was introduced to this place, oh, it must be almost twenty years ago, when I was still politically active. I was a known rabble-rouser, as they say. I spoke out against anti-abortion laws, supplantation laws, anything that threatened a person's ability to govern their own body and their own fate. One of the leaders here contacted me in secret, and I immediately became involved. The Haven has been in existence since 2050 or so, not long after the supplantation ban. It started as the very maintenance closet that was here after the subways closed. Over the last twenty years, it has grown into what might even be called a town. It has required the help of many good people."

"That's insane. How do they even keep this place running? No one's ever noticed a working city underneath Chicago?"

"Carefully, Mikolaj. And slowly. Building this place has taken time, as I said, as well as knowledge. We are lucky to have engineers here that have helped make it structurally sound helped siphon power from the city grid to keep the lights on. People don't just show up here. They are carefully vetted by the leaders before they're brought in. One mistake, and the whole operation could be exposed and destroyed. Now, enough with the questions. I'm sure they'll all be answered later. You're exhausting an already exhausted old man. We are almost there."

"Almost where?"

"To where you'll be living from now on."

"What are you talking about? I have an apartment already. Once we deal with whoever has been looking for me, I can go back, right?"

"I wish it were that simple, Mikolaj. It'll only get worse. They were looking for you because you are ex-military. A loose end. When you left the Army, they didn't care as much. They forgot about you. But when you showed up on the system at that police station, they remembered. And with what has been going on, the killer on the news, it has re-energized whoever wants to rid this city of supplanted people. You were the first target in this new hunt but far from the last. It's not safe out there anymore."

"Goddamnit. What do I do now? I just live in this underground bunker forever?"

"I don't know the answer to that, Mikolaj. And for that, I'm sorry. We're here."

They arrived at an entirely new area of the Haven. The massive marketplace had given way to a sort of residential complex. There were no individual structures here but a winding, cavernous beast of metal and concrete. At a momentary glance from the outside, it looked like a construction site, blocks and scraps of material haphazardly placed about. However, inside there was a maze of hallways and bedrooms and kitchens that seemed to go on forever. Mik used his supplanted vision and saw rows upon rows of people going hundreds of yards farther. He immediately thought of looking into an infinity mirror.

A woman wearing a welding helmet was busy soldering pieces of metal together in front of the complex. When Mik and Filip got close, she got up, turned toward them, and switched off the soldering iron. She raised the faceplate of the helmet. She was middle-aged but extremely fit with sinewy muscles. "Hello, Filip," she said, her voice smoky and rich. "Been a while."

Filip nodded. "Jade." He gestured at Mik, a cross between a point and a beckon. "This is Mikolaj. Mik."

Jade looked Mik up and down at least three times as if looking for flaws and then grinned a wide, genuine smile of perfectly white teeth. They were a shocking contrast to the dust and grime on the rest of her face and body, not to mention her darker complexion and clothing. "Well, nice to finally meet you, Mik. Filip couldn't say enough about you." She extended her open hand.

Mik was almost caught off-guard by the sudden gregariousness but managed to smile back and shake hands. "Only good things, I hope." A corny line, but forever useful.

Jade's smile vanished, and the look of serious inspection returned. "Hmm." She paused, peering into his eyes. "Mostly." She was beginning to make Mik feel uncomfortable again, but then she burst out laughing. "Yes, yes, all good things. Welcome to the Haven, my new friend."

Mik felt a nearly overwhelming sense of relief. It must have been obvious on his face because Jade started laughing even harder. "Thanks," he said.

"Just some good-natured ribbing is all," Jade said. "Filip has already told me everything, well except about today, of course, and we've been expecting you to show up here at some point soon either way. I'll be showing you to your room if that's all right."

Mik looked at Filip for guidance. Filip nodded. "Now's a good time for that," Filip said. "Thank you, Jade." He turned to Mik and whispered closely to him. "Listen, Mikolaj. I know this is hard. Everything has happened all at once, faster than we thought. But you'll be safe here for the time being until we get things sorted out. I have to go back up to the surface, back to the shop. It is vitally important to keep up appearances to keep them off your trail. What would they think if we both vanished? No, I must go back but don't worry, I'll return soon to check on you. I promise this much."

Mik's mind was indeed racing, but he felt a sense of deep appreciation for the old man. He really had become sort of a father figure since his dad had passed away, even if neither of them wanted to admit it. "Thanks, Filip. I'll be all right. I'll see you soon."

Filip smiled and patted Mik on the shoulder. "See you soon, my boy." With that, he turned around and headed back toward the Haven entrance.

CHAPTER 30
CALL SECURITY

JULY 28, 2071

Albert had spent the better part of yesterday staring at the ceiling of his bedroom through the overlay of his HUDPhone. He had played with the dimming controls and scrolled through the menus of contacts, navigation, and system settings. He had browsed through at least a hundred internet sites and watched plenty of stupid videos. Those features were only available when the HUDPhone detected zero user movement in order to prevent people from watching videos while walking or driving. It was a failsafe put in by law after the initial release when people would literally run into each other on the street. Albert had gone through every feature a dozen times, always fixated on the paint strokes on the ceiling.

He couldn't do anything to shake himself from what had happened when he called Mr. Colson and got booted from Genovas within minutes. All that goodwill that he had built from his meeting with Colson and then with all the big wigs was destroyed in a flash. That was surely disappointing. He had worked his ass off to get to a place like that with the company. It paled in comparison, however, to the guilt that coursed through him about what he had allowed, nay encouraged, to happen. Within days, those prisoners would be sent to a fate not of their own making but of his. Of course, he was not the only one to put it into motion, but he was the final straw in any argument against it.

Now, a day later, he woke up, looked at the paint strokes on the ceiling, and decided that he wouldn't spend another minute wasting time. He was going to go into the Genovas headquarters, regardless of his current employment status, and fight like hell to get them to stop the experiment before it was too late.

When he arrived, no one seemed to notice, and if they did, they didn't make a stink about it. He took the stairs up to the sixth floor this time, partially because he didn't want to take even the smallest chance with the elevators and partially because he could use the walk to warm up a little and think about what he was going to say. He was starting to breathe heavily about halfway up, and the sweat started soon after. No matter. This wasn't about appearances anymore. When he exited the staircase by loudly bashing open the door, the secretary jumped in her seat. For some reason, seeing her helped Albert clear his head a little. A friendly face in all this mess. He took a deep breath and walked over to her, using his fingers to comb through his hair on the way. The secretary smiled when he walked over, but he could tell she was still recovering from the initial shock of him barging into the area.

"Hello, Mr. Murata," the secretary said with a slightly puzzled look. "I didn't know we were expecting you this morning."

Albert suddenly felt terrible that he never once asked for her name. So *damn selfish of me*, he thought, *and exactly what got me into this in the first place. If I truly cared about other people, I wouldn't have to be here right now, would I?* "Um, hi, yes, sorry. I don't think I made an appointment, but I was hoping Mr. Colson was available."

"I'm sorry, Mr. Murata. He's booked up the whole day. If you'd like, I can make an appointment for you to see him later this week. I'm sure I can squeeze you in."

"No, um, that won't be necessary, thanks." *Damnit.* Of course, he couldn't just waltz in here and—

The phone rang at the desk. The secretary looked surprised. "Hello? Mr. Colson? Oh, sir, it was nothing. The door to the staircase just opened really loudly. Oh, not a big deal at all. Everything's fine. Oh, it's just your employee. Mr. Murata. Oh. Oh, I'm sorry, sir. I can just tell him to—"

The heavy wooden doors at the end of the hall flew open and out stormed Colson, possibly angrier looking than ever. "Murata! What the fuck are you doing here?" Ah, that was a familiar tone. This time, Albert wasn't nearly as afraid.

"Mr. Colson, I had to see you in person. I don't care about the job or even my reputation. You need to put an end to the—"

"I'll tell you what I need to put a fucking end to, Murata. You. We are way past the negotiation stages here. I'm not even going to explain why this time. Get the fuck out, right now."

"You need to stop this experiment!" Albert's anxiety was gone. His fear was pushed way down deep. He already lost his job, the one thing keeping him from fighting. "You're going to kill people or worse!"

"It's over, Murata. You're over. Hannah, call security and have Mr. Murata here escorted out." *So that was her name, after all.*

"No need," Albert said. "I'm leaving."

"No, I fucking insist," Colson responded. "Hannah, call them now."

Hannah looked at Colson and then at Albert and hesitated for a moment. She winked at Albert almost imperceptibly. She pressed on her earpiece. "Hi, yes, security? Your services are requested to escort our former employee, Albert Murata, out of the building. Yes. Sure. Yes, that would be fine." She removed her finger from the earpiece. "All set, sir. Security will meet Mr. Murata downstairs."

"Why didn't you have them come up here?" Colson asked, clearly annoyed. "Ah, fuck it. Get the hell out, Murata. Trust me when I say you don't want to see me ever again."

Albert started walking back toward the staircase. "No!" Colson yelled. "Take the elevator. I want to make sure you're actually fucking leaving." Albert pressed the elevator button. Within a few seconds, it arrived, and he stepped in. He turned to face the doors, seeing Mr. Colson staring back at him. Albert pressed the button for the first floor, the doors closed, and he headed down. When the doors opened on the first floor, there was no security personnel to greet him. *Hannah saves the day again*, he thought. He took the staircase up to the second floor, where the logistics department was located. He placed his hand on the palm pad to enter the department, but it flashed red. They must have disabled entry when he was terminated. Panic started to creep up his spine, but he pushed it back down and knocked on the door. A young man in a cubicle looked up curiously and squinted his eyes behind his glasses. Then, the man smiled and waved. Albert smiled back. It was someone he recognized. He couldn't remember his name, either, just like the secretary, Hannah, but it was a person with whom he had always exchanged a hello and a nod in the hallways. The man walked over to the door and opened it, letting him in.

"Hey, um—" the man looked at the employee badge hanging from Albert's belt. "Albert, how are you?"

"Hey, Victor," Albert responded, taking a cue from him to look at his badge. "I'm doing well, thanks." The last thing he wanted to do was let on that anything was out of the ordinary.

"What brings you all the way over to logistics?"

"I just wanted to go over some of the details of an upcoming project. I was hoping I could solidify some of the logistical information. Make sure everything is where it should be."

"Oh, no problem," Victor said. "Follow me over to my, um, office." He pointed at the tiny desk in the cubicle. "Here, have a seat." He pulled over a flimsy office chair for Albert. "What project did you need the info on?"

"It's a research project with the state prison system. Not exactly sure what it would be under."

"Let me take a look." Victor pressed a few keys and scrolled through the files. "Ah, here we go. We have a research protocol in place at Stateville Correctional Center in Crest Hill. Client is Correcticorp. Never even heard about this. Project Manticore?" He laughed. "Sounds ominous."

Albert tried to laugh in return, but it came out more serious sounding than he would have liked. "Yeah, that's the one. Can you pull up the details on it?"

"One second. Oh, this is strange."

"What?"

"Almost all the information is encrypted. That is a first for me. Funding, contracts, participants, methods, all unavailable. Usually, all this stuff is open to us so we can do our jobs, but it looks like they're trying to do this with just a small team of Genovas staff. I see here that only the big guys have access. Colson, some doctor named Isaac Cross. Whoa, you're on this list. But, wait, hold on. You're restricted. What kind of project is this?"

"An important one. What information *can* you give me?"

"Um, like I said, you're restricted from all the details, but I can give you the information that's available."

"Please."

"All right, well, it says here that enrollment is complete. Um, looks like it goes live July 29. Isn't that tomorrow?"

"Yes. Damnit."

"What's the problem?"

"Nothing, sorry. Please continue."

"Okay, so yeah, when it says 'live,' that usually means the next phase of research. Intervention. The actual experiment starts then basically."

"Is there anything else on there?"

"Hmm. Just that it all seems to be taking place at Stateville. The prison. That's also strange."

"Why's that?" Albert was getting more and more worried.

"Because we almost always bring participants here, to our in-house research facility. I can't remember the last time we did it on-site with a contracted client."

"Okay, is there anything—"

"Murata!" The booming voice scared the hell out of Albert and of Victor too, by the looks of it. Albert jumped out of his seat. "Get out here right fucking now!" Colson was yelling, running to catch up with four security guards who were already just outside the department. Albert felt the pins and needles of fear up and down his spine. Victor just sat there with a look of pure surprise on his face. When Colson got closer, Albert could see his face was red, either with exertion or anger. "Get the hell out here, Murata, you sack of shit!"

Albert had no choice but to walk out of the logistics department at this point. He mouthed *thanks* to Victor before he did. "All right, I'm coming. All this security is totally unnecessary."

Security escorted Albert downstairs and out the front door of Genovas, with Colson close behind. When they got outside, Colson followed him, then waved off security so it was just the two of them. "I was nice to you before," he said, his voice quiet but dripping with malice. "But you have no fucking idea what I can do to you. Just you wait. I know people, Murata. Your internet and phone calls will be monitored. Your every step fucking traced. If you so much as whisper a word of the project to anyone, so help me God, you will wish you were never fucking born. If you have any desire for self-preservation, you'll fuck off right now and forget about everything forever." With that, Colson re-entered the building, leaving Albert alone outside in a cocoon of terror.

CHAPTER 31
CLIENT RELATIONS

The buzzing of the phone woke Zen from the most peaceful sleep she could remember in some time. The fact that Aiden was gone forever was not lost to her when thinking about why she slept so well. *Pretty messed up,* she thought. She answered. The call was from her workplace, Guardian Hill.

"Hello?" Zen did her best to take the sleepy tone out of her voice and somewhat succeeded. She was feeling surprisingly energetic today despite everything that had happened. A good night's rest really worked wonders.

"Hey, Mrs. Thomas?" The perky voice was instantly recognizable as Julia, the secretary.

"Hi."

"It's Julia from work. I was wondering if you were coming in today."

"Oh, sorry, Julia, I woke up late. I was planning on coming in this afternoon. Why, what's up?" The last thing she wanted to do was tell Julia about her husband's death. That would only spur an endless conversation.

"Oh, I didn't mean that!" Julia laughed awkwardly, but her voice was perky as ever. "It's just that Mr. Gant told me to call you to come in and talk with him." Benjamin Gant was the head of client relations at Guardian Hill. Zen had worked with him on occasion, but her role was tackling the nuts and bolts of an operation, not smooth-talking clients, so they rarely needed to collaborate.

"Why? What about?" She was trying to figure out why he would want to talk to her, especially face-to-face.

"Something about an old client. He asked me if I'd seen you, and I told him you stopped by yesterday, and I helped you with those files."

"Is he there with you now? Why doesn't he just call me?"

"No, he just dropped off the message and left. He said it would be best if you just came in and made sure to bring that tablet back with you."

Zen was starting to get an uneasy feeling. "Okay. Can you tell me how he seemed?"

Julia laughed awkwardly again. "What do you mean?"

Zen had to put this in terms Julia might understand. "Like, did he seem hurried at all, or angry, or anything like that?"

Julia giggled. "Now that you mention it, he seemed like he was in a rush. And he looked, I dunno, scared or something, I guess? I didn't think anything of it at the time, though."

"Okay, would you let Benjamin, I mean Mr. Gant, know that I'll be in shortly?"

"Sure thing, Mrs. Thomas. I know I'm not supposed to ask, but what's going on?"

"It's all fine, Julia. Thanks for the call."

This was not good. She had no idea what was going on, but there was something in motion. Of that, there was no doubt in her mind. Benjamin Gant calling out of nowhere and making sure she brought back the Genovas files after what Aiden had told her and his alleged suicide? There was no way in hell she was going into work today.

She found that her fists were balled in anxiety, just like the day she waited for the doctor's appointment to confirm the bad news about her infertility. Her mind raced, trying to find options. Her parents were at work. That was a good thing. The last thing she needed was to involve them in something like this. But she definitely couldn't go into the office. She doubted very much that Mr. Gant just wanted to shoot the shit about some old client. She pulled open the drawer in the nightstand next to her bed and took out the tablet. She scrolled through everything again, just as she had until late the night before until she fell asleep. All the security files were outdated, and all the personnel files were encrypted. There was nothing of use on here, but it didn't stop her from looking once more.

She brainstormed for at least an hour and came up empty of

ideas. She couldn't think of anything. She had no one to tell about this. If she went to the police, what would she say, that she had a hunch something was maybe about to go down at work, but she had no idea what that might be? And fuck them, anyway, for claiming that Aiden committed suicide. What a crock of shit that was. She started to get hungry despite the anxiety or possibly because of it. She quickly put together a peanut butter and jelly sandwich and ate it, washing it down with a large glass of milk.

As soon as she finished the last sip, she heard the doorbell. She wasn't sure why it made her so afraid, but that uneasy feeling just wouldn't go away. She took a breath. This was all probably nothing. She was just losing her mind. She walked to the front hallway, quietly just in case, and checked the video feed at the front door, her rational mind expecting to see some salesman or a delivery guy. But that wasn't what she saw at all. What she saw were two men, dressed in black fatigues, and she was sure they were not there to deliver anything good. Her fight-or-flight response kicked in, and she scurried as quietly as she could toward the back entrance of the house. Her hands were shaking, but she managed to open the door, exit, and lock it behind her.

She was completely unfamiliar with the area. Her parents had just moved here, and she hadn't taken the time to explore at all. Tem Tem District was a far cry from the sense of luxury and safety offered by Oasis District. She darted down an alley, not daring to look back for a second because that would only slow her down. She turned the corner to the right and headed down a side street, wanting to keep off any main roads in case those men had backups or other patrols out looking for her. There were people out here bustling about, so she slowed to a fast walking pace to blend in. It also gave her a moment to catch her breath.

She continued until she heard yelling behind her. She spun her head around, and there they were. Men in black fatigues and they definitely had guns at their hips. She hadn't noticed that before, but the silhouette was clear as day. They were pointing directly at her. She took off running, adrenaline fueling her. She spun down another alley, careful to avoid the garbage bags piled high and indiscriminately along the sides. It gave way to another side street off to the left, this one devoid of people, a one-way with trucks lining the sidewalks shrinking the street to a narrow lane. Her feet pounded the pavement, and she felt the pain in her hips and shins and the dull ache of her exhausted lungs. She could still hear the yelling, but it was more distant. Perhaps she had lost them, but she couldn't take the risk of slowing down. Her legs kept churning, the burn of lactic acid slowly building inside them.

"Hey!"

Zen looked ahead of her in the direction of the voice. She scanned the area but saw no one.

"Hey, what's going on?"

Finally, she saw the origin of the voice, a man around her age standing behind the open door of a truck. The view had been obstructed by another truck that was parked along the street. She wasn't close enough to answer him, not with her lungs feeling like this. She barely had enough breath to keep running.

"What are you running from?" The man's voice sounded light, almost like he was joking around with her. "Wow, you're fast!" Goddamn it, he *was* joking around with her.

Zen heard a door slam open behind the man as she ran past. She didn't bother to even acknowledge it.

"Wait!" It was a different voice now, older, coarser, quieter. "Come here, quick!"

She turned her head to see an old man holding open a door that led into one of the buildings. "Please!" The man's voice seemed much more serious. She quickly thought of her options. Either listen to him or run until she fell over and got caught. She slowed, turned around, and ran toward the two men, right past them, and into the building. "Ollie, you fool," she heard the man say as she collapsed to the floor in utter exhaustion.

CHAPTER 32
CHANGE OF SCENERY

Jose was kind of looking forward to this. He had been locked up at Danville medium security for nearly two years now, and it had already gotten old after a few months. This was his second stint in the wonderful Illinois correctional system, and this one was as much bullshit as the first. The first time he was nineteen and thrown in for six months for having barely a teenth of shitty coke. It wasn't like he could afford some kind of fancy lawyer, and the public defender didn't really seem to care all too much. He was scared shitless that time. This time, it was eight years for illegal gun possession. Well, that and an ounce of black tar. But still, you needed a gun to protect yourself in that kind of business, and it's not like he was going to get hired for any decent-paying job. Not after he had to fill out the criminal history part of every employment application. On the bright side, he wasn't afraid. Just bored as all hell, and today was an opportunity for a little change of scenery.

It seemed a little early for the annual flu and COVID vaccinations since those were usually in the fall and in the prison infirmary, but he wasn't complaining. Being able to take a ride somewhere else in an open-windowed bus afforded him at least a fleeting moment of a summer breeze on the road. The door to his cell opened with a loud buzz, and he and his bunkmate, Sean, stepped out just like at every mealtime and cell inspection. A few of the other cells were also open, with their occupants standing outside, but not everyone. The guards commanded them to move, so they shuffled along until they got outside.

"Why isn't everyone out here?" Jose asked, directed at Sean in front of him.

"Fuck if I know," Sean responded. "Who gives a shit, though. We get to go for a ride."

"Truth. I'll take it."

Two buses were parked outside, flanked by guards at each end with mean-looking weapons. Jose and Sean were assigned to the first bus and shared a seat near the back. It was like they specially designed the seats to be as uncomfortable as possible. It was a hot day, and when the bus wasn't moving, it was quickly becoming unbearable, especially with all the prisoners stuffed in like sardines. Jose's face was already dripping sweat onto his jumpsuit despite being right next to the window.

After what seemed like forever, the doors shut, and the bus started moving. The breeze was an incredible relief, and he let out a contented sigh. He looked out the window the whole drive there, feeling the air and sun against his skin. It was wonderful, but it made him ache for the free world. Then he remembered what his free world was like, living in a state of stress and fear, and he suddenly no longer ached for it. Prison was miserable and boring and gray, but it was simple and structured, and there was a tangible benefit to that. Still, he loved that open air.

The trip was reasonably long, but it felt way too short. The buses rolled up the driveway to the front entrance of Stateville Correctional Center. Jose peered outside and noticed a large cohort of prison guards along with a few people dressed in expensive suits and a man in a white lab coat. This was substantially more than the usual welcome party.

"Check this out," Jose said.

"What?" Sean seemed faintly annoyed and aloof.

"Look at all those guards. And some doctor or something."

Sean leaned over and looked out. "Mothafuckas really rolling out the red carpet for us. Don't you feel special?"

"Don't you think this is kinda weird?"

"Man, it's always fucked up in some kinda way. I learned to just say 'yes sir' and not look around so much. Easier that way."

"Yeah, I get it, but those guys in suits? Just saying this isn't the usual shit."

"Man, you're acting like this is the first time they switched all the shit up on you for no fuckin' reason. I think the mothafuckas get a kick out of fuckin' with your head."

"Truth." Jose shook his head. Sean was right. There was always a new rule or protocol put into place just so they could catch you slipping up.

"Open 'em up!" A guard yelled from outside. The electronic doors of the buses slid open, and a guard from the front row of seats stood up. He directed the prisoners out in an orderly fashion. Jose and Sean followed the men from the rows in front of them down the steps and out into the open air. Armed guards lined their path to the prison. Quite the welcome party indeed. They walked until they were right outside the entrance to the intake building.

"Stop!" A guard yelled. Jose wasn't sure if it was the same one or not. "Line up, move to the right!" Jose couldn't see him too well, but he was motioning the first prisoners toward the far end of the area. The prisoners lined up next to him, and finally, Jose and Sean were lined up alongside everyone else, almost exactly in the middle. When all the prisoners from both buses had been unloaded and lined up, the man in the white lab coat and two men in suits walked in front of them, using the shade of the arched entrance to shield themselves from the sun. Of course, they left the prisoners out there exposed.

"Hello, everyone," the man in the lab coat spoke. "I'm Dr. Isaac Cross. I know some of you must be wondering why you've been brought all the way here for your vaccinations. For the purposes of record-keeping and making sure that every inmate in the Illinois correctional system receives the proper healthcare, we are conducting them only at specific sites where we can properly monitor and record them. I want to apologize in advance for what may be a slightly crowded living situation for a little while. We will, unfortunately, need you to stay here for a few days to make sure that the vaccinations have the desired results. We don't want to send you back without the proper protections. Now, please follow the instructions from the helpful staff here so you can get situated. Thank you." With that, he walked into the prison complex through the intake building, flanked by the men in suits.

"The fuck was that?" Jose asked in a whisper.

"Told you, man," Sean answered. "They just wanna fuck with you."

A guard stepped in front of Jose and looked at the tablet in his hands. "Gutierrez, Danville inmate number 921065, you are assigned to block C, cell 516." He then spoke to Sean. "Teague, Danville inmate number 965037, you are assigned to block C, cell 516. Well, look at that. Looks like you two will be rooming together." Jose rolled his eyes, making sure the guard couldn't see. He didn't think that was much of a coincidence since they probably just kept all the living arrangements more or less the same.

Another guard spoke up. "All right, all those assigned to cell block C, follow me. If you are assigned to block C and do *not* follow me, you will instead be staying in solitary confinement. If you are *not* assigned to block C and you *do* follow me, you will instead be staying in solitary confinement. Have I made myself clear?" He was answered with a cacophony of *yeahs*, *sures*, *yes sirs*, and *whatevers*. "Now, let's move!" He walked into the intake building, and Jose and Sean followed.

CHAPTER 33
SMALL SACRIFICE

Zen guzzled down the first glass of water and the second in quick succession. She had tried to sit on the stool, but she was so dizzy that she ended up just sitting on the floor leaning against the cabinets. "Why'd you help me?" she asked, still catching her breath.

"I saw them out the front window," the old man said. "Men with guns yelling and running." Zen noticed he smelled like almonds, not altogether unpleasant.

"I don't get it. Why'd you help me? For all you know, I'm running from the cops or something."

"And if you were, I would like to think I'd still help you. But I recognized their outfits. They were after my—" He paused. "They were looking for my employee just yesterday."

"What employee?" the younger man interjected. "What the hell are you talking about, Filip? You talking about Mik?"

"Yes, Ollie."

"Is that why he's not here today? You told me his HUDPhone broke. I knew that sounded ridiculous, but you're an old man so I thought you'd never lie. Is he all right?"

Filip shook his head. "Yes, Ollie, that's why. But he's safe, so don't worry."

"Whoa," Zen said incredulously. "Who's chasing me? Why did they want your employee? What the hell is going on?"

Filip must have noticed that both Zen and Ollie were looking at him with obvious impatience and cleared his throat, coughing a couple of times along the way. "All right. Fine." He sighed deeply.

"Well?" Ollie whined. "Out with it, old man."

Filip glared at Ollie and continued, turning to Zen. "I don't know why they're after you, miss—"

"The name's Zen."

"Ah well, nice to meet you, Zen, under such unusual circumstances. I'm Filip, and this here is Ollie." Ollie waved sheepishly. "Maybe you'll be able to shed some light on why they might be after you once I explain what I know so far. Now, Ollie, I was hoping that Mikolaj could eventually be the one to tell you, but I wanted to make sure he could trust you."

"What the hell are you talking about?" Ollie grimaced.

"Well, you know Mikolaj was in the Army. What he didn't tell you was that he was supplanted."

"Like gene supplanted?" Ollie responded. "No way. He woulda told me."

"I wouldn't let him until I knew you were trustworthy."

"Until you knew I was trustworthy? I've been Mik's best friend here for over five years. I've worked for a grumpy asshole just as long, and I didn't even quit. How is that not trustworthy?"

"Anyway," Filip said, paying no mind to Ollie's tantrum. "Mik was supplanted as part of a voluntary experiment while he was in the service in exchange for a stipend to pay for his father's cancer treatment."

"Holy shit," Ollie said.

"Yes, well, when you two bumbling idiots decided to get into a barfight and then taken to the station, his supplantation was flagged in the system, and therefore, everyone's minds in the military and government. I don't know what he told you about what happened in China—"

"He never wanted to talk about it," Ollie interrupted.

"Well, in China, every other supplanted soldier on his mission was killed. He was the only one who made it home. I'm sure he was lost in the shuffle in the years after, but when he was back in the system, they remembered."

"Why'd they even care?" Zen asked, and Ollie nodded, indicating he was going to ask the same question.

"The government doesn't like loose ends. Especially when there is such a public outcry against supplantation with that killer going around."

"That can't be it," Zen said. "If those are the same people who were after me, there has to be more to it. I'm not supplanted. I don't know why they're after me. But—"

"You can't think of anything?"

"Well—" Zen paused, stood up, feeling the blood rush to her head, and filled up her glass with water from the sink. "It's just too crazy. But I guess it can't hurt to tell you. Can't be worse than guys with guns. I'm gonna skip the preamble, but long story short, my ex-husband calls me from jail on Sunday. Rambling on about some kind of experiment that they were gonna do on prisoners. That night, his lawyer calls me. Says he committed suicide in his cell. I say to myself there is no way in hell this guy killed himself. And if you're wondering why I'm not crying right now, it's partially because I was just chased down the street and partially because he had a knack for beating me. Anyway, this experiment. He says it's some kind of gene supplantation thing. Company called Genovas. I didn't get much more out of the conversation. So I go to work the next morning. I work in legal at a private security firm. Anyway, I knew that we worked with Genovas in the past. So, I go in and transfer the Genovas files to a tablet and head home. Next thing I know, these guys with guns are at my front door, and I make a run for it. That's it."

"Hmm." Filip scratched his chin. "Anything in those files?"

"I looked for hours. Just old junk. The personnel files are all encrypted. Plus, I left it at—" Zen put her hand on her left pant pocket and felt its rectangular shape. She pulled it out. "How—I didn't even know it could fit in here. I must have stuffed it there when those guys came after me. Either way, there's nothing on it."

"What the hell is going on?" Ollie asked. He had been sitting there with his jaw slightly open while she told the story.

"Hold on, Ollie," Filip said. "Zen, you said that the experiments were in gene supplantation, right?"

"Yeah."

"Well, it seems to me that you either know something they didn't want you to know or have something they don't want you to have. Or both. I don't think we'll be able to figure that out sitting here, and it isn't safe to go anywhere until tonight. I would venture to guess that the men are still out there looking for you. So, it might be some time until we have answers. Now, I need to remove your HUDPhone implants. Both of you."

"Huh? Why? I don't have one." Zen's brow wrinkled in confusion.

"What the fuck are you talking about, Filip?" asked Ollie, clearly nervous.

Filip ignored Ollie and looked at Zen. "You don't have a HUDPhone implant? I find that hard to believe. Now, we need to remove it quickly. We've already waited too long mired in conversation."

"Look," Zen said. She pulled her phone out of her right pocket and shook it in the air for effect. "I never got the implant. I was never gonna let them put a chip in my head."

"Give it to me," Filip said. "We need to destroy it before anyone locks on to your location. Ollie, we will still need to remove yours."

"What the fuck are you talking about?" Ollie repeated. "I'm not removing my HUDPhone from my goddamn *head*. You're out of your mind, old man!"

Zen hesitated for a moment and then handed Filip the phone. Filip put it on the butcher's block and smashed it a few times with a meat tenderizer until it was a mess of frayed metal and silicon. "Now," he said. "We need to remove your implant, Ollie. No more whining."

"Absolutely not. This is all ridiculous. People with guns after Mik. After you." Ollie nodded at Zen. "How about we just take a minute here and think through our options? There's gotta be a better way than going into my head. Let's be reasonable."

"I already removed Mikolaj's implant," Filip responded, with as much calm as he could muster. "He managed to get through it just fine. Unless you want all of us to be captured or killed, I think it's high time you make the small sacrifice of your stupid HUDPhone. You'll barely feel a thing." Zen could tell that Filip was beginning to lose his patience.

"Are you—" Ollie said and then immediately sighed and slumped his shoulders. "Fine, whatever. If Mik did it, I'll do it. If it means that he'll be safe. That we'll all be safe. Fine."

"Good. Now rest your head on the block, left side down."

CHAPTER 34
TOUR

"This is where we tap into the power and internet from the city grid." Jade pointed at a massive array of transformers, cables, wires, and other unidentifiable devices.

"Wow," Mik said. He had never seen anything like this. Much like the residential complex, the depth and size of it were almost overwhelming. "You guys have internet?" He quickly realized how dumb that question sounded.

Jade laughed. "Yeah, we have internet. Obviously, we can't tap into the satellite networks since we're so far underground, but we found a way to hardwire into the mainframe. HUDPhones aren't gonna work too well down here, though. But this system allows us to refrigerate and cook food, shower with hot water, and, like I said, keep the lights on. C'mon, I want to show you around some more."

Mik had spent a fitful night's sleep on a bed deep in the residential complex and hadn't dared try to explore the Haven on his own. A woman named Gayle had cooked him a phenomenal breakfast when he finally decided to get out of bed just before noon, and he had spent the better part of the early afternoon meeting some of the people in the complex. Jade had come by and offered to show him around a little and allow him to stretch his legs and shake out some of yesterday's jitters.

Mik followed Jade to a large open area lined with long tables and hundreds of chairs. Behind it was a large, almost industrial-looking kitchen, filled with massive ranges, steam kettles, convection ovens, and all sorts of equipment one might find in a large commissary. People were working away in the kitchen, and the smell of sauteed vegetables, braised meats, and all sorts of spices and herbs aroused his appetite even though he had eaten only a few hours ago.

"This is the cafeteria," Jade said. "Everyone in the Haven comes together for dinner here. Every night. This way, we can make sure that each person is fed and healthy. Plus, it fosters a real sense of community. I can see you eyeing the kitchen over there. Smells good, doesn't it?"

Mik nodded. "Sure does. I can't believe you got all this equipment down here. How do you even ventilate this place with all that smoke and steam?"

"Good question, Mik. We've built ventilation shafts that connect with the sewer system. It was quite the feat of engineering, but it allows us to vent out all the nasty stuff. It all just goes out the manholes as the steam you always see. We also have separate air siphon shafts that bring in fresh air. Without those systems, we'd all suffocate and quickly. Too many people in such a closed space without it."

"This is like something out of a book or movie. Some giant underground civilization right under our noses the whole time. Speaking of having too many people in a closed space, how do you deal with stuff like disease?"

Jade nodded with an impressed look on her face. "Look, I'm not gonna lie. Disease transmission is absolutely an issue down here. There's no getting around nature in that aspect. Where there are lots of people, there's a lot of passing bad stuff around. We have a couple of things going for us, though. One, we put a very strong emphasis on sanitation. We have a crew that scrubs down all the public surfaces regularly and makes sure all the plumbing is in working order. Two, and you might not believe this, but we have quite the medical wing."

"If you told me that when I walked in here and just saw the crazy marketplace, I wouldn't have even dreamed of it. But after seeing the power hub and the kitchen and everything, I would have to give you the benefit of the doubt."

"Glad to have it, Mik. There's someone I want to introduce you to later if you don't mind. Filip told me about your supplantation. You were in the Army, right?"

"Yeah."

"He told me about the experiment. What you did for your father and your country. And now he says it's the reason they're hunting you down. Makes no damn sense to me. It's bad enough that they don't take care of you after, but to—" Jade paused and regained the composure she was starting to lose. "We have a number of vets down here, too. I'm sure you'll get a chance to meet them if you want. You mind telling me about what happened? What was the experiment? It's all right if you're not comfortable."

Mik shook his head and waved his hand dismissively. "It's fine. If Filip trusts you, I'd be a fool not to. I had no idea what the supplantation was gonna be beforehand, but it turned out they were kind of resurrecting the 121st recon division. That was the one that started the whole thing back in the day, you know, the fruit bat echolocation squad that captured Hans Schlemmer."

"Oh, yeah, of course. That was the beginning of everything. Dr. Larry Needleman. Going under the needle. Crazy."

"Yeah, so this time, they were trying a new supplantation. Pit viper genes."

"Pit viper? Why?"

"I don't know if you can see it, but—" Mik pointed to the freckle-like mark on his chin. Jade leaned in to inspect it. "This little thing is a pit organ. Allows me to kind of see infrared light, heat signatures. It's not quite vision. It's hard to explain."

"Wow, that little thing," Jade said. "You can hardly notice it."

"Yeah, so they created a new company under the 121st. You can probably guess at the name, Viper Company. Eighteen of us all with the same supplantation. We were sent out to China to scout a compound they said had WMDs." Mik sighed. "I'd rather not get into the details, but I was the only one who made it back home."

"I'm sorry, Mik. Truly."

"Thanks."

"Like I said, though, there's someone I want to introduce you to. I know you have a complicated past with supplantation, to say the least, but I don't know, if you have any questions about it, he could be the one to answer them."

"Yeah, to be honest, I've come to a peace with it. Despite everything that happened, it did pay for my father's medical bills for a while, and it's gotten me out of a couple of tight spots. Sometimes I wish I never joined up to begin with, but I'm not really the type of person to sit around and regret everything. Life goes on, I guess."

"I understand. Listen, is there anything I can help with? Show you around some more?"

"No, it's okay. I appreciate everything you're doing for me. I'm probably just going to explore on my own a bit if that's all right. Say, any idea when Filip is gonna be back?"

"Of course, this is your home now, for better or worse. I'm not sure when he'll be back, though. He didn't say. I'll leave you alone for a bit. Give you a chance to catch your breath. By the way, dinner's at six." Jade smiled and put out her hand. Mik took it in his, and Jade put her other hand on top. "If you need anything, Mik, anything at all, please let me know."

Mik smiled back. "Will do."

CHAPTER 35
SPECIAL GUEST

"This is Speedy Powers, and I'm coming right at you, Chicago, with another edition of *The Power Hour*! The word on everyone's tongues these days is *supplant*. With the Killer Frog on the loose and seemingly murdering at will, demonstrations throughout metropolitan Chicago have ramped up to a fervor. Reports of violent clashes between noble anti-supplantation protesters and radical pro-supplantation groups have dominated the headlines. While supplanting has long been discouraged, many are now calling for the outright criminalization of supplanted people in general. I, for one, am tired of hearing about the innocent victims of the Killer Frog, a monster who uses his supplanted genes to commit unspeakable acts on poor young women. I stand behind these protesters, and I wholeheartedly support the criminalization of supplanted people. Enough is enough, and I encourage all my amazing and loyal viewers and listeners to do the same. Humanity is for humans, not for these creatures! Now a word from our sponsors, Oasis. Bringing hope to a struggling world.

"And we're back. Thank you to all our sponsors who make *The Power Hour* possible. We have a very special guest here today. He's one of the leaders in charge of the great state of Illinois. Please welcome our governor, Bill Peters!"

"Thanks for having me, Speedy. Glad to be here."

"Absolutely, governor."

"Please, call me Bill."

"All right, Bill. I couldn't think of a better time to have you on our show than at such a crucial moment in our city's history. I'd like to get right down to business, so our audience can get as much power in their hour as possible. Now, as we all know, much of the public sentiment is pushing toward stricter regulations concerning supplantation and supplanted people. Meanwhile, you've long been known as a *live and let live* type of politician. Some might even call you a libertarian—"

"Listen, Speedy, I do believe in basic rights and freedoms for everyone. That's what our great country was founded on, but I'd hardly call myself a libertarian."

"Fair enough, but your voting history clearly points to more of a pro-supplantation stance. You've repeatedly voted for equal rights for supplanted people and stood against anti-supplantation legislation, notably the mandatory installation of gene sensors in corporate districts."

"For one, I respect the deals we made with our corporate partners. They're allowed to run their districts as they see fit, so I would never force them to install gene sensors or anything else, for that matter. I've never wavered on that stance. Secondly, I'd like to address the whole issue of supplantation. You're absolutely correct that I've supported the rights of supplanted people. I've always supported the rights of every man, woman, and child in our entire state. But I condemn anyone using their supplanted genes to commit crimes against the people of this great city."

"Duly noted, but I'm sure my audience wants to ask you one thing. What do you have to say concerning the rumors swirling around that you're involved in some sort of military supplantation project?"

"Just that, Speedy: they're rumors. Nothing more. I'll admit that I was involved in preliminary discussions in the past about such a project. I mean, we owe it to those troops who captured Hans Schlemmer back in '43. But I was merely investigating the possibility of that sort of project should the need arise when our country is threatened. Any current project, though? Absolutely not."

"Well, governor, ah, Bill, you not so long ago put a message out there that you, and I quote, 'support the exploration of our scientific frontiers, in technology, defense, medicine, and even gene supplantation.' What do you have to say about that? Don't you think gene supplantation is simply immoral and wrong?"

"Well, Speedy, let me answer your questions one at a time. In terms of the message I was trying to convey, I stand by that. I think it would be pretty short-sighted to all-out condemn an entire field of research when it could hypothetically lead to some sort of benefit in the future. To your other question, yes, I do believe going through illegal gene supplantation is wrong. Trust me when I say that's not the easiest thing to admit. I've always been a governor who's valued the freedom of the people. But in the light of current events, that answer is quite clear to me. Illegal gene supplantation is wrong."

"As governor, what do you say to the people who are suffering at the hands of the Killer Frog? What do you say to their mothers and fathers? Their sisters and brothers?"

"Like I said before, I condemn anyone using supplantation to commit crimes against their fellow man."

"That's it? What about justice for these poor families? What will you do about apprehending this monster and putting him away for good? Will you pledge your assistance?"

"I feel like I'm under fire here, Speedy, and I'd like to put this all to rest. We're all on the same page here about the senseless crimes occurring in Chicago. I *will* be pledging my assistance. Of course, I will. I will be allocating special reserve funds to the Chicago Police Department and the state troopers to apprehend this criminal. New equipment, more men. And I encourage the corporate district owners to do the same for their law enforcement and public safety officers."

"Why won't you call him what he is, a monster? The Killer Frog?"

"I'm not here to sensationalize the facts, Speedy. I'm here to explain my position and do my best as governor to make sure the people of Chicago and all of Illinois are safe."

"When the Killer Frog is caught, will you call for the death penalty?"

"I will leave it to our fair and qualified judges and jurors to come up with a decision for sentencing."

"I have to say, Bill, I'm a bit disappointed with your lack of conviction in this matter. Why won't you call him what he is and condemn him to die?"

"People of Chicago and Illinois, I, Bill Peters, governor of Illinois, pledge all the necessary help to capture and punish the Killer Frog. He must be stopped. He's a monster, and he must be punished accordingly for his crimes. I want to make sure, Speedy, that your audience understands that I do have the conviction to put this man away. I will do my best."

"Thank you, governor, ah, Bill. My audience desires justice above all else. It's about time we had someone in a position of influence willing to come out and say it in plain English for everyone. You heard it here first, folks. Governor Bill Peters will do his best to capture the Killer Frog and bring him to brutal, swift justice. I want to thank him for coming on our show, and as always, thanks to everyone for watching. I'm Speedy Powers. And this was *The Power Hour.*"

CHAPTER 36
MOSQUITO BITE

Last week was just simply glorious, and this week had been shaping up just fine as well. That is until Governor Bill Peters went on *The Power Hour* and said to the whole world that he was going to help track down the Killer Frog and bring him to justice. That didn't make him happy at all. In fact, it made him angry. Very angry. And when he got that way, there was no real accounting for what might happen.

When he got bored, the urge slowly returned. It was like a mosquito bite, where, no matter how much you scratched, the itch would come back stronger, begging for more scratching, more and more until the skin was raw and bleeding, and the only thing that dulled the itching was the sharp, sweet pain of destruction. The only thing that he could do that would cause him that sort of pain along with that intoxicating relief was to go through his little ritual. The choosing of the target was exciting, but it barely whetted his voracious appetite, an amuse-bouche to a grand banquet. The hunt was even more glorious. The talk, the games, the flirty gestures that mimicked reality. Then came the possession, the taking, the violation. It was so beautiful how his prey wilted to his desires, how it succumbed to his poison and his dominance. The extinguishment came next, the taking of not the body, but the soul, the lifeblood. For many who were like him, but entirely unlike him, this was the greatest moment. The moment when he took a living person and ferried her across the barrier of death. It was undoubtedly delicious, but it was not what gave him satisfaction. The only thing that could do that was the crescendo, the blinding orgasm of bliss and salvation, the presentation of his work to the world.

Tonight, though, he was angry. It was not an emotion he felt often. Boredom, yes, accompanied by those great urges and pure and utter euphoria from completing his rituals. But in general, he had little to be angry about. His life had afforded him the comfort and freedom to listen to and satisfy those urges, and he could only imagine what it would be like if he could not. But tonight, the anger coursed through him, and it was all-encompassing as if his hand touched a hot stove, but he couldn't lift it up until the burning consumed all of him.

He couldn't sit still any longer. He left his pristine, palatial house in demonic haste, and he bounded down the streets of Oasis District. Tonight, he appreciated nothing of its luxury and splendor. His vision was tinged blood red, and his mouth was dry, so dry that he felt like he couldn't remember the taste of water. He kept a torrid pace as the buildings and streets passed him by. He could hear the labored inhales and exhales of his burning lungs, but he was entirely undisturbed by it. He had hoped, deep in his mind, that this would remedy some of the excruciating anger, but it did nothing. So, he continued, past block upon block until he ended up in Tem Tem District. Normally his target selection was meticulous, driven by primal desires. Age, gender, and hair and skin color, all things that mattered so dearly to him. But that was when he was bored, and the urge returned. Tonight, he was purely angry, and he had no desire to spend valuable time choosing his next victim, not to mention the studying and planning.

He was moving so quickly that he almost missed him. Against the side of an old restaurant to his left was an old man huddled in a worn blanket, gently coughing and quietly humming a tune to an unknown song. When he slowed down, the old man noticed and called out. "Hey, man!"

He turned to him. His piercing blue eyes belied vision still muddied by anger. He tried to focus on the old man and said nothing.

"Hey, man!" the old man repeated. "Why're you just standing there? Come over here!"

Perhaps this would help. Maybe, just maybe, it would temper the rage. At least for a little while.

"Come over here, man! Could you help me out?"

He started to feel the burning of his lungs now that he stopped and turned his attention to something else. It was almost pleasant in that it took just a touch off his fury.

"Are you just gonna stand there, man? C'mon, please? Could you help me out?"

Yes, perhaps this would help. He walked over to the man, slowly, cautiously. He was not afraid. He was never afraid. But his mind was attempting to weigh his next moves, and the thought process was still so very clouded.

"Hey, wow, you finally heard me. Thanks, man. Hey, could you help me out?"

He reached into his pocket and pulled out a small handful of shiny coins. He reached out toward the old man, his palm upturned. The coins glimmered in the light of the streetlamp.

"Hey, man, do you have more than that? C'mon, please? Could you help me out? Just a little more?"

He retracted his arm and reached his hand back into his pocket. He pulled out his wallet. He sifted through it and took out a few crisp bills. He extended his arm again, once again his palm upturned. This time, the old man reached out in kind. Their hands met as the old man took the money. He flipped through the bills. All hundreds.

"Hey, man, thanks. You really helped me out."

He stood there watching the old man smiling at his new small fortune.

"Hey, man, what are you still doing here?"

He didn't move. He just watched.

"Hey, man, I don't need your help anymore, got it?"

He didn't move.

"Hey, man, get outta here, okay? I'm all set, man. I don't need your help!"

He just watched.

"Hey, man—" the old man stumbled over his words. "What's going on?"

The veil of anger started to lift.

"What'd you do to me, man? I don't feel so good."

He breathed deeply of the cool night air, fueling his empty, burning lungs.

"I don't—" The old man wobbled and fell to a knee on the pavement with a loud crack. "Ahh—"

He closed his eyes, his senses of smell and taste returning.

"Man, I—" The old man shivered and collapsed to the ground, his eyes staring up at him.

He opened his piercing blue eyes and looked down at him. When the old man finally stopped breathing, he did not feel joy or satisfaction. Nor did he feel the urge to complete the ritual. He only felt a bit of relief as his anger was partially abated. His hand was still stuck to the stove, but someone had turned down the temperature. The burning was at a simmer. This would have to do for tonight. But tomorrow, the anger would come back violently, and he would have to do something to get rid of it for good.

CHAPTER 37
CHOW TIME

It was a damn tight fit. They weren't lying. Jose and Sean shared a small cell in C block, and the place was crawling. The waiting was torturous, and that wasn't helped by the constantly high volume of the other prisoners. Some were new arrivals like them, but mostly, they were men who were already serving time there. A new batch of inmates was always a cause for mock celebration, and today was no different. It didn't matter that they were only supposed to be there for a few days for the vaccinations. The veterans always loved messing with the newbies. They had heard all the jeers and insults as they were walked to their cell, but now it had devolved into a mess of voices and sounds.

An alarm blared. It would have normally jolted Jose to attention, but it only added to the cacophony filling his ears.

"Chow time! Get your asses up!" a guard yelled, and everyone quieted down dramatically. Jose almost laughed at the change of atmosphere. The hierarchy was clear. He and Sean stood up out of their beds and walked to the front of their cell.

"Shit, I could eat," Sean said.

"Truth; me too," Jose replied. "All this sitting around has made me fucking starving."

"What you think? Prime rib? Side of mashed potatoes?"

Jose smiled. "Man, I'll be happy with something that doesn't resemble what I did in the bathroom this morning."

"You're a gross mothafucka. Anyone ever tell you that?"

"Yeah, my ex."

Sean laughed. "Yeah, I bet she did. Nice girl too, huh. You probably go for them twisted ass bitches."

"The heart wants what the heart wants." Jose winked at him.

Another alarm sounded, this time a loud buzz, and the cell gates slid open. The guard was standing a few cells down from theirs. "Get your asses out of the cell and into line. If you don't move your feet, you don't get to eat. Let's go!" With that, Jose and Sean shuffled into line and quickly started the slow march to the mess hall. They poured in, along with the rest of the prisoners, and lined up to get their food. They were basically being pushed by the men behind them, so they didn't have to think about where to go. They picked up their plastic trays, and when it was their turn, they placed them on the metal rail in front of the kitchen. An entirely disinterested prisoner wearing a hairnet unceremoniously dumped a chunk of meatloaf on their platters, followed by one ladle each of steamed corn and mashed potatoes. They had to quickly pick up their trays again as they were hurried from behind and exited the tray line.

Jose scanned the mess hall for empty seats and found stools near the end of a long metal table that was already half-filled with inmates. "Follow me. I see a place that's not gonna be too close to anyone." He and Sean walked over there and placed their trays down and sat. "Looks like you got those mashed potatoes you wished for."

"Yeah, but this mothafucka don't look like prime rib."

Jose cut a piece of meatloaf with his fork and held it up with a disgusted look on his face. "No, I don't think it is."

"Yeah, the moment you think maybe somethin' good is gonna happen, they just shove it in your fuckin' face. That's what prison's designed to do, man. Fuck with you until you just shut the hell up and do what they tell you without even thinking. And that's when they fuckin' have you."

"You don't have to keep telling me that, you know. I've been in here almost as long as you have."

Sean smiled. "Yeah, just don't forget it, though. They're always just fuckin' with your head. Don't ever believe 'em."

"Don't worry. I never do."

Sean seemed satisfied enough with that answer because he dove into his unappealing meal as if it were that very prime rib he had wished for. Jose joined him. He was suddenly hungry despite himself, and the food smelled a hell of a lot better than it looked. They tore through the meal and were on the last few bites when Jose felt a hard tap on his shoulder. He turned in his stool and looked up. A large man, with sharp features and a completely shaven head, was accompanied by three others. Jose squinted. "Hey, guys, can I help you?"

"What's goin' on?" Sean chimed in, holding a fork with the last piece of meatloaf still on it.

The large man folded his arms across his chest. "We just wanted to welcome you fellas to our little neck of the woods."

"Oh, I appreciate that," Jose said. "I was starting to feel a little homesick."

Sean leaned over the table and whispered to Jose. "These mothafuckas are fuckin' with you, man. They ain't trying to welcome shit."

The large man laughed. "Ain't that just the thing? Whispering sweet nothings into your ear. I know a lot of fellas who would like that."

"Listen, man," Jose responded. "That's cool. I've got no problem with anyone's preferences. In fact, I never understood the obsession over it in the prison system. Always behind the times in here, huh?"

Sean grimaced. He whispered again. "What the fuck you doing, man? You tryin' to get us into a fight? Shit, we're only here like two fuckin' days."

Jose nodded at Sean. "Fair enough," he said and turned back toward the large man and his friends. "Listen, guys; we appreciate the welcome. We really do. But if it's all the same, I'm not quite done with my meal here." The large man said nothing and unfolded his arms. He smiled wide, showing a row of broken yellow teeth. Jose turned back toward the table and picked up his fork to eat. It was almost to his mouth when he felt his abdomen slam against the edge of the table. His face almost ended up in the remnants of his meal. He dropped his fork, and it clattered onto the table, flipped over, and fell to the floor. The wind was forced out of his lungs, leaving him gasping for air.

He turned around, still trying to get his wind back, when a right hook smashed against the side of his face. His vision blurred, and his equilibrium spun, but he recovered quickly, and his wind returned. Sean was already out of his seat, running to engage one of the large man's friends. Jose stood up and brought his hands up to protect his face. He successfully dodged a looping haymaker and responded with a left jab and a straight to the large man's nose. It immediately started bleeding. The man bared his yellow teeth and pressed the attack with another haymaker. Jose ducked under it and tackled the man with a burst of energy, slamming him to the ground. He got on top of him and rained down punches and hammer fists, his adrenaline fueling the assault. Sean was busy wrestling against the wall with the other inmate, each of them holding on to the other's shirt. Jose grinned devilishly as he continued to punish the man, but he suddenly felt a jarring sensation at the back of his head. His vision danced again, and he immediately felt like vomiting. He felt another blow to the back of his head, and he saw blackness for a few seconds before slowly returning to consciousness. He rolled over onto the floor, covering his head with his hands when he heard it in the back corners of his mind.

Alarms. Blaring loud above the chants of the inmates in the mess hall and above his threatening dive into oblivion. "Stop now, you pieces of shit!" A guard bellowed. "Everyone get on the fucking ground and put your hands on your head. Don't fucking move!" Jose did his best to oblige, trying not to pass out. He glanced over to see Sean and the other inmate with their hands locked behind their heads, staring angrily at each other.

Guards surrounded them. One of them pulled Jose roughly up to his feet, and he tried to maintain his balance on shaky legs. The guard spoke loudly to him from point-blank range. "If you weren't here for a vaccination, I'd throw you in the fucking hole. Now, move your ass. Back to your cell." Jose was half-pushed back to his cell, with Sean being hurried along behind him.

"I need to see a doctor," Jose said, his eyelids drooping. "I think I have a concussion."

"You should have thought about that before you got yourself into a fight in my prison. Count yourself lucky that we're under strict orders to keep you lot in your assigned cells, or you'd find yourself feeling a hell of a lot worse than you do now." With that, the guard pressed a button, closing the cell doors behind them. Jose collapsed onto his bed.

"You all right, man?" Sean stood over him, clearly concerned.

"I'll be fine. Thanks for getting my back out there."

"Shit, you know I will. You gross mothafucka."

Jose tried to laugh, but his ribs, and everything else for that matter, hurt him too much to do so. He closed his eyes, feeling the room spin, but quickly found a restful sleep.

CHAPTER 38
ZIGZAGGING

"Quit your whining, Ollie. The bleeding stopped hours ago."

"I'm just saying it kinda sucks that I can't even watch a video or anything while we're just sitting around."

"We're not just sitting around. We've been waiting for it to get dark enough to make our move."

"It's already dark."

Zen had been thoroughly entertained by the banter between Filip and Ollie that she didn't need any other distractions. She nodded at Filip. "I think he might be right, Filip. It does look pretty dark outside, and you said that we couldn't just wait for the men to show up again."

Filip cleared his throat and nodded. "Yes, it's dark enough now." He turned to Ollie. "I only listen to people when they aren't being selfish."

Ollie shrugged and relented. "Fine, I'm sorry. But I want to go meet up with Mik. This is all just crazy."

"Good, yes; that's the plan." Filip slowly rose from his seat and stretched out his stiff back. "Are you both ready? Make sure. I don't want anyone slowing us down."

"If anything, you'll—" Ollie started but stopped when Filip glared at him. "Never mind. Yeah, I'm ready."

Filip turned to Zen. "And you? Are you ready to make a run for it?"

Zen nodded. "I got some practice in earlier. I'm good to go."

"All right, both of you. Follow me, and stay on my tail. I know the best route to get there, and we can't afford to get split up."

They exited the back door of the shop, the same door that Zen ran through at the behest of Filip. Filip was first, followed by Zen and Ollie closely behind. The night was cool with a slight breeze, the perfect sort of night for a beer or margarita on an outdoor patio. Zen felt the hairs on her neck stand up and goosebumps form along her arms. She tried to tell herself it was just the cold. The repartee inside the shop allowed her a momentary reprieve, but now, the fear came rushing back.

"Stay close and stay quiet," Filip whispered. They stealthily moved along the one-way street, crouching behind the trucks that were parked alongside. When they reached the corner, Filip held his hand up as an order to stop. He quickly peered around the building and gave the go-ahead. They walked along the sidewalk, adjusting their stances to blend in a little better. Most of the shops were closed, but there were still a few convenience stores and late-night eateries open in the area, so they weren't totally alone. They walked for a few blocks down the street until Filip gave the signal to move into an alleyway. "If we can avoid the roads, we will," he said. "Don't worry. I know where we're going." Zen nodded. Ollie looked a little less convinced.

The going was slow. The distance to the abandoned Division station wasn't too far as the crow flies, but they were zigzagging through alleyways and quiet back roads. So far, there was no sign of the men who were looking for them. The night was quiet and growing emptier and stiller as the minutes passed. The breeze had stopped, and the air took on a stagnant warmth. Zen felt sweat begin to trickle down her neck. She tried to tell herself it was just the heat. When they reached another intersection, Filip gave the stop signal once again. He turned around. "We're almost there," he whispered, between somewhat labored breaths. "It shouldn't be more than five or ten minutes. Keep your eyes open and stay quiet."

They continued until they could see, in the distance, the border between Tem Tem District and the downtown area still controlled by the city government. They ducked down an alley to the left and walked until it led into a larger side street. Filip stopped at the corner and turned around. "Down this road, about five blocks is the fence opening that will allow us to get to the station. We're almost there. Don't do anything stupid. We need to move quickly but quietly. Now, once we're inside the abandoned area, we should be safer. I've hardly even seen anyone patrolling in there. But it's a straight shot to the fence from here on out. So be wary and be watchful." Zen and Ollie nodded. "Okay?" Filip apparently wanted a verbal response. They responded with affirmative whispers. "Good. Now we go."

They scurried down the street, making their steps as light as possible while maintaining a near jog. Even at this pace, time seemed to stretch, each block longer than the last as the fence got ever so slowly closer. Four blocks, three blocks, two.

"*There!*" The shout rang out into the stillness of the night, piercing Zen like a dagger. "Over there! I see them!" She turned her head for just a moment while running and saw them. Four men. It was dark, but she knew in her heart exactly who they were.

"Go ahead!" Filip said urgently. "You two are faster than me. You can outrun them."

"Hell no," Zen said. "We are not leaving you behind after what you've done for me. For us."

"Yeah," Ollie said. "No way, Filip."

"Run, you idiots," Filip growled. "The opening is just ahead. You can see it on the fence to the right. Go to the sign for the Division station, move the concrete blocks out of the way and go down until you see a maintenance closet door with a small helix on it. Now go, and stop arguing with an old man."

"Please, Filip," Ollie cried.

"Go!" Filip stopped running and turned around. Zen and Ollie slowed down but continued running; their heads turned back to Filip. The men drew closer.

Zen looked ahead and scanned the fence for the opening and found it off to the right. "There it is. Ollie, we have to get through."

"We can't just leave Filip like that. They're gonna kill him."

"You heard him. They'd kill all of us if we stayed. We don't have weapons." Zen and Ollie arrived at the opening and crouched down to get through, making sure their clothes didn't get snagged on the severed chain links. They turned around again and looked back toward Filip. The men were there in front of him with guns pointed squarely at his head.

Zen and Ollie stayed low to the ground. In the darkness, it was anyone's guess whether the men could see them or not. "Hands up!" one of the men yelled. "Where are your friends?" Filip put his hands up but said nothing. "Tell us where they are, and we won't have to shoot you." There was a pause that seemed to hover in the darkness.

"C'mon, Filip," Ollie whispered to no one in particular. "Don't do this, you old bastard."

"One last chance," the man said. "Tell us where the fuck they are, and you don't die in the street. Your call."

"All right, all right," Filip said. "I'll tell—" A massive plume of smoke burst forward from his mouth. The almond smell that Zen had noticed on him earlier permeated the air. The plume engulfed the men. She could hear them coughing and hacking and gasping.

"What the fuck was that?" Ollie asked, his face a picture of shock.

"I have no goddamn idea," Zen said, then thought for a moment. "What the hell just happened?"

The plume of smoke dissipated. The men were lying on the ground, shuddering and gasping for a moment, and then completely still and quiet. Filip was standing there, slowly lowering his arms to his sides.

"Holy shit," Ollie said. "Holy shit, holy shit."

Filip turned and walked toward them. When he got closer, Ollie blurted out, "What the fuck was that? What did you just do to those guys?"

Filip put up his hand in a stop gesture and sighed. "I had hoped it would never come to this. Come, follow me. I'll tell you while you're moving the blocks." He crouched through the opening, and the three of them headed to their destination. As Zen and Ollie started preparing their entrance down to the abandoned subway station, Filip spoke. "I wanted to go my entire life without needing to use it."

"Use what?" Ollie asked impatiently. "What are you talking about?" Zen motioned for him to stop talking.

"I was very reluctant for a long time. Even though I was past the age of fathering children, the very idea of supplantation always bothered me. Not for others, but for myself. But I knew that one day the Haven would be threatened, and I would be called upon to help save it. Unfortunately, that time has come. Ten years ago, I went to the supplanter in the Haven. He's a very old man now, but he is still there. He had compiled genes from thousands of different species. Although I could choose anything, I decided on one that could truly help defend us."

"Which one?" Ollie asked, unable to remain entirely silent.

"The dragon millipede. They have a gland that allows them to breathe out a burst of hydrogen cyanide gas."

"Did you just say cyanide?"

"Cyanide! Almonds!" Zen finally made the connection in her head. "I remember reading about cyanide smelling like almonds."

"Yes, cyanide," Filip said. "Anyway, I figured the small price of smelling like almonds would be worth it if I ever needed to use it."

"Holy shit," Ollie said. "Never knew you were supplanted."

"Now, you know. Let's go. You've moved enough blocks. Let's get to the Haven before the night's over."

CHAPTER 39
SOMETHING IN COMMON

"Hey, new guy, pass the beer pitcher would ya?" A man wearing a tank top and covered in grease beckoned impatiently. Mik pushed the nearly full container across the table.

"Don't mind him," Jade said. "Caleb can't be bothered to remember people's names—" She raised her voice for dramatic effect "—or *wash up* before coming to *dinner*."

Caleb smiled. "You know a shower would be a damn waste of time, Jade. Just because you go home and get all cozy doesn't mean I get to punch out. I gotta finish with the auxiliary vents tonight. Plus, I knew his name. Mike, right?" He laughed.

Mik couldn't help but return the smile. He was feeling contentedly stuffed. A whole helping of roasted chicken with a side of grilled peaches did wonders after so many days where he didn't know which way was up. He now understood why Jade had been so adamant about everyone eating dinner together. You got to know everyone and how each person had their role to fill in keeping the Haven going.

Caleb poured a beer for himself and grabbed Mik's glass and poured him one as well. "Welcome to the hole in the ground, Mik!" He raised his own glass in the air.

"Thanks, Caleb." He raised his as well, and Caleb clinked them together, perhaps a bit too hard. No beer was spilled, however, so no harm done. He drank it as quickly as he could, which was slower than his last glass. He felt the walls of his stomach tightening under the strain of excessive food and drink. He brought his hand to his face and burped as quietly and politely as possible. It helped a little. "Caleb, Jade, I think it might be time for me to head back to my room. I feel like I'm about to explode."

"Nonsense," Caleb said. "Stay for another."

"Thanks, but I don't think it'll fit."

"Suit yourself."

Mik grinned. "See you later, Caleb."

Jade stood up. "Mik, how about I walk you back? In case you fall over and actually do explode."

Mik laughed, but it only served to put more pressure on his stomach. "Sure." They left the cafeteria and started walking back to the residential complex. "Caleb didn't bother me, you know."

"I know," Jade responded. "It was just a good opportunity to give him shit about coming to dinner without cleaning himself up."

"I guess I can't blame you on that one. He *was* a little ripe. Smelled kinda like what you want the vents to take out of—"

"Jade! Jade!" A young woman was yelling. Mik could see her running toward them. She stopped and caught her breath for a second. "Jade, Filip's back!" Mik's eyes lit up. *Hell yes.* He was worried that Filip might never return. Their talk and goodbye were almost too perfect. It crossed his mind that it could be the last time they ever said anything to each other because it was just so damn heartfelt.

"Mik, you wanna—"

"Yep." Mik answered the question before Jade could ask it. They followed the young woman in the other direction, past the cafeteria, the sprawling marketplace, and finally to the entrance of the Haven, just inside the doors of the old maintenance closet.

Filip was there talking to a couple of people. *Was that—yes! It was Ollie!* Ollie was looking around, completely dumbfounded, his eyes wider than Mik thought possible. When his eyes met Mik's, the biggest shit-eating grin came over his face.

"Hey, Ollie. What in god's name are you doing here?"

"Oh, you beautiful son of a bitch," Ollie responded and ran over. "First, what the hell is this place, and second, Filip told me everything. Why didn't you tell me that you were supplanted? And you're in this Haven place in an old subway tunnel because men with guns were chasing you. And now we're all here. Plus, some girl ran into our shop because she was being chased by the same people you were. Then

Filip ripped the HUDPhone out of my head. Please tell me he wasn't messing with me, and he actually removed yours too. Then we were sneaking all across goddamn Chicago to get here and guess what, the damn men with guns showed up. I thought we were all dead until Filip blew deadly almonds out of his mouth or whatever so we could escape." He doubled over, trying to catch his breath.

"Relax, man. I only understood about half of that. Do you want a beer? Maybe then you can tell me more slowly about what happened."

"Hell yes, I want a beer. I don't think I've ever had such a good excuse to drink. Not that I've ever needed one."

"All right, come with me. The cafeteria has plenty. Say, who's the girl? Did she come with you?"

"Did you say cafeteria? Jesus. This whole bazaar here is, well, friggin'—bizarre. What else is here?"

"I have a lot to show you. You didn't tell me who the girl was."

"Oh, do you need me to talk to her for you? Break the ice?" Ollie winked. "She was the one who ran into our shop. Men were chasing her. Name's Zen. Apparently, the same people who were after you. Not that I knew anyone was after you until Filip told me. You guys really kept me out of the loop, huh? Was that why you ran like a psycho out of Old Tom's last week?"

"No, not at all. I didn't know what the hell was going on that night. I saw a guy staring at me in the bathroom, and I just freaked out. Next thing I know, I went to work, and Filip started telling me about the men who are after me and that we have to come here. I'm barely ahead of you, man."

"You *are* supplanted, though, right?"

"Yeah, sorry I never told you. Just didn't know what you'd think."

"Filip said he didn't know if I was trustworthy. Did you feel that way too? If you did it for your father, that's pretty badass. Ah, it hurt me to say that."

"Thanks, Ollie. And no way. I told him I trusted you completely."

Ollie seemed satisfied. "So, you wanna meet her? You two clearly have plenty in common."

"Um, sure, but didn't you want that beer?"

"It can wait a few minutes."

Mik and Ollie walked over to where Zen and Filip were talking with Jade. Filip finally seemed to notice Mik. "Mikolaj, my boy. How are you?"

"Glad you're back, Filip. I was worried I'd never see you again."

"I told you I'd be back soon. Now, who's the one who doesn't trust?"

"Yeah, yeah. Well, either way, I'm glad you're here. Do you have any more of an idea of what's going on? And what's this I hear about you blowing almonds on people? Is that just Ollie being nuts or what?"

"Ollie can't keep his mouth shut. That's what I was worried about. I'll tell you about that later. I'd like you to meet someone." Filip turned around. "Zen? Come here. I want you to meet Mikolaj. Mik."

Mik looked at Zen and held out his hand. "Nice to meet you, Zen."

"You too, Mik." Zen took Mik's hand. "Filip told me a lot about you. About your service, what you did for your dad. And apparently, the same people are chasing both of us."

"Sounds like we have something in common." Mik immediately regretted saying that since it came off as a bit of flirtation. "Why are they after you? And Filip sure talks a lot for someone who doesn't like other people talking a lot."

Zen smiled. "I'm quite sure I have some information that they don't want me to have. Anyway, I think we can forgive him. He basically saved my life. And Ollie's, too."

Mik sighed and nodded. "And mine. The old man is undoubtedly useful." He tapped Filip, who was now deep in conversation with Jade, on the shoulder. "So, what do we do now?" Zen and Ollie joined Mik in waiting for his answer.

"We all get some rest," Filip responded. "Jade, would you mind showing them where they'll be staying?"

"Of course," she said. "C'mon, guys, let's get you a bite to eat and a nice warm shower."

"We will discuss our next moves in the morning. I think we've all been through too much today to focus on anything else. Zen, Ollie, you need your rest."

"What about you?" Zen asked.

"Yeah, what about you, Filip?" Ollie interjected. "You're an ancient man running through half of Chicago and blowing deadly almond gas. You need rest more than any of us."

"Oh, be quiet, Ollie," Filip said, but his tone was anything but chiding. "I'll be fine. I'm in better shape than you think."

Mik and Ollie shook their heads unbelievingly at the same time. "I think you need some damn sleep," Mik said.

"Bah." Filip waved dismissively. "Fine. I'll get a bit of sleep. See you all in the morning. Perhaps we can find some answers."

CHAPTER 40
SHOTS

JULY 29, 2071

The same alarm blared as last night. Jose was never going to get used to that sound, no matter how often he heard it. He rubbed the sleep out of his eyes and yawned twice. He wasn't sure what time it was, but he knew that it was too damn early. It took him a couple of minutes to feel the bruising on his head and face, but luckily, he didn't have as much of a headache as he had predicted. He was, however, extremely thirsty. He got up slowly and turned on the sink. He put his mouth below the faucet and drank. He couldn't wait to get the vaccinations done so he could go home. Ha, home. Amazing what a shitty prison turns into when you're introduced to a shittier one. Jose and Sean knew what to do. They stood at the door of their cell. Much the same as at dinner time, they were ordered out and shuffled along to their destination. The longtime residents cat-called them all the way. If there was one thing that every prison had in common, it was the abundance of routine.

This time, along with the rest of the inmates that were bussed in with them the day before, they were brought to a large gymnasium. It was almost nostalgic with its hardwood floors and paneled walls. If prisons didn't need to spend money on updates, they surely didn't bother. It was fitted with makeshift white medical tents and plastic partitions. Men and women in white lab coats shuffled around. Jose wasn't sure if they were doing much or just trying to look like they were. The same man who had greeted them outside walked in through the back doors of the gym, still flanked by the men in suits, and moved up to address the inmates.

"I do apologize for all the trouble. I'm aware that the lodging situation is less than ideal, so we are trying to make this process move as quickly as we can. If everything goes smoothly, you should be out of here by tomorrow afternoon and back to your usual, ahem, place of residence. As I mentioned yesterday, I'm Dr. Isaac Cross, and I'm the vaccination coordinator. I'm in charge of making sure that each of you receives your vaccines and that your health and wellbeing are being looked after. You're all in line already, so you've already finished step one!" His attempt at a joke was met with dead silence. "As I was saying, one by one, you will be checking in with me, and I will be assigning you to one of the tents here behind me to receive your shots. Hold on a minute." He walked away for a short time to talk with the men in suits.

Sean whispered to Jose. "What kind of shit is this? We have to be assigned to tents now?"

"Look, man, I don't know. I've seen so much crazy shit in the system that I've long since stopped looking into everything. Maybe it's just so they can do this faster."

"Yeah, *maybe* it's just another way of fuckin' with us."

Dr. Cross returned. "Ah, yes. Sorry about that. You will meet with me, and you'll go to your tent for your shot. Then, you will return to your cell with a special monitoring bracelet so we can measure your vitals and immune response remotely. I apologize in advance. They will be locked onto your wrist; although, I do suppose you're used to that sort of thing by now. So, without further ado, let's begin."

"You heard him, shit birds. Stay in line, and shut your mouths!" the guard nearest to Dr. Cross yelled. "Failure to do so will end badly for you."

"Yes, well—" Dr. Cross grimaced. "Thank you for that, officer. I hope that won't be necessary."

The line moved at a decent pace. Jose could see each prisoner being assigned to a different numbered tent. After fifteen or twenty minutes, it was Sean's turn in front of him. Dr. Cross smiled at him politely. "What's your name?"

"Sean. Sean Teague."

"Ah, yes." Dr. Cross looked down at his tablet. "Danville inmate number 965037. Teague. All right, Mr. Teague, please walk over to tent number five. The nurse there will get you situated and administer the vaccination." Sean looked like he wanted to say something but thought better of it and walked over to the tent with a red 5 on a standing placard next to it. "All right, next?" Dr. Cross looked at Jose. "What's your—"

"Gutierrez. Jose. Danville Correctional Center. Inmate number 921065."

"Hmm." Dr. Cross glanced at his tablet briefly. "Good. Tent number two, please."

Jose walked over to the tent, where he was stopped by a woman who asked him to once again confirm his identity. He followed her inside. It contained the same type of chair one would see in any phlebotomy lab and a plastic folding table. On the table was a white cube, perhaps a foot and a half in each direction.

"Please, Mr. Gutierrez, would you have a seat?" The woman placed the tablet she was carrying next to the cube on the table. Jose sat in the slightly reclined seat and stretched his legs out, flexing his calves. It felt good to finally sit down again. The woman donned gloves and wiped his outer shoulder with an alcohol swab. She pressed a button on the side of the cube, and the top raised with a pronounced hissing sound. What looked like smoke or steam billowed from the opening.

"What is that thing for?" Jose asked, quite taken aback. He immediately thought of Sean's notion that they were always messing with your head.

"Oh, I'm sorry about the theatrics," the woman said. "In order for the vaccines to maintain their potency, we have to store them at extremely low temperatures. The syringes are pre-loaded in a bath of liquid nitrogen for easy transport. The evaporation really puts on a show." She giggled. "Nothing to worry about, though. Are you ready?"

"Yeah, I guess." Jose was never one to be afraid of needles. He figured he would have been quite the hypocrite as a heroin dealer. "Let's get it over with."

The woman smiled and took out one of the syringes. The cube automatically closed again with another hiss. She punctured Jose's shoulder and squeezed the plunger, then immediately threw the syringe into a biohazard bin. She took out a clear nano-fiber bandage and placed it over the area. He could immediately feel it tightening and going to work repairing the microscopic damage left by the shot. "You're all set, Mr. Gutierrez," the woman said matter-of-factly. "Please leave through the exit flap of the tent, and a corrections officer will escort you back to your cell."

When Jose got back, the cell was still empty. *Strange*, he thought. *Sean was right in front of me in line.* He sat on the edge of his bed for a few minutes, and then he saw Sean being brought back to the cell.

"Shit, you beat me," Sean said as the cell door opened, and he stepped in.

"Yeah. Probably didn't spend all that extra time crying over the big, scary needle."

"Ha, you mothafucka." Sean laughed. "I asked the bitch in there to stab me twice I liked it so much. See?" He showed Jose the bandages, one on each shoulder.

"The fuck?" Jose's brow furled in confusion. "You serious?"

"Nah, man, what you talkin' 'bout? We got two shots. One for flu and one for corona."

"Huh? I only got one shot. Look!" Jose showed him the single bandage. "You think they forgot to give me one of 'em? That's fucked up."

"Shit, what isn't fucked up in here? Mothafuckas probably did it on purpose just to fuck with us."

"Fuck, now I'm gonna get COVID or something."

"Nah, man, you'll be straight. I'm immune to it now, so I can't give it to you." Sean laughed again. "Man, sometimes you just gotta laugh about all this shit just to stay sane."

"Yeah, easy to laugh when you get both your shots." Jose shook his head. "And what was that shit about the box with the fuckin' liquid nitrogen?"

Sean nodded. Then he slowly smiled. "Fuckin' with your head, of course."

CHAPTER 41
PAUSE THE GAME

Zen woke up with a start. Panic immediately set in when she saw the unfamiliar surroundings. Then the events of last night came flooding back, and she relaxed. The place was unfamiliar indeed, but it was the safest feeling place she'd been outside of her parents' house, and even that felt so very different after the men showed up. She never felt safe with Aiden in Hinsdale, and she never felt safe growing up in Roseland with its gangs and just-a-little-racist police officers. She achingly wondered about her parents. *Would the men come back and hurt them? But it was me they wanted. Maybe there's a way to call them to make sure they're safe.* Her full faculties returned after the flood of waking emotion. She washed up, got dressed, and wound her way out of the residential complex, more than once making a wrong turn.

Just outside the entrance, Mik, Filip, Ollie, and Jade were sitting at a table, talking away. "Hey, good morning," Jade said, the first person to notice Zen.

"Morning. What time is it?"

"It's about ten. We let you sleep a little. I know it's kind of hard to sleep here without any natural light, or darkness, for that matter."

"But you are all up already."

"I've lived here for years," Jade said.

"I'm an old man," Filip added. "I've learned to sleep in just about any circumstance over the years. And I woke up these two lazy bastards only about half an hour ago." Mik and Ollie smirked.

Jade beckoned Zen over. "Come have something to eat. Breakfast will be out here shortly. Figured we could all eat together."

Filip cleared his throat. "And figure out a plan. Any ideas, anyone?"

Mik put his hand up. "Whoa, Filip, relax. How about we get a little food in our bellies before we start all that."

"Yeah," Ollie chimed in. "I haven't even had my coffee yet. Plus, the lack of sunlight is freaking me out a little. I'm not even hungover."

"You get used to it pretty quickly," Mik said.

"We don't have time to waste," Filip said impatiently. "With you two talking about coffee and sunlight, we could have been formulating our plan. Now, Zen, you still have that tablet, yes?"

Zen walked over. "Yeah, still have it in my pocket." She pulled it out and placed it on the table.

"You said it contains encrypted personnel files for Genovas. Potentially some kind of supplantation experiment on prisoners." Filip rubbed his chin. "Jade, we think this is why they were after her. The information she has, and what the tablet might contain."

Jade nodded. "We could bring it over to our tech guys. Have them take a look."

"What about it? What does the experiment have to do with us?" Mik remained skeptical.

"We don't know anything beyond that," Filip responded. "I hope we find some answers. And quickly."

Breakfast arrived at the table. Coffee was poured to the appreciation of many, along with oatmeal, toast, reconstituted scrambled eggs, and thawed frozen fruit. All in all, it was a veritable feast. They all scarfed it down voraciously, and they were done within minutes.

"Follow me," Jade said when the table was cleared. "Let's find out what they can tell us. Zen, don't forget the tablet."

Zen was still so tired that she almost left it on the table when she got up. The coffee hadn't quite kicked in yet. She put it back in her pocket and followed the group, shaking the cobwebs out of her head. They headed down past the cafeteria and kitchen and took a right down a dimly lit hallway of sorts. Lined with steel beams on each side and wires and tubes running along the ceiling, it was almost like an unfinished basement. The hallway opened up into a room that was bathed in the blue-white glow of artificial light. Two men and a woman were staring intently into their personal monitors while a large wall-based unit was mounted in front of them, showing satellite images and maps.

Jade knocked on the open door. "May we come in?"

The woman looked up and nodded. "Of course, Jade. What brings you around here?"

"We have some new friends with us. Mik, Ollie, Zen." She gestured to each of them in turn. "Maria, we were hoping you might be able to help us with something."

"Sure, what's up? These two are just playing games against each other. It only looks like they're hard at work." The two men didn't even acknowledge the callout.

"Zen here has this tablet from work. It contains information about Genovas. A genetic research company, right, Zen?"

Zen opened her mouth. She was suddenly very thirsty. "Ahh, yes, uh huh. We worked with them years back, but I wasn't involved then. I don't know exactly what's happening, but there might be some kind of experiment going on at some prison. That's what we think, at least. I looked through the thing, but it was all encrypted or outdated."

Maria didn't take the tablet from her. Instead, she plugged *Genovas* into the internet search engine. "When in doubt, just look it up. Always a good place to start." She scrolled through the information online. "Yeah, genetic research, involved in the infant gene-editing industry, nothing about any prison experiment. The only new info that's up there is this press release about some employee leaving the company."

"Damn," Jade said.

Filip grunted. "We are not off to a good start."

"Who's the employee? Maybe we can look *them* up?" Ollie had moved to the front of the group, mainly fixated on the monitors. Everyone looked at him. "What? What if they're connected to this experiment or something?"

"Can't hurt to look," Jade said.

Maria pulled up the press release. "Okay. This was posted yesterday. Albert Murata, a senior finance officer, has resigned from Genovas today, blah blah, whoa, wait, look at this." She pointed at the screen. "Resigned due to allegations of corporate malfeasance, we've decided not to pursue further charges. Holy shit."

"Goddamn, Ollie," Mik exclaimed. "You just might be onto something here!" He slapped him on the shoulder, which was met with an *ouch* and a smile.

"I'm not just a pretty face, you know," Ollie said.

Filip waved them off. "Anything online about this—"

"Murata." Maria finished his sentence.

"Anything online about him?"

"I'm looking. Not much else on here, really. Pretty strange nowadays to have such a small digital footprint, but then again, when people join these big corporations, they usually have teams that go around and wipe everything online for liability purposes. Can't even find his contact info."

Zen was finally fully awake. "Well, there are personnel files on this tablet. That's what's encrypted. I couldn't look at them, but maybe you guys could."

Maria nodded. "Let me see what we can do. May I?" She put out her hand, and Zen gave her the tablet with assuring nods from Jade and Filip. "Hey, morons, pause the game and help me out here."

"We can't pause it," one of the men answered. The other laughed.

Maria pressed a button, and their monitors went black. "There, I paused it." The men sighed deeply in unison and walked over to her terminal. "We're trying to find information in this tablet. Personnel files are encrypted, and I need you two to undo all that for us." That was answered with a frustrated huff. "Sooner you're done with that, sooner you can go back to shooting each other."

"Thanks for doing this, Maria," Jade said.

"No problem. They need to do an honest day's work for once."

"What do we do now?" Mik asked.

"We wait and stay safe for now," Filip responded. "Nothing else we can do until we have a plan."

"What if they don't find anything on that tablet?"

"Well, we can't just go around trying to stop an experiment we know nothing about, can we?"

"Is *that* the plan? To stop this experiment? How would we do that?

And why? I get that Zen has information they don't want her to have, but it seems pretty insane for us to anything about it."

Zen felt hurt. "I don't know what we should do, but telling me about this experiment is what killed my husband, as much of an asshole as he was. They chased me from my own home because of what he told me and what's on that tablet. I don't expect anyone to do anything, but I need to know why this is all happening."

"I'm sorry." Mik suddenly felt like a petulant child. "I didn't mean to make light of what you've gone through. We just need a decent plan."

"It's all right."

Filip shook his head at Mik, making him feel even worse.

"Got it!" One of the tech guys yelled, almost comically high-pitched.

"You got it?" Maria looked down at the monitor. "You got it. How about that. Unencrypted. All right, go back to your games. But you'd better pause it when I need you again." The two men slinked back to their own terminals, their excitement already clearly gone. "Come 'round, guys." She beckoned everyone over, and they huddled together behind her as she worked through the files. "Okay, here we go. Let's see. James Colson, CEO. Address blanked out, personal phone number, email, financial records, insurance forms. Damn, what kind of company do you work for, Zen? Not everything is available, but this is a hell of a lot of information about a corporate CEO, especially these days."

"I work. Or worked, not sure. For Guardian Hill. We do private security. I'm a lawyer, though, more on the boring stuff like contracts and things. Nothing super interesting, but we have pretty detailed records on some clients out of necessity." Zen laughed suddenly. The sudden burst of relief and purpose quickly brightened her mood. "If I wasn't dying, almost literally, to know what was on this tablet, I'd be a little disappointed with how easy it was for you guys to crack it."

Maria smiled. "They're lazy but good at what they do."

"A lot of that around here," Filip said, eyeing Mik and Ollie intently and then winking at them.

"All right," Maria continued. "Nothing too special in here, but here we go, the file on that Albert Murata fellow. Most of the stuff is blanked out again, but we have an address and phone number. What do you all wanna do?"

"I don't know," Zen said. "All the information on there is like five years old or more, so we don't even know if the number works, but I say we try it. If the experiment really starts this week, and he was let go yesterday? That seems like too much of a coincidence."

Mik nodded. "I agree. We should call him. Nothing to lose, and it's our only option, the way I see it."

Jade looked at Filip. "Gotta say, I agree, too. Filip?" She was met with an affirmative nod and then addressed the group. "Who wants to do the honors?"

"I guess I should," Zen answered. "I have the only in with him, really. I could say something about updating our files and that we need more info or something. It's a long shot, but does anyone have a better idea?"

"All yours." Maria handed her a phone. "Don't worry; the lines here are completely secure. Hardwired in. They can't track us."

Zen wasn't sure if anything could be truly secure, not after her experience at Guardian Hill, but this was worth the risk. She dialed the number.

CHAPTER 42
HELLO?

Albert stared at the cup of coffee in front of him. It had been piping hot when his wife placed it there, but the steam was already subsiding. His wife had taken the kids out into the living room to play and watch some shows and left him in the breakfast nook alone with his thoughts. A patrol car was parked outside, unmarked, because the squeeze on him was unofficial. His internet service and HUDPhone signal were tapped. There was no one he could reach out to for help without immediately alerting those in charge of keeping him quiet. He knew that if his wife and kids left the house, they would be tailed by men watching their every move. When he had told them of that fact last night, there was a lot of crying and yelling, but, in the end, they had decided to stay put for the time being. He had lost his job and potentially his reputation, his pleas had fallen on deaf ears, and here he was, mute to the world.

He sat there until the coffee was too cold to even try, then he picked it up and walked over to the sink to pour it down the drain. He could hear his wife playing with the kids in the other room, but he knew how scared she was, and it made him sick. He sat back down in his seat at the table and put his head in his hands and started to cry. When his HUDPhone started ringing, it barely registered in his mind. He was trying so hard to keep quiet so he wouldn't disturb his family. Then the image popped up, UNKNOWN CALLER, and he stopped crying immediately. His first instinct was to decline the call. To ignore it because there was no hope left. Mr. Colson had ruined him and now watched his every move. Plus, it was probably some spam marketer or worse. He let it ring three times. Then there was just that glimmer that maybe it was someone he could speak to and tell his story. There wasn't much else to lose. Visions of the men who Colson had employed murdering him and his family flashed through his head, but rationally, he knew that the worst had already happened. There was only one option. Answer the call.

"Hello?" Albert felt a mixture of fear, hope, excitement, and trepidation, expecting nothing and everything at once.

"Mr. Murata? Albert Murata?" a female voice questioned on the other end of the line.

"Uh, yes, this is Albert." Talking on the phone was so automatic. "Who's this?"

"Hi, I'm Zen, um, shit," the voice said, followed by fevered whispers. Albert thought he heard *shouldn't use your name* in the background. "I was hoping you could help me with updating some of your information in our systems."

"What? Who are you? What systems?"

There was a long pause. "I work for Guardian Hill, private security. I was hoping you could help me update our information about some current experiments that Genovas is conducting—"

They're testing me, Albert thought. *They're testing me. This is a fucking test. If I say anything, they'll take me away or worse, my wife or kids or all of us. They'll take us away and dispose of us. Loose lips sink ships. They want to know if I'd talk.* He hung up the phone, feeling a wave of relief as he did so. *Yes, that was a test, and I passed. There's no reason to do anything to us now.*

The HUDPhone rang again. UNKNOWN CALLER. *What are they doing to me? I already passed the test. Why are they doing this again? Unless—unless this wasn't a test. You're a fool to get your hopes up.* He ignored the call. Three rings. Four. He couldn't say exactly why, but he picked up the call just before it went to voicemail.

"Hello?"

"Hi, Albert?"

"Is this a test?"

"Huh?"

"Is this a test? Are you testing me to see if I'll say something about the experiment? What are you gonna do to me?"

"Um, Mr. Murata? What test? What do you mean?"

"Oh, you know! If I tell you about the experiment, you'll do something to me or my family!"

"What? Men were chasing me because I found out about an experiment that Genovas is doing, and I need your help!"

Oh, man, they're good, he thought. *They weren't just going to test me by simply asking. They're going to pretend that they need my help. And what's this about men chasing them?*

"I'm not saying anything. You're not just content to let me sit here trapped in my own house, you actually want—"

"Mr. Murata, Albert, please! I don't know what you're talking about with me testing you or something. I need your help. My husband was a prisoner, and he told me about some experiment that was happening with gene supplantation. Run by Genovas. And—"

Wait a minute. He shook his head as if he had just been in a stupefied haze. *Am I just being paranoid? Maybe this isn't a test after all. But test or not, they're listening. This is my only chance to tell someone what I know. Maybe it's worth the risk. Maybe, just maybe, they can help before it's too late.*

"Okay. Yes. I'm sorry. They're monitoring all my communications, so I have to hurry. Genovas is running an experiment at Stateville Correctional Center. Supplantation research on prisoners. They are calling it Project Manticore. They're testing a new procedure to deliver multiple supplantations on people. You need to hear this. I think they're trying to create super soldiers for the military. Super. Soldiers. They're using prisoners as test subjects without their knowledge. They don't care if they live or die. Everyone's involved. Governor Peters, Army generals, Correcticorp. Help, please! It's already—" The low buzz on the other end of the line went quiet. "Hello? Hello?"

The call ended automatically. Albert sat there at the table. Test or not, those who had tapped his HUDPhone *had* listened, and they had heard everything that he told this Zen person on the other line. He sat there and waited for the men to come inside and take him and his family away to some unknown hell. He knew there would be consequences. But this time, he didn't cry.

CHAPTER 43
ONE THING AT A TIME

"I'm sorry, Zen," Mik said. "I'm sorry for taking it lightly. For doubting just how terrible this is. I keep thinking they won't stoop so low, but I guess I should be realistic about it. They already sent my entire company to their deaths. Didn't hold up their end of the bargain when I got home. Now they're hunting me down years later for no goddamn reason except they want to shore up loose ends. They're hunting you for finding out about it. And now this? Fucking super soldiers? They could kill these prisoners, and for what? To create monsters out of the same kind of men that I called my brothers and send them to kill or die? You're right. We have to stop this. But how? What's the plan now, Filip? Now that we know what the experiment is, where it is. What the hell can we do?"

Filip glanced at Mik sympathetically. "Well, Mikolaj, I understand—"

"We have to save *him* as well," Zen said flatly.

"Hmm?"

"We have to save Mr. Murata. Albert. The guy on the phone. You heard him as well as I did. He could be killed for telling us about this."

"I'm sorry, Zen," Filip said. He gently placed his hand on her shoulder. "We can't do that."

"Why not?" she snapped. "We have his address. Let's go help him!"

"If people are indeed listening to him, it may very well be the same people that are after you and Mikolaj. He knew about the experiment. And now all of us do. They'll be waiting for us to make a move like that. They're probably watching his house right now."

Zen was about to argue then realized that Filip was right. "Fine. We can't save him yet. But what *can* we do?"

"Seriously, Filip, what can we do about this?" Mik asked anxiously. "We can't just go to the press or police, can we? For all we know, they could be involved. Albert said everyone was. The governor, the military, god knows who else. This goes all the way up the chain."

"And the experiment started already," Ollie said. "When the phone disconnected, he said *already*, and I knew what that meant."

Zen started pacing around. "We can't just sit here. I don't know if you all forgot, but we left four dead bodies out there on the street. They're probably looking for us right now. It's only a matter of time before they find the entrance at the subway station."

Mik rested his chin on his fist. "It's not like we can drive down to Stateville and break into the damn prison."

Filip put up his hand, and everyone stopped talking. "We can't save the man on the phone. And we can't just sit here either. Zen, Mikolaj, you're right. We have to do something. But they are looking for us. And likely not just with men anymore. I would assume they've employed Prowler drones with thermal imaging to scan the streets and look inside the buildings. The only reason we made it here is that someone wanted to keep it quiet. If they used the drones before, it would have caused a panic. But now they know that *we* know about everything. And I killed their men. They'll stop at nothing to find us now."

Mik let out an exasperated sigh. "If we can't go outside, what the hell can we—"

"I may have an idea," Jade said.

"For what?"

"For getting out there. For avoiding the drones. And don't worry. I made an announcement telling everyone not to leave the Haven until we are sure there are no drones in the area."

Mik scrunched his eyebrows. "Yeah, I heard. Even if we do get out of here, where would we even go? We can't break into the prison. Are we just going out for a stroll in the hopes we stumble upon something that exposes the whole thing?"

"One thing at a time," Filip said. "Jade, what's your idea for avoiding the drones?"

"Normally, I wouldn't have any idea, but I was talking with Caleb earlier. He's really tight with the guys doing R&D. He said they've been working on ways to avoid detection, to keep the Haven safe from prying eyes. I'm not totally sure of the technology, so don't quote me on it, but he said they came up with a prototype for thermo-reflective shielding. You know those Prowlers work with thermal imaging. Kinda like you, Mik. Anyway, he said they came out with a way of bouncing back thermals, so the drone is blind to anything underneath the shield. It's a way to use the drone tech against them. It's visible to people. He says it looks sort of like an umbrella or tent. But to the drones, it looks like nothing."

"That could work," Filip said. "Very good, Jade. Would you mind talking with Caleb? Seeing how ready they are to put the prototype into action?"

"No problem."

"Before you go, we need a plan. Are we all on the same page that we need to stop this experiment?"

"Yeah, you're damn right," Mik said. "But how the hell are we gonna do that? Even if this thermal shield thing works, where are we gonna go?"

"What he said," Ollie added.

Zen took a deep breath. "We need to help those prisoners, but I need to ask one thing before we go. I don't even know if my parents are okay. I want to talk to them and make sure."

"We can make that happen," Jade said. "Just like we called Albert. On a safe line."

"Once I can do that, I'm on board for whatever you all want to do."

"We need to stop the experiment," Filip said. "But you're right, Mikolaj; we can't just break into prison. But perhaps we can break *them* out somehow. Get the subjects out of there before it's too late."

"How are we gonna do that?" Mik asked.

"I don't know."

"How about we talk with Maria and those tech guys?" Ollie asked. "They figured out that tablet in like two seconds."

Mik's mood brightened a little with the forward motion of plan setting. "Can't hurt, Ollie. See what they can find out. They could at least give us a layout of the prison, maybe blueprints. Plus, we need to know how to get there, and we don't have HUDPhones for GPS anymore."

The group walked back to the tech room, where the two men were hard at work playing against each other in a shooting game, and Maria was aggressively scrolling through files. She looked up as they entered. "Back again so soon? What can I do for you?"

"What information can you get us about Stateville Correctional Center?" Filip asked.

"Are you thinking about—you know what, never mind. I don't wanna know. C'mon guys, stop playing that stupid goddamn game and help us out."

"Zen wants to call her parents," Jade said. "Can she do that now?"

"Yeah, sure thing. Here you go, Zen. Just plug in the number."

Her mom's number was one of the few that Zen knew by heart. There was really no need to remember anything when it was all on her phone, but there had been a time or two that she was stuck at a friend's house and lost her phone and needed to call home for a ride. She dialed the number on the weighty corded phone. Two rings, then three. Zen started to feel sick to her stomach. Then, "Hello?"

"Mom?" Zen's spirits lifted instantly.

"Zen? Is that you? Where are you? What's going on?" Her mom's voice was hurried and breathless.

"I'm fine, Mom. I'm safe."

"Where are you? We tried calling! George, it's Zen. She's safe!" A quiet grunt sounded on the line.

"I can't tell you where I am. Just know that I'm safe."

"What's going on? These men showed up looking for you, and you were gone. We were worried sick." This was followed by a grunt of disagreement in the background.

"I'll tell you everything later, Mom, but I can't say where I am. In case those men are still looking for me. In case they're listening to our conversation."

"What? What the hell is going on, Zen? Honey?"

"Please, Mom, just relax. It's okay. I'm in a safe place, and everything will be all right. Listen, I love you, but I have to go."

"Don't hang up. I love you too. Promise you'll stay safe."

"I promise, Mom. I'll call you later."

"You'd better!"

"Bye, Mom." The call ended. "Thanks for letting me call them, Maria. I'm just so glad they're okay."

"Of course, Zen. Guys, what do you have for me about Stateville?" The two men were busy arguing with each other, most likely about the scores of the last game they played.

"Here," one of them said, and images started populating the main screen on the wall. "Maps. Satellite images. Architectural blueprints. Sewage and sanitation plans. Building contracts. Government prison contracts. Security systems. Power grids. About everything you can think of except this experiment you're all talking about. That's all we could find."

"Is that enough?" Maria asked Jade and Filip. "I can throw all that info on some tablets, and you could look at it."

"That would be perfect," Filip said. "Everything you found. Do you have enough for all of us?"

"I think we can manage that. Give me a few minutes. Where will you all be meeting?"

"We'll meet at the cafeteria. It will give us room to spread out and analyze everything. Does that work for everyone?" Filip was met with sounds of agreement.

"Perfect. I'll bring them out to you when I have them all ready."

"Thank you. It's time we come up with a solid plan."

CHAPTER 44
CUT-RATE BULLSHIT

Jose opened his eyes, sat up at the edge of his bunk, and tilted his neck in each direction, feeling the satisfying cracks of release. "Ahhh." Then he coughed a few times.

"You all right, man?" Sean asked. "How's your head?" He was sitting in his bunk, his back propped against the concrete wall and his feet still under the blankets.

"It's good. How long was I out?" Jose squeezed his eyes shut and opened them a couple of times, trying to acclimate to the lights.

"You passed out like a minute after they locked us back up in here. Your concussion is way worse than you thought. That mothafucka really beat the shit outta the back of your head. No offense, man. I know you were smacking that bitch on the ground. I saw you. Mothafuckin' cheap shots, all it was. I was yelling at the fuckin' guards for a doctor to come see you after you passed out, but they just did their usual shit like their ears just magically stopped working all of a sudden. Mothafuckas. This shit is the same no matter where we go. Told you."

Jose took a few deep breaths to test if anything else was hurting, but it was just his head. *Not like you need that for much*, he thought. "Yeah, man, I didn't blackout. I'm good, though, truth. Just let me sit here for a bit. Any of 'em come by to tell us what the fuck is going on?"

"When I was yelling for a doctor, one of 'em just told me to shut the fuck up and sit fuckin' tight, like I was his fuckin' kid or something. Anyway, I don't think we're doing much until dinner. Hope they let us out to eat. Also, check this shit out. What is with these fuckin' bracelets, right? Checking on our health, like they suddenly give a shit whether we live or die. Not even like one of those old fitness watches, either. Can't even measure my own heart rate." He held his arm up for effect. The watch was all black with a green LED light on the face. "Cut-rate bullshit."

Jose stood up slowly. Waves of dizziness threatened to overcome him, but he steadied himself, shook his head, and found his equilibrium.

"Yo, I saw that shit," Sean said. "Sit your ass back down until that concussion is better."

"Nah, man, I'm good," Jose responded. "Seriously, it was just my blood pressure. It's always been low." He thought that part might be true, but altogether, the statement was patently false. He knew his concussion was a bad one, but he wasn't about to act that way. Not here. Not where all those pieces of shit in the other cells could see him, just waiting for a moment of weakness to attack again later.

"All right, I'm just saying. You're swerving like you just had a few, and I don't see top-shelf whiskey anywhere around here."

"I'm good. Don't worry about it."

"Suit yourself. Maybe I'm just getting dizzy watching you stumble around, but I'm not feeling too fuckin' hot either."

Jose closed his eyes and grabbed onto the bars of the cell door to steady himself. "What do you mean?"

"Shit, I don't know. Just feeling a little off. Can't place it. Not like a stomachache or cramps or anything but feeling something. Started a little while you were passed out on your bed and snoring like a fuckin' jet engine. Now it's worse."

"I snore?"

"Fuck yeah, you snore. I'm just a nice mothafucka, so I never mentioned it before. But damn, you're lucky I'm a heavy sleeper, just saying."

Jose opened his eyes and turned around. The dizziness hit him again and almost brought him to his knees. "I'm good, I'm good," he repeated and sat back down on his bunk.

"I know you're all kinds of fucked up," Sean said quietly. "But I know you gotta look tough around here."

"Yeah, just let me chill for a bit."

"You know I got you." Sean adjusted in his seat, trying to get comfortable. "Ah, fuck."

"What is it?" Jose looked at him, but his eyes were threatening to close again.

"Fuck!" Sean yelped. "Shit, it is fuckin' cramps. On my right side. Fuck, they're bad." He gritted his teeth, clearly in pain.

"That time of the month?" Jose was feeling like shit, but he didn't want to let an easy joke pass him by.

"Fuck you, man," Sean grimaced but tried to smile. "It hurts really fuckin' bad." He held his arm across his abdomen.

"You said you wanted prime rib."

"Yeah, no shit, and they gave me fuckin' poison meatloaf. My stomach's used to the finer foods. Caviar, foie gras, whatever the fuck that is, champagne, you know."

Jose laughed. "You've been locked up for how long? You got mules smuggling in Dom Perignon for you?"

"You know it, man. I got connections." Sean laughed but then coughed—a wracking, sharp, heaving cough that had him nearly drooling phlegm. "Fuck, it hurts, man."

"You want me to call a guard?" Jose was getting concerned now. Those coughs looked painful as hell.

"You know what good all that does, man," Sean replied. "They didn't even bring your ass in after you got fucked up. Think they're gonna listen now? Nah, I'm all right. It'll pass."

"You sure? That looked like it hurt."

"It did fuckin' hurt, but they—ahhh, *fuck*!" Sean gripped his right side like a vice.

"Okay, that definitely hurt. I'm calling a guard."

"No, man, they won't do shit." Sean gritted his teeth and breathed a few times, at first shallow then deeper. "Okay, okay." He let out one more breath. "I'm good. Cramp's gone."

Jose shook his head. "I don't know, man. That looked bad."

"It's all good. It passed. How's your head?"

"Still attached. At least, I think so. Been dizzy as fuck, if we're being honest."

"Yeah, no shit. Just take it easy. Last thing we need is—*fuck!*" Sean grabbed the blanket on his bunk with a talon-like grip, making his knuckles turn white.

Jose saw him grab the blanket like he wanted to murder it and noticed that the LED on Sean's watch had turned from green to yellow. "Okay, that's it. I'm calling a guard."

"No, it's nothing, it's—*oh shit!*" Sean doubled over in pain, almost falling off the bunk.

"Guard! Guard! My friend, he's in fucking pain!" Jose got up despite the dizziness and hurried over to the cell door, yelling out into the nothingness beyond. His calls were greeted with a hail of laughter and insults from the other inmates in the block. He turned his head to see Sean attempt to get up and fail, flipping over onto his side on the floor. "Shit. Sean, man, you all right?" He knew he wasn't, but if he could keep him talking, maybe he could help him through this.

"*Aaaagghh!*" Sean's cry of agony was deep and cutting. He crawled on his hands and knees on the floor, shaking with pain.

Jose knelt down and put one hand on Sean's back. "Let me help you up. C'mon, let's get you—guard! *Guard!* Someone fucking help us! He needs a fucking doctor!" The storm of jeers continued to rain down unimpeded. "C'mon, man," he said to Sean. "Let me get you up and back to your bed."

"I can't fucking see," Sean said, shaking his head wildly from side to side. "I can't fucking see anything. I can't—" He jerked forward and heaved, spewing vomit onto the floor and across the cell. "Those mothafuckas!" He vomited again. "They fuckin' poisoned me!" He vomited a third time, then breathed rapidly in little gasps.

When Jose looked down at the floor, it was brown and red. Food mixed with blood. Lots of blood. "He needs a doctor! Please! He needs a fucking doctor!" He cried out, unanswered except for the painful storm of crude comments.

Sean was lying on the floor, shaking and spasming. "Please—" he said, barely a whisper. "Please—"

An alarm rang loud, cutting through all other sounds. Two guards rushed over and opened the door. They were followed by two men in white lab coats who were carrying a stretcher. The guards held their bully sticks out threateningly at Jose in case he would dare to use this to try anything, while the men in the lab coats hoisted Sean onto the stretcher. Jose just stood there and stared at them as they picked him up and slowly carried him out of the cell. As they passed, the watch on his wrist turned from yellow to red. The guards backed out, holding their sticks in front of them until they were out of the cell. The door automatically shut behind them. The men and the guards disappeared, and the nothingness outside returned. This time, Jose was all alone.

CHAPTER 45
REFLECTION

"This is disappointing," Filip said and pointed at his tablet.

"What? What is?" Mik responded. Filip was generally disappointed as a rule, so Mik thought it could be next to nothing even despite the situation.

"It's quite solid. Guards and cameras at every entrance to the entire campus. High walls with razor wire. Not to mention the prisoners are housed in what amounts to giant concrete blocks."

"Well, it *is* a prison," Ollie jibed. "That's kind of par for the course."

"We weren't going to break in, anyway," Mik said. "So what's the big deal? Thought we were gonna find another way to do this."

"Well," Filip said, then coughed into his hand, followed by a wipe of his mouth with a napkin that was on the table. "My initial plan consisted of shutting down the power to the whole prison, but it's fed by secure underground lines. Since we don't have the means to target them, we have no choice but to get inside and somehow trigger the system manually."

"It doesn't matter," Zen said.

"Hmm?" Filip looked up like a disappointed professor.

"What do you mean?" Mik asked.

"I've seen my fair share of security systems," Zen responded. "Even in prisons. I never paid too much mind to the particulars, but it was important that they were always up to code. And one of the main regulatory musts was that the place would not have security failures in case of power outages. Even if we did have a way of shutting down the power from the outside *or* the inside, all that would do is delay them a bit until they got the power back on. The prisoners would be locked in their cells. The doors wouldn't just magically swing open. Plus, they'd know someone was tampering with it, and we would be out of options."

"Well, shit," Ollie said. "I guess we're screwed."

"Not necessarily. Filip's power idea got me thinking. There was something that happened once, right when I started at Guardian Hill. It wasn't a prison—it was an industrial shipping plant—but it had a similar power plan tied to the security systems. When power was shut down, everything would stop and lock up, so no one could come in and mess with it. But what they didn't know was what would happen when there was a massive surge of power. You remember that insane electrical storm we had like five years ago that put half the city out of power for a week? Well, during that storm, lightning directly hit one of the internal transmitter systems. The grid couldn't handle the massive voltage, and it sent the whole place haywire. Cranes dropping cargo crates, alarms going off, conveyor belts running at crazy speeds, but most importantly, all the gates opened. All tied to the power grid, and they all opened."

"So, you're saying all we need to do is wait for a lightning storm, and we're good?" Ollie smirked.

"You're extremely unhelpful," Filip said to Ollie. "Keep your mouth shut unless you have something productive to add."

Mik crossed his hands across his chest. "I don't suppose the Haven has any EMPs laying around, do they?"

Jade, who was listening intently, broke out of her stupor at Mik's question. "Unfortunately, not. We have some pretty cool tech down here, but it stops just short of EMPs."

"We need to think on this some more," Filip said.

Jade nodded. "While we do that, we should meet up with Caleb. I didn't get a chance to talk to him before, so how about we have him introduce us to R&D and have a look at that new thermal shield? No plan is going to work unless you can actually get to the prison, anyway."

"Fair point."

They headed over to where Caleb was working on a ventilation duct outside the residential complex. As usual, his face and clothing were caked in soot, dirt, and all manners of foul materials. He smiled when he saw them approach. "Hey, Jade. Filip. Mike. I mean, Mik. The rest of you, who I've never met before, I'm Caleb. Resident grease monkey. I've taught Jade everything she knows."

Jade laughed. "Sure thing, Caleb. Well, maybe *some* of the things I know."

"Always so literal. Anyway, judging from your announcement over the broadcast system and the anxious looks on your faces added to the fact I just recently told Jade about what the R&D team was working on, I suppose you want me to bring you over there to show you their new toy."

"Sorry to be so obvious about it. Some of us might need to leave, and we can't take any chances of being caught so close to the entrance and exposing the Haven."

"That would definitely not be good. I guess the least I could do is make the introductions. All the really hard work is already done here, so the rest of 'em can finish up. C'mon, follow me."

The group followed Caleb through a hallway that was to the deep left of the residential complex, tucked near what one could call the frontier of the Haven, the far wall where they were ever-expanding. Through there was a moderately sized warehouse-like room with fiberglass walls and corrugated steel flooring to prevent slippage. There was a small team of people helping lift what looked to be a modified drone onto a large workbench near the center of the room. They hadn't noticed that the group had entered and was watching them perform the task.

"Aloha, team!" Caleb nearly shouted. It was lucky for their sake that they had finished moving the drone onto the table, or the shock may have caused some damage. They quickly looked over to Caleb and the group, more than a little annoyed. "Sorry to bother you. Ladies and gents, this is our greatly esteemed R&D team. R&D team, this is the group of misfits and vagabonds that I recently met and befriended. Word has it they might want to take one of your newest creations out for a little spin."

"What are you talking about, Caleb?" A thin man wearing work gloves walked forward. A touch of impatience was evident in his tone.

"I'm not privy to all the gory details, but it might just be vitally important for some of them to leave the Haven for a while."

"So what?"

"Well, there's a bit of an issue that's come to light recently. Not sure if you heard about it." Caleb waited for an acknowledgment, and receiving none, he continued. "There was an incident, and there just might be Prowler drones outside near the entrance."

"Yeah, we heard Jade's announcement earlier. What the hell?" The man looked stunned.

"Nothing anyone needs to be overly concerned about," Filip said. "It's only a temporary issue and one that we are hoping to deal with shortly. But we were told that you might have a solution for avoiding detection by those drones."

"It's not ready yet," the man snapped.

"C'mon, Wes; you already told me it's perfect," Caleb argued. "You were basically bragging to me earlier that it passed all the quality tests."

"It's *Wesley*, Caleb. Wes was my father. I told you that before. Anyway, yes, it passed all the tests, but we still can't know 100 percent that it'll avoid Prowler detection. And I can't in good conscience send anyone outside and risk them being caught and the whole place going up in flames. Not gonna do it. We need to do more testing. More testing to really, positively make sure."

"What kind of additional testing does it need?" Filip interjected. He was well-known enough to be listened to even by those who didn't want to listen.

"We have infrared cameras here with thermal imaging, but we can't be totally sure that the Prowler drones don't have more advanced systems, higher density mapping or something, that could pick up on tiny flaws in the surface reflections."

"Maybe I could help," Mik said.

"How?"

"Sorry, we haven't met yet. I'm Mik. New here. Long story short, I have a supplantation that allows me to see infrared light and thermal images. I would think better than any rudimentary camera or drone system could."

"How?" Wesley repeated himself.

"I was in the Army. Pit viper genes. I have a pit organ that allows me to tap into that wavelength. It's not so much seeing as detecting, but it's pretty similar."

"I see."

"Would it work or not?" Mik was trying not to get impatient, but time was of the essence, and Wesley was extremely stubborn for his taste.

"Well—" Wesley took a way-too-long pause to think about it. "Yes, it would. That's as pure as it gets. All right, let me go get the shield." He shuffled over to the back of the room and opened a large drawer in a metal cabinet. He pulled out the shield.

"Holy Jesus fuck," Ollie exclaimed. The rest of the group looked on in shocked silence, their jaws agape.

"You didn't tell them? Caleb, seriously?" Wesley was holding the shield in his hands. It reflected all the lights in the room drastically, like a moving mirrored kaleidoscope. It was nearly blinding to look at it for any length of time. It had the look of a tarp, but every surface was a bright multiplication of the room's lighting.

"I may have neglected to mention that aspect of it," Caleb responded.

Wesley sighed. "It refracts infrared light in a way that prevents detection in that wavelength, but as you can see, it draws quite a bit of attention."

"So," Jade started. "If this catches the eye of anything *except* a drone, the cover is completely blown. We'll have to find a way around that. Wesley, if it would be all right, can Mik test it now?"

"I guess so. I'm not sure how it works for you, Mik. What do you need?"

"It's separate from my normal vision," Mik responded. "So, I can close my eyes and still see in infrared. But it's way too bright in here, especially with those reflections. Mind turning off the lights?"

Wesley gave the signal, and another member of the team flipped the switches, engulfing the room in darkness, except for the starry sheen of the shield that still managed to brightly reflect even the smallest and dimmest light sources. Mik nodded and closed his eyes. He concentrated, scanning the room with his supplanted trait. He could easily make out all the other people. They radiated like fire to him. But the shield was invisible, only noticeable in the way that other things around it reflected light.

Mik opened his eyes. He gave a thumbs up to the great relief of Wesley. "Couldn't see a damn thing. It works almost too well. It's completely dark."

"That'll work well enough for the drone cameras," Jade said. "They're not going to be sophisticated enough to relay an absence of vision. But even traveling in the dead of night, that thing will reflect normal light like a beacon."

"We will figure that out," Filip said. "Wesley, would you mind if we borrowed the shield?"

Wesley nodded and handed him the shield, holding on a bit too tight on the exchange. "Don't rip it, okay?"

Filip nodded. "We'll do our best." That was met with a cringe from Wesley. "Now, we need to have a discussion. Mik, Zen, Jade, and Ollie, follow me. We may have found a way out of the Haven, but we have much to figure out. How to get to the prison, how to get inside, and what to do when we get there. Get some lunch from the vendors and meet me in the cafeteria."

CHAPTER 46
A VERY IMPORTANT DECISION

Filip was waiting at the table after Mik and Ollie finished their sandwiches. They had grabbed them from a makeshift food cart in the marketplace and scarfed them down while making crude jokes that would most likely piss off Filip.

"Hey, Filip," Mik said and waved. Filip was busy scrolling through what looked like maps on his tablet and didn't notice.

"Hey, old man!" Ollie said much louder. This time, Filip looked up to see Ollie smiling and Mik still waving. He cleared his throat and went back to looking at the tablet.

Mik and Ollie sat down opposite him at the table. "What's going on?" Mik asked. "Did you get anything to eat?"

"No time," Filip replied. "I've been searching for some ways of entry. I talked with Jade, and we may have a plan of how you'll be able to get to the prison and perhaps release the prisoners. She had to go off to attend to some other matters, so she won't be joining us here."

"How *I'll* be able to?"

"Yes. You're the obvious candidate or at least one of them. Your ability to scout the area without extraneous equipment will be essential. You also know how to drive. You're not going to get all the way to Stateville on foot. This will require great planning, as well as stealth and speed. I'm far too slow to be of any use on this sort of mission, so I won't be going with you."

"That's true," Ollie added to the immediate chagrin of Filip.

"Also," Filip continued, ignoring Ollie's comment. "A small team would be best. Fewer people mean less risk of getting caught. We will also need a way of overloading that circuit, or whichever words Zen used when describing that. I want to wait for her to discuss this further, as it will require a very important decision and not one that should be taken lightly."

"What do you mean?" Mik was curious.

"Not for you. Now, do you have your tablets?"

"Yeah."

"Good. You'll need them so we can formulate our final plan."

Zen showed up a few minutes later, holding a light brown drink. "Who knew that they would have such a good coffee milkshake underground?" She feigned a smile, but she actually felt sick to her stomach. "Sorry if I'm late. Got caught up talking with Jade."

"Ah, you saw her?" Filip asked. "She said she had to go."

"Yeah, she was on her way out, but she told me about the plan, at least to an extent." Her smile faded, and she tossed out the rest of the milkshake, having completely lost her appetite after the conversation.

"Did she tell you about—"

"Yeah, she did. I'll do it if I have to. We don't have much choice, do we? And it *was* my idea."

"What are you guys talking about?" Ollie asked.

Filip cleared his throat again and coughed twice. "I told you that a very important decision must be made, and apparently, it already has." He gestured to Zen.

"Huh?"

Filip sighed. "You're off the hook, Ollie. Have a seat, Zen. What was it? Overloading the—"

"Internal transmitter systems," Zen finished. "From what I've read, an electric burst that goes beyond its voltage capacity has the potential to create complete chaos."

"We don't have EMPs, so we need a way to accomplish that. Zen will do it. If you're sure about it, that is. If you need more time to think about it, that's completely fine."

"I'm sure. I'll get the supplantation."

"Whoa, what?" Mik was in shock. "What are you talking about with this supplantation?"

Filip closed his eyes for a moment. "Jade told me she wanted to introduce you to him, Mikolaj. There just hasn't been any time."

"You mean the person she said I could talk with about my supplantation? What does that have to do with this?"

"Down here he goes by Noah."

"What do you mean he goes by Noah?"

"I don't know his real name, Mikolaj. I'm not sure anyone does. But he's provided the Haven with gene supplantations since I've been here. Jade was hoping that he could answer your questions if you had any. Or at least he could be someone you could confide in."

"I don't think my questions matter anymore. Anyway, why do they call him that?"

"I think that will become very clear once we go to him." Filip looked at Zen. "If you're completely sure you want to go through with this."

Zen nodded, then suddenly burst into tears. "Yes."

"Go through with what?" Mik asked. "Go through with *what*, Zen?"

"The supplantation," Zen answered, still sniffling.

"What supplantation? Filip, what is she talking about?"

Filip looked at Zen sympathetically and then answered. "Jade and I discussed ways to overload the power systems at the prison. As you said, Mikolaj, we don't have any EMPs. The only thing we could come up with was—"

"Supplantation," Zen finished again. "Jade told me she had spoken with Noah recently. He has a way of supplanting with—" She cut herself short and shook her head. "I can't have kids, so I'm the one who should get it. The only real side effect is what it does to children, so it should be my responsibility. You know, I always wanted them. Children. We tried so damn hard. I thought it would bring Aiden and me together, but in the end, it helped break us apart. I'm almost thankful for that, as strange as it sounds. We were wrong together. He was a good man in his heart; I really believe that. But he took out all his anger and frustrations on me, and the news from the doctor that I could never bring a child to term was too much for him. For us. I guess that led me here, for better or worse."

"Well, that's good," Ollie said. "I'm not getting any damn supplantation, that's for sure."

"Shut up, Ollie," Mik said.

"What? I wanna have kids someday!"

Mik felt rage quickly build up. He nearly rose out of his seat. "Read the fucking room, Ollie," he said almost venomously. Ollie looked totally ashamed.

Zen put her hand on Mik's shoulder. "It's okay, Mik. Ollie's right. It's not his place to do this. He can still have children. I can't. I brought this whole problem here. If it wasn't for me, we wouldn't even be in this situation."

Mik looked at Ollie, still furious. "I brought it here, too. It's not just on your shoulders."

"That's why we're both going to fix it." Zen smiled reassuringly.

Mik took a deep breath to calm himself down. "So what supplantation are you getting then?" His impatience had gotten the better of him as his anger subsided.

Zen cringed thinking about it. It was pretty damn crazy and quite the long shot, but she had spoken with Jade, and they had decided it was the only chance they had. "Guess."

Mik let out a sudden burst of laughter. The playful answer took him by surprise, and it felt good to relieve some of that tension. "Ha, seriously? All right, well, we need to overload the transmitter thing with electricity. So, let me guess. Electric eel?" Zen's stone face and pursed lips said it all. "No shit, really? An electric eel? You're kidding."

"That's kind of badass," Ollie said. "Now I kinda wish I was getting a supplantation. Screw kids, I don't want 'em; they suck." He laughed, and Mik and Zen joined in despite themselves. "Also, did you know that the electric eel isn't an eel at all but a kind of fish?"

The only one not to crack a smile was Filip, who was still busy poring over the maps on the tablet. "We should head over now. Jade will meet us back here after the procedure, and we will figure out the rest of the mission details. Don't forget your tablets."

"You're really, really sure you want to do this?" Mik whispered to Zen as they started following Filip out of the cafeteria.

"Yes, now stop trying to convince me otherwise." She playfully pushed his shoulder.

"Hey, ouch, all right," Mik said, dramatically feigning injury.

"Wow, you're a bit more fragile than you look. Speaking of, I think Ollie's still a bit hurt from when you snapped at him."

"He seems fine to me."

"That's his defense mechanism. Trust me on this one."

Mik frowned and nodded. "All right." He turned around to Ollie, who was quietly following the group from behind. "Sorry I yelled at you, man."

Ollie seemed to be staring out into space but quickly returned to action when he heard this. "It's all good, you mean son of a bitch."

CHAPTER 47
NOAH

With Filip in the lead, they walked toward the medical wing that Jade had told Mik about. It was equipped with the same light diffusion technology found in modern operating and procedure rooms, but this time, it was throughout the entire hallway. The lack of shadows always took some getting used to. In the back, past the triage areas and supply rooms, was a hallway that distinctly did not have the same lighting. Instead, it was rather dark, bathed only in a dim orange glow. It was quiet here, unusually so for the Haven. Even in the areas removed from the marketplace and cafeteria, there was always the murmur of humanity. This place was the exception as if the walls were covered in sound-dampening foam. The only sound other than the almost imperceptible hum of electricity was violin music. It was sweet and clear and magical.

As they walked through the hallway toward the room at the back, the music slowly got louder. It drowned out everything else. The room was dark, much like the hallway, but it was lit only with candlelight. The smoke from the candles twisted in the air, eventually vanishing up the ceiling vents. The beautiful music was coming from a violin played by an old man who was facing the far wall, his ashen hair cascading down past his shoulders. Against the wall was a stand that held what must have been ancient sheet music. The old man's wrinkled fingers danced on the strings. His foot tapped along with the notes, keeping the rhythm. He didn't seem to notice the group's entry into the room, continuing the melody on and on.

Zen, Mik, and Filip stood at the doorway, entranced. Mik noticed that Ollie was about to send out one of his patented loud greetings, so he put his hand on his shoulder and shook his head. They waited until the song came to its resounding conclusion, and when it came, they couldn't help but break out into applause. The old man didn't seem surprised by the sudden reaction. He slowly got up to his feet and turned around, holding the violin in his left hand and the bow in his right. Upon seeing them, he smiled a toothy grin and took a deep bow. "Thank you! It's rare to have an audience these days. Hello, Filip. It's been a long time."

"Yes, it has," Filip responded. "I apologize for rarely coming over here to see you. You know you're always welcome to join us for dinner in the cafeteria or for drinks. I know they'd love to hear you play."

"I appreciate the gesture, but you know how I feel about crowds. I greatly prefer my solitude. It allows me to think. Anyway, where are my manners? Welcome, everyone, to my little hole in the wall. Inside a much bigger hole in the wall." He placed the violin and bow into a case on the floor and stood up.

"Noah, this is Mikolaj, Zen, and Ollie."

"Ah, Mikolaj! You go by Mik, yes? Jade told me about you. You can feel free to bend my ear anytime. So, what brings you all here? You must have heard about my mediocre violin playing."

"I definitely wouldn't call it mediocre," Mik said. "I haven't heard anything like that in what feels like a very long time. I wanted to come talk with you before, but a lot of things have happened very quickly."

"We're here because we're in a dire situation," Filip said. "I don't want to waste time with the whole story, but Zen has made the decision to get a supplantation. And you're the man to see about that."

"A supplantation?" Noah asked. "That's not a decision to take lightly. While I've made great progress in reducing the initial side effects and speeding up the process, there is no way to eliminate the inevitable. I'm sure you know what I'm talking about."

"I do," Zen replied. "Trust me; it wasn't an easy decision, but it was made easier because of my situation. And what's at stake."

"I see. I want to give you a little information about what's going to happen, just so you're totally aware of the consequences of the procedure. This will grow organs inside of you, much like it did for Filip.

You will feel very unusual during this process, especially since I've discovered a way to make it take only a scant few hours to complete. You'll also want to increase your electrolyte intake, namely sodium and potassium, so no low-salt diets. The organs rely on sodium ion channels, ah, I don't want to get overly scientific, but any excess sodium or potassium you eat will be stored in the organs first. The good news is you won't have to worry about high blood pressure. Your brain will take care of the rest. There will be the added bonus of electro-sensing, as I like to call it. Being able to pick up sources of electricity by location, including people. I digress. Are you still certain you want to do this?"

"I am."

"Well then, I'm ready when you are."

"Before we do this, I know I'm not the only one who's been wondering. Filip won't tell us. Why do they call you Noah?"

Noah smiled just a little. "Follow me to my procedure room, and I'll show you." He was met with curious glances from everyone but Filip. "I hope you didn't think I perform supplantations by candlelight." Zen, Mik, and Ollie smiled, mildly embarrassed by their initial assumptions. "Wouldn't that just be perfect to set the mood? Please!" He gestured for the group to follow him.

They walked back down the hallway until it was once again bathed in diffuse light. Noah opened the door to the left and beckoned once again for everyone to enter. "Here we go." He walked over to a white cabinet that spanned almost the entire far wall. It looked as if it was built into the structure, but the sturdy, large wheels on the bottom gave it away. A retina scanner was built into the cabinet itself for security purposes. It wasn't lost on Mik that only the most important places in Tem Tem District had them at their entrances, and this cabinet had one just for opening the damn thing. Noah stood in front of the cabinet and turned to face it. He pressed a button, and the retina scanner identified him. He quickly turned back around to face the group as the cabinet slowly began to open.

"I give to you, the Ark." As the door swung open, what looked to be steam billowed out from it. A faint blue glow emanated from behind. As the cloud settled, rows upon rows of tiny black canisters were revealed, each digitally labeled with a Latin species name, the corresponding English name, and underneath, the genetic trait to be used in supplantation procedures. Zen's jaw dropped, and by the looks of it, so had Mik's and Ollie's. *Chamaleo zeylanicus, Indian Chameleon, Camouflage. Lagenorhynchus obliquidens, Pacific White-sided Dolphin, Ultrasound. Desmoxytes purpurosea, Dragon Millipede, Hydrogen Cyanide Gas.* Filip's supplantation. *Trimeresurus gramineus, Bamboo Pit Viper, Infrared Pit Organ.* Close enough to Mik's. *Canis familiaris, Dog, Precognition.* Wait, was that even a real thing? It was easy to get lost in the possibilities. It was as if a whole other dimension of being was introduced, and all Zen had to do was choose which door to walk through.

She had to stay focused. The Ark was fantasy. Superpowers. Beyond human. The allure had always been there, especially for those who were kids or young enough to dream unabated during the time supplantation was legal. The choices then were almost bland compared to these, but they were still magical, and it didn't take much imagination to think of the potential of different species and different traits. Now, it was here before her. One of those dreams could be made a reality with just a needle. But she was here to follow through on the mission. She was nothing if not resolute, and she had resolved to get the necessary supplantation to give them the only chance of completing this mission.

"Where's the electric eel?" she asked.

Noah quickly scanned the hundreds of canisters, which were in some sort of order, but definitely not alphabetical. "Ah, here it is." He pointed with his bent and wrinkled index finger. *Electrophorus electricus.* The name was enough to give anyone a good jolt. "Please, Zen, have a seat." He gestured over to a white adjustable chair that blended so well with the white of the room and its lack of shadows that Zen almost tripped on it when she went to sit down. As she sat, Noah pulled the canister out with a loud hiss, flipped the cap, and pulled out a single syringe. Holding it dramatically aloft in one hand, he closed the canister and replaced it in the cabinet. The cabinet door automatically shut, locking up all those dreams once more.

"Are you ready?"

"Yes."

CHAPTER 48
RATS

Jose woke up. He couldn't remember falling asleep. His head pounded like a jackhammer. This was worse than any concussion he had ever had, and he had to deal with his fair share. It was made worse by his anger and confusion. One minute, he and Sean were shooting the shit, and the next minute Sean was throwing up blood and being carried out of the cell on a stretcher. All he could think about was his watch going from yellow to red. It was clouding his thoughts, almost haunting them. That wasn't any goddamn vaccine he ever had before. This headache was a thunderclap, and he vaguely remembered nearly recovering from the concussion anyway. *Wasn't I only dizzy when Sean was taken away? It had to be a side effect. And there was something to Sean receiving two shots to my one. Was that it? Some allergic reaction to different mixtures?* His head hurt so much that he couldn't follow a single train of thought. *Is it going to kill me too?*

The only thing he could keep his focus on was his anger. His rage. And he slammed on the bars of his cell with his open palms until they would have screamed in pain, but since his head hurt so badly, he barely felt it. He yelled until his throat was dry and ragged and his voice began to give out. "Where the fuck is he? What did you do to him? Fuck you! Did you kill him? I'M GOING TO KILL YOU, YOU MOTHERFUCKERS! WHERE THE FUCK IS HE?"

He was about to give up and slump back down onto the floor when two guards showed up, along with a man in a white lab coat. Jose's headache dulled his mind, but he remembered the man from before. *Yes, it was that doctor.* Dr. Cross. And now, he hated him more than anyone in the world. "Where the fuck is he? Where's Sean? What did you do with him?" He was no longer yelling, but his voice remained aggressive.

"First, I'm going to need you to relax, Mr. Gutierrez," Dr. Cross said, simply and calmly, as if Jose hadn't spent the last ten minutes making an extremely loud racket. "You're referring to your cell-mate, Mr. Teague. Unfortunately, he had an adverse reaction to the vaccination."

"What the fuck are you talking about, an adverse reaction? We've all had flu and COVID vaccines before. What happened to him? What did you do?"

"I'm sorry to be the bearer of bad news, Mr. Gutierrez. Mr. Teague did not recover, despite our best efforts to save him."

Jose's rage found new life. "He's fucking *dead*? You killed him, you motherfucker! Open this door so I can fucking see you up nice and close, you piece of shit!"

"I *told* you to be calm," Dr. Cross said as if he was a headmaster disciplining an unruly student. "If you continue your outbursts, this conversation will be over. We attempted to resuscitate him, but we are using a new version of the vaccines, and they can, rarely, have undesired consequences."

"You mother—" Jose was about to unleash a new tirade, but Dr. Cross's warning sounded in his head. The conversation would end, and he would get no answers, no nothing. "Is that why my head hurts like a fucking bitch?"

"Yes, that might also be a side effect of our new, more effective vaccination, but don't worry. You'll be fine." Dr. Cross seemed to nod subtly at Jose's watch, which still shone bright green.

"I'm not worried," Jose said, as calmly as he could with his blinding rage and blinding headache competing for his attention. "I'm pissed off. You killed my friend. My only friend for the last two fucking years. All because you wanted to test some new vaccine. You treat us like fucking rats. But you don't understand. You're the fucking rats." His anger slowly started overriding his faux calmness. "You're the ones who hide behind your white, marble walls, in your perfect modern rat holes. You lock us away so you can go about your little rat lives without thinking about anyone who has it different from you, without thinking about what life must be like for us. And now, you have the fucking audacity to come to me and tell me to be fucking calm? You tell me to be fucking calm after you kill my friend with a fucking vaccine? Open this fucking door. *Open this fucking door so I can see this fucking rat right up close!*"

The guard to the right of Dr. Cross whacked his baton against the bars of the cell and Jose's hand that was holding onto them. Jose felt the fingerbones of his left hand shatter into pieces. The pain put any headache to shame. There was an excruciating burst of agony followed by a grinding throb as blood and sensation rushed to the area of injury. His headache momentarily overtaken, his anger doubled. He pulled his right arm back from the bars and balled his hand into a fist, not sure what he could even hit outside the bars of his cell but knowing that he wanted to destroy the people standing there with every fiber of his being. The feeling in his right hand was almost unnoticeable at first, attempting to compete with the crumpled horror that was his left hand and his still-present headache. But the feeling grew until his right hand also exploded in agony. *What the fuck is happening?* Was he so out of it that he still had his right hand on the bars without even realizing it? Was he only imagining bringing his right hand back to strike? He broke his animalistic stare outside the cell to take a quick glance at his hand. It was no longer just a fist. His bones had broken the skin, dripping crimson on the concrete floor of the cell. How did his right hand break? *What the fuck?* He looked closer. His knuckles had somehow rearranged, re-mineralized. What was recently a closed fist was now a claw with four white talons protruding forward. He was surely hallucinating; that was it. The pain in his left hand had been too much, and now, he was semi-conscious, half in reality, half in fucking dreamland. But his anger never subsided, and the men outside his cell were now staring at him in bewilderment. So, he bared his teeth in a menacing scowl and shot his right arm forward, aiming his new bony claw directly between the bars into the chest of the guard who had shattered his other hand. The four daggers pierced the man's shirt and flesh with frightening ease until they were embedded four inches deep. Jose could feel the man's blood pushing out around his claws and onto the rest of his hand. He pulled his arm back, and the blood gushed out like faucets. The guard still stared at him, but this time he was afraid, so afraid, and he maintained that expression until he collapsed onto the floor on his back, the blood still shooting out in little geysers. The life left his eyes, and the staring ended.

Jose looked at his right hand, the four sharp bones still red and slick. He looked at the guard, dead on the ground, and back at Dr. Cross and the other guard, both of whom had backed far enough away from the cell to avoid similar retribution. The guard called on his radio for backup, and Dr. Cross was immediately talking rapidly on what must have been his HUDPhone. Within seconds, a group of guards appeared, armed with rifles and pistols. Three of them pointed their weapons at Jose, but he could see that they couldn't totally keep their eyes off their fallen comrade and the bony claw that protruded from his right hand. Dr. Cross finally ended the call and walked up to the cell, within range of another potential attack, but he seemed to sense that Jose valued his life enough not to do it again. He looked directly at him and whispered.

"It would seem to me that someone gave you something they shouldn't have. There was supposed to be a very particular set of—you know what, never mind. It doesn't really matter anymore. I have the necessary results, either way. I appreciate your participation, even if it did get a little messy." Dr. Cross then turned around and addressed the guards at a higher volume. "I assume you would generally put an inmate who has assaulted and killed a correctional officer into solitary confinement." He was met with a few affirmative nods. "However, I must insist that you bring this particular inmate to one of the cells that are specifically designated for those who are here for the vaccination program."

While a few guards had their guns leveled at Jose, two others opened the cell door and cuffed his hands behind his back. One was shattered and broken, and the other one was a bony claw that was covered in a guard's blood. One guard grabbed each of his shoulders and roughly pushed him through the block. Only now could Jose hear the calls of the other prisoners. They had noticed what had happened and saw his grotesque hands cuffed behind his back.

One of the inmates in the cell across from his yelled out. "What the fuck *are* you, man? The Mexican Wolverine?"

"I'm Puerto Rican, motherfucker."

A guard smacked Jose in the back of the head, and the world spun into darkness.

CHAPTER 49
DOWN TO BUSINESS

Jade was waiting for them in the cafeteria when they got back. She was busy looking at her tablet when a small coughing bout from Filip grabbed her attention. She looked up at the group and noticed Zen had her sleeve rolled up and a nano-bandage on her shoulder. "How'd it go?"

"That Ark was crazy," Ollie replied.

Jade laughed. "I meant to ask Zen how it went, but the Ark definitely catches the eye."

"It was the anxiety of it more than anything else," Zen said. "Felt like getting any other shot minus the theatrics."

"I'm sure they told you already, but I've heard the process can be a little unnerving, especially for a supplantation that grows organs or glands."

"I can tell you first-hand that it kinda sucks," Mik said. "But Noah did say that he came up with some new methods to lessen some of those side effects and make it go quicker. I'm sure you'll be okay."

Filip shook his head. "Back in my day, it was a real son of a bitch. You'll barely feel it with all the new technology he's been working on."

Jade grinned. "Yeah, maybe. So, I was talking to some people down here who know this stuff better than I do. I want to go over a potential plan. Mind having a seat?"

The group all took their seats at the end of the cafeteria table and pulled out their tablets. "What do you have for us?" Filip asked.

"I've been looking at the prison blueprints along with Caleb and a few others. We're lucky enough to have the whole 3D model so we can see every level. I think we may have found you a way in." She pressed a button, and the images populated everyone's screens. "One of the common threads of all prisons is that their number-one priority is to keep their prisoners from getting out. In this case, it might be doing us a big favor. According to the image here, their transmitter systems are heavily fortified from prisoner interference. From the inside. However, they have a much easier access point from the other direction. Before you start asking questions, I don't mean that it's easy. Just that it might be possible." The image changed again. "The best and only way in without setting off all the security systems and being seen is through the sewer system."

Mik and Zen groaned simultaneously. "You know," Mik said. "I just had a feeling we would have to do that. I don't know why, but I knew we were gonna get dirty."

Jade looked amused. "It's the only way in that's not through the front door."

"I know, I'm just getting my complaining over with."

"Glad I'm not the one going," Ollie said. "It would just be unseemly for someone like me to not look their best."

Jade did her best not to smile, but she did quickly and got back down to business. "The sewers are not only a way in, but if you follow the lines up toward the main campus, they eventually connect to a hub *here*." The image changed once more. "It's a two-level spiral staircase that has access to different maintenance rooms. The only way down here from the inside is through the guard station, and I don't recommend that. *This* door here is to the electric room. That's the most likely spot for the transmitter system."

"What do you mean the most likely spot?" Mik asked. "You mean you aren't sure it's there?"

"Look, these blueprints, while detailed, are from ten years ago when the place went through its most recent construction project. I would assume that they went by the blueprint when they assigned the rooms, but we can't be totally sure. Assuming it's there, that's where Zen will overload the systems. Then you get out of there the way you came, as quickly as humanly possible. The place is going to melt into chaos, and I don't want you to get caught."

Mik was trying to remain calm, but the cynic in him took over, and to a slightly lesser extent, the military tactician. "Hopefully, that room has the transmitter system, although that's a big *if*. Then we have to hope that Zen will be able to overload those systems with the amount of voltage she can produce. Another big *if*. Then, we have to hope that the overload actually causes the system to go haywire and open everything up. Sorry, Zen. I'm 100 percent in this with you. Just stating facts. Let's say all those things work. What's our plan for getting to the prison? We're talking like forty miles of packed city streets and open roads between us and there. Sure, the thermal shield might protect us from the drone cameras, but from what I've seen from those reflections, any asshole with a working set of eyes is gonna see us coming from miles away."

There was a long pause in the room as reality set in. Then, Filip cleared his throat, probably louder than he needed to, and grinned. "Jade, we still have that old clunker in the warehouse, don't we?"

Jade smiled in response. "We sure do. Good old American muscle. It was still running last I checked. Then again, that was about two years ago. You might want to bring a jump start." Then she nodded at Zen and laughed. "Never mind, you already have one."

"You have a car?" Mik asked.

"That we do. The old girl runs on gas if you can believe it. Good news is I replaced the canisters back when I checked on it. You just need to fill it up. Oh, and there should be a jumpstart battery in the trunk. Let's not waste Zen's voltage."

"I'm all good with that. Back in the Army, most of our vehicles still ran on gas. Hard to find a plug in the middle of a desert or forest."

"About the thermal shielding, the good news is it's late July, just after the new moon, so any ambient reflections should be at a minimum except for streetlights and such. Still, you'll want to haul ass and get to the car as fast as possible."

"What if we run into a patrol? On the way to the car, at the prison, wherever. I don't want to go empty-handed."

"I'll get someone to outfit you with what we can, but the key to this whole thing is to get in, overload the transmitter system, and get out. We're in a world of hurt if you get caught. It could lead back here to the Haven. So, I recommend traveling as light as possible."

"Good point."

"You'll park the car *here*, out of sight of anyone in the guard towers, so you can drive it back afterward."

"Got it."

"So, we have our plan," Filip said. "Are there any other questions for Jade or myself?"

Jade raised her open palm. "Before any questions, I want you two to remember the plan and the blueprints by heart. You can't take these tablets with you."

"Fair enough," Mik said. "When do we leave? We have to wait for Zen's supplantation to finish, don't we?"

"We should be ready to go by tonight, right, Filip?" Jade asked.

Mik was shocked. "What do you mean, tonight? Already?"

"I don't even feel anything yet," Zen added. "We can't leave before it works."

Filip attempted a reassuring gesture. "We can't wait any longer. Noah informed me that the supplantation should only take a few hours to set in. I'd recommend you two get as much sleep as you can. Report back here at two a.m. Jade and I will get you outfitted and ready."

"Well, shit," Mik said. "This is getting real."

"You're telling me," Zen replied. "It wasn't even a week ago that I was going to work and thinking about getting a divorce. What the hell happened?"

"A bunch of greedy, evil bastards, that's what."

"Isn't it always?"

CHAPTER 50
I JUST WANT TO TALK

In the end, he was right. The anger was back, violently. But he didn't imagine it would be this bad. He had hoped the vagrant down in Tem Tem District would calm it down enough so he could at least think. But his mind was clouded, and his rage was electric. It had to be assuaged completely. As difficult as the hunger was between kills, this was so much worse. He left his luxurious house in Oasis District and walked down the long front steps into the twinkling stillness of the night. It was cool for the dead of summer, but he felt so hot that he was sweating.

It was a short trip, so there was no need for a car. Heading south down a main street, he paid no mind to the people passing him by. The lights of the shops and restaurants did little to distract him. He was singularly focused. He arrived in less than twenty minutes, but his dress shirt and carefully pleated pants were already sticking to his skin like flypaper. The place was massive and an architectural rarity. A holdover from the pre-districting days, it was a row of three old Chicago graystones, only semi-remodeled to fit the ultra-modern aesthetic of Oasis District. It looked peculiar as a standalone building, but its occupant had desired a place that was mostly untouched by the demolition and wholesale rebuilding that Oasis brought to the area. Only the center unit served as an entrance, while the others were converted to only having massive windows where the doorways once stood.

He stood outside the entrance and stared at the video doorbell button. The rage acted as blinders, like tunneling darkness, and he focused on it. Now was the time to finally put it to rest. He pressed the button, then stood there unblinking. The black lens of the camera watched him, impartial to his beautiful face with its chiseled jawline and piercing blue eyes. There was no response. The night was still, but now it felt even more so as if even a slight gust of wind would ruin the clarity of the moment. He squeezed his eyes shut, now conscious of their burning. Two small tears fell out onto his cheeks. He took a deep breath. He had not even remembered to breathe since he had arrived. He pressed the button again. He waited, rage boiling up inside of him like a cauldron. His eyes were on fire, but he didn't dare blink. Every sinew was coiled like a spring. He could feel his heartbeat thumping desperately inside his head.

Then, finally, he was answered. "What are you doing here?" The voice was cold and distant, but he could sense its fear.

He forced his own voice to be calm despite the great urge to scream and yell and destroy. "I want to talk to you." It came out measured and reserved. Good.

"Go away. I'm not talking to you."

How dare he reject him? What right did he have to shut him out as if he were a salesman or, God forbid, one of those wretched souls that begged you for charity? He would not accept this outcome, but he was partially in charge of his fate. He put every fiber of his being into the effort of appearing calm despite the rage threatening to burst through the seams at every moment. Measured. Reserved.

"I just want to talk." The tone of the voice was so far removed from his emotions that it sounded like someone else.

"I told you. You're not welcome here."

Again. Keep focused. "I just want to talk. I promise."

There was a long pause that seemed to stretch an eternity in the heavy air. The rage pulsed, ebbing and flowing at the corners of his vision. No response? He felt his hands going numb as the adrenaline coursed through his veins. This is not how this story was going to end. Not with quiet admonishment. Not with silence.

"Fine."

There it was, the first page of the night's next chapter. The relief of getting a response threatened to dampen his dry rage, but he focused and maintained it. The door buzzed and unlocked. He gripped the door handle and pulled, feeling the cold bronze against his hot palm, the nerves coming back to life with the sensation. He walked inside the massive front hall. The air conditioning blasted frigid against his sweat-soaked skin. He started to shiver. He would have found it refreshing at any other time, but the rage was hot and did not have any regard for temperature. He heard footsteps upstairs, faint and slowly getting louder. Then he saw the man at the top of the curving marble staircase, dressed nicer than anyone who had the right to be dressed while alone at home. The man began walking down the stairs, never taking his eyes off him, like a deer eyeing a hunter in the woods.

"Hello, Dad."

"Hello, Jacob," Governor Bill Peters said as he took his last step down the stairs into the hall. "You said you wanted to talk."

"Wherever you'd be most comfortable," Jacob Peters said. He was getting good at this. Appearing calm as the rage danced red in his piercing blue eyes.

"The kitchen, then," the governor replied. He turned his back to Jacob, but Jacob knew that it was the last thing he wanted to do. The urge to turn his neck to make sure he was still far enough away was so powerful. But he was the leader of the whole damn state, and the last thing he wanted was to come off terrified of his own son, no matter what sort of monster he might be. When he reached the massive island in the center of the kitchen, he quickly swiveled back to face him, his face alight with palpable relief.

"So, what did you want to talk about?" he asked. Jacob was almost impressed. There was no hint of wavering in his tone. It was as strong and projecting as ever, no doubt honed by his years in politics.

"I wanted to talk about what you said on *The Power Hour*. You once promised me something. You promised me that you would never condemn your own son. But on that show, you told the world that you'd pledged every resource to help capture and punish me. That I *must* be stopped."

"Goddamnit, Jake. What else could I do? He had me between a

rock and a hard place. I've been trying everything to help you. I love you, son, but you need help. It's gone too far. When Speedy Powers asked me about my ties to the military gene supplantation research, I lied. I'm involved in that. And do you know why? Because Dr. Isaac Cross told me that he's been working on a way to reverse supplantation. If I helped fund his research, he would give me what I needed to help you. To bring you back. To make you *you* again. My only son, who I watched sleep in his crib. Watched playing sports in school. God, it feels like only yesterday we played catch in the backyard. I didn't want it to come to this. When you were nineteen, you came home one day saying you got supplanted. I went to hug you, and you jumped back. You screamed at me not to touch you. That you got supplanted with poison dart frog genes. Your mother and I cried so hard that night. Then we found Lucky's body under the front porch, and when I went to pick him up, you screamed at me not to touch him. That you held him and made him stop barking, made him stop barking forever. He was a good dog, goddamnit. I told you I'd always help you. I promised you that I'd never condemn you. That I'd never stop loving you because no matter what you've done, you're still my son. I bought you a house in Oasis District. I let you rape and murder those poor women. But now I have a way to help you. If they capture you, I can get Dr. Cross to help me turn you back because I know you'd never do it willingly. Maybe if we can turn you back, maybe, just maybe, you'll be *normal*."

The governor's words hacked away at his rage, like a lumberjack to a great sequoia. He almost felt sorry. He almost felt *love*. Did his father truly love him? Did he love him back? He felt the emotions start to fray the edges of his rage, but there was only one way to do that. He knew better than anyone that taking away his supplantation wouldn't make him normal. He would just find a new way to kill, a new supplantation. He had come to peace with what he was a long time ago. His father was earnest; he gave him that. But he was misguided. And now, despite his best intentions, he threatened his way of life.

"Shake my hand, Dad."

"What? No. I told you, Jake. I'm trying to help you. Let me help you."

"I understand, Dad. I know you meant well. But you broke your promise. There's nothing that can be done now. Shake my hand."

"No!" The governor turned and ran through the kitchen and the living room. He stopped at the glass-paned bay doors leading out to the back patio. He fumbled with the lock and handle. Jacob caught up with him in a sprinting fury, and they shattered the glass and fell onto the patio outside. The governor was splayed out on his belly, shards of glass sticking out of him, leading to little rivers of blood against the cold cement. He turned over. He had taken the brunt of the damage. There was a piece of glass in his forehead, pooling blood on his face, covering his eyes, nose, and mouth. He took his right hand and wiped his eyes.

Jacob was standing over him, having been cushioned by him on the way down. "I forgive you, Dad. Let me help you up."

"No." The governor coughed and spat. "Get away from me."

"It's too late, Dad. It's over." He could feel the anger subsiding. It was like jumping in a backyard pool after playing basketball at the park. He tingled with relief.

"What are you—" the governor tried to say as his muscles began to tense up. He stared up at Jacob as the blood pooled in his nose and mouth. He tried to spit it out, but he was getting weaker and weaker. The blood continued to pool. He tried to breathe, but the blood in his nose and mouth was now too heavy. The end came shortly after.

Jacob looked down at his father. He took off his shirt and used it to wipe away the blood on his father's face. He wiped until his forehead stopped bleeding. He stood back up, looked at his father's face, now cleaned of blood, and smiled. He really did love him, after all.

CHAPTER 51
SEE YOU LATER

JULY 30, 2071

Zen had spent the late hours of the evening tossing and turning in bed. The side effects of the supplantation were mild as advertised, but she could still feel the changes occurring inside her body. That by itself was enough to put anyone on edge but coupled with the anticipation of what was going to happen, there was no way she was going to get any sleep. Mik didn't fare much better. It reminded him a bit too strongly of the night before his mission to the compound in China back in the Army days, and what happened there had kept him up many a night since.

They met with Filip, Jade, and Ollie at about five minutes before two in the morning. Filip and Jade looked focused, if not a bit nervous, while Ollie looked like he had been roughly awoken in the middle of a beautiful dream. Mik thought that was probably exactly what had happened.

Jade handed Zen the thermal shield, the brilliantly reflective tarp that seemed extremely counterintuitive to providing any sort of stealth but might just save them in the unique situation they found themselves in. Filip handed Mik a pistol, a silver and black hammer-fired 1911. A firearm like this was getting somewhat rare, usually found in display cases and safes. Most mechanical guns had been replaced with biometric grips and smart triggers to fit into the sweeping gun law reforms.

"I've had this in my possession almost my whole life," Filip said. "And I want you to have it. I think you'll be able to use it more than I could. Here's a holster. Bring it with you this morning, although I hope you won't need to use it."

"Oh, man," Mik replied. "Thank you, Filip, but I can't take this. Wasn't this your father's?" Mik's guns were still at his apartment, which seemed thousands of miles away now.

"It was. He brought it with him to Desert Storm in 1991 when I was two years old. On my twenty-first birthday, he gave it to me. Well, he waited until I got my license, but I went to the range with him to shoot it that day. I've never been one to go all rah-rah over the 2nd Amendment, but it was fun as hell."

"Thanks, Filip, it means a lot." Mik pulled his belt out from his pants, slid the holster on, and cinched it back up. He then placed the pistol in, met with a satisfying click in the molded plastic.

"That could be especially useful on this mission," Jade said. "There's no telling what will happen when Zen sends out that electric pulse. It just might disable any smart triggers or grips anyway. Speaking of, no electronics at all on this. That means radios and any other form of communications, GPS, tablets, phones. Nothing. We can't take that risk. What's the point of all this if we lose the both of you?"

"Everyone knows the plan, right?" Filip asked. He was met with nods from Zen and Mik.

"We go over to the warehouse," Mik said. "Making sure to cover ourselves with that shiny beacon. We grab the car and drive safely and slowly down to old Stateville, where we park it behind the ridge so the guards can't see us. We head through the sewers, the exact place of which I know like the back of my hand from looking at all those satellite images, then Zen does her EMP impression, the whole place goes up like Independence Day, and we haul ass back here, job done and mission complete."

"I remember where everything is in case he forgets," Zen said with a wry grin.

"Mik, can I talk to you for a sec?" Ollie asked. He looked over at Filip, who gave him a permissive nod.

"Sure thing, Ollie. What's up?"

They walked out of earshot of the rest of the group.

"Listen, I can tell you're nervous as hell. You get, well, a little interesting when you're nervous. Always did you wonders with the ladies. Now, get your ass back here in one piece. I've met the people here, and well, they're nice enough, but they can't throw 'em back and shoot the shit with me like you can. We'll have a beer or ten when you're back. I'll reserve us seats at the bar."

"There's no bar here, Ollie, but you got it. We'll have a good time when I'm back."

"Hell yeah, we will. Now, enough talking. Go crank that place up."

"We're gonna try, man."

Mik and Ollie walked back to the group. Outfitting was completed with bulletproof vests, waterproof boots and pants, and not much else aside from Filip's old 1911. It was time to go.

"Good luck," Jade said. "We'll see you back here in a couple of hours."

"I'd say it was great meeting you, Zen," Filip added. "But that has a negative connotation. I'll talk to you later this morning. You'll have earned yourself some breakfast and a nap. Mikolaj, my boy, I'll see you later."

"Later, Filip," Mik replied. "Later, Jade. Ollie." He nodded and smirked at him.

"Thanks for everything, guys," Zen said. "Got pancakes or waffles or anything for when we get back?"

"I'll see what they can scratch up," Jade answered.

"Sounds good to me. Mik, are you ready to go?"

"Ready when you are."

Mik and Zen left through the Haven entrance into the cool darkness of the subway tunnel. This was the first place they'd been where the thermal shield wasn't reflecting ambient light like a disco ball. Zen placed the shield down for a minute to start helping Mik remove the concrete blocks that separated the abandoned station from the outside world. As soon as a few blocks had been moved, they draped the shield over the entrance so they could move the rest of the blocks without being noticed by drones.

The air had cooled off drastically over the night, but the wind was still dead. It would have been one of those perfect nights around the fire pit in the backyard with a beer or whiskey in hand. Mik could see through the shield with his infrared vision, but it left Zen blind in any practical way. Neither of them wanted to think about the reflections that the shield would be giving off even in the nearly moonless night. It was a good thing that there were no businesses or exterior lights in the abandoned area of Tem Tem District that housed the Division station.

Zen pressed a button on the interior handle of the thermal shield, and it stretched out from a loose tarp to a deep umbrella-like shape. That was precisely what was needed, with the drones potentially scanning from overhead. She held it with her left hand as she put her right hand on Mik's shoulder, following him from close behind. She was relying on him for navigation as she could only really see the ground in front of her.

"This way," Mik said, looking ahead. "I can see the warehouse from here, about a hundred yards away. We should be there in no time."

Then came a dreaded sound, the low whirring buzz of a Prowler drone. Without sight, Zen's hearing was slightly enhanced, and she could hear the quick movements of the motors and cameras from above. "There's a drone right above us," she whispered. "I guess we'll know very quickly whether this thing works."

"I hear it, too. Let's move slowly. Last thing we need is something messing up the shield. Thank God it's not windy tonight."

"I don't think it sees us." Zen breathed a deep sigh of relief that Mik could feel on the back of his neck. It made him relax as well.

In less than a minute, they arrived at the warehouse. The door was rusted steel, but Mik could only make out the general shape of it. He pulled out the keychain with the warehouse and car keys. After searching partially with his eyes and partially with his fingers, he felt the keyhole. He inserted the key and turned. He grabbed the doorknob. It opened as he knew it would, but there was always the inkling of anxiety in the back of his head that said it wouldn't. Zen pressed the button again, and the tarp collapsed on them so they could enter.

Mik wasn't going to risk turning the lights on in here, mostly because he knew that the shield would reflect them blindingly. There was just enough light so they could see with normal vision, at least by squinting intently. There it was, right in the middle of the large square room. A 2039 Dodge Kodiak. One of the last big-engine gas guzzlers ever made. A goddamn classic. He smiled despite himself and unlocked it. He entered the driver's seat, put the key in the ignition, and attempted to start it. As expected, there was nothing but a barely audible click. The battery was dead.

"Looks like we'll have to jump it." Mik opened the trunk and grabbed the jumpstart kit. He popped the hood and placed the two leads on the alternator. He turned on the kit, which lit up, and got back into the car. He tried it again, and this time the engine roared to life, deep and throaty. "Get in," he said with a big shit-eating grin. "Let's see what this baby can do."

CHAPTER 52
GET ME OUTTA HERE!

Jose's headache was gone. That was the first thing he noticed when he woke up. It had been there as a symptom of his concussion after the prison fight at dinner, and it had come roaring back after Sean had died and that doctor and guard had come over, and *oh shit!* He had been so focused on the relief in his head that he momentarily forgot what had happened. He had grown claws out of his hand and stabbed that guard to death through the cell bars. He quickly looked down at his hands. They were completely normal. Nothing out of place. No claws, no blood pouring from the open wounds in his knuckles. Even his left hand that had been smashed by the bully club looked as good as new. Did he imagine the whole thing? It was so damn vivid, though. Plus, he was pretty sure he remembered getting walloped in the back of the head while being escorted away from his cell.

He looked around his room, if you could call it that. A ten-by-ten concrete cell with a single hanging light and a tiny window in the door made of some kind of plexiglass-type material. No window to the outside and no bars. All the ventilation must be from above because he sure as hell wasn't getting any air from outside the cell. He had avoided solitary confinement so far in his prison career, but he was sure this was it. He slowly stood up and walked over to the window. He half-expected to see an empty hallway with rows of other similar cells, but the opposite was true. It was bustling out there. Men and women in lab coats scurried around, calling out orders and requests. The sound dampening was quite strong, but he could still hear the gist of it all. He seemed to be in a solitary wing, but it had a huge central area, and it was filled with people and machines, and—*are those bodies?* They weren't near him, rather on the other side of the area, but he could see them laying on examination tables, some nude and some with sheets pulled over them. *What the hell is going on here?*

Jose tested the door by hitting it with the palm of his hand. The world outside didn't acknowledge his actions. He started hitting the door harder and yelling. "Hey! Hey! Come over here! Get me outta here!" Still nothing. He changed his tactics. He slammed his heel into the door with a strong front kick, his laceless shoes threatening to slip off. He moved back to the window and continued smacking the door with his palm. "Hey! You!" There was a young woman in a lab coat working on a computer nearby. "You on the computer! Get me the fuck outta here!" He smacked his hands into the door again, repeatedly, until they started to go numb. Just when he was about to give up and rest, he caught her quickly glance over and then immediately go back to work. "No! I saw you! You heard me! Get me outta here!" He resumed kicking the door and smacking it with a renewed vigor. He saw her curse to herself and look back over to him. She walked off out of his limited field of view.

"What the fuck!" Jose yelled. "You can't just leave me in this cell without telling me what's going on! Come back! Come back, god-damnit!" He kept attacking the door until he saw the woman re-enter his vision. This time she was flanked by two men in suits and none other than Dr. Isaac Cross. She said something to them and pointed to the cell and to Jose's face pressed up against the window. Dr. Cross nodded at the woman, and she left to go back to work. He began coming toward the cell. Something about him gave Jose the creeps, and that was beyond the whole situation with Sean dying and him coming up with some bullshit vaccine excuse. He could see it in his eyes, even through the tiny window. Once you knew what to look for, you could always spot crazy.

"Mr. Gutierrez!" Dr. Cross exclaimed. Jose could tell that he said it loudly, but it came through rather soft and muffled. "I'm glad you're awake. I must apologize for your new living situation. You were creating quite the ruckus over in general population, and we just can't have that while conducting this experiment. I wanted to thank you for doing that, by the way. It gave me the crucial insight needed to modify some of our protocols for future subjects."

Jose flushed with anger. He had known for quite a while now that this wasn't some simple vaccination, but the audacity of Dr. Cross to blatantly admit it in front of him now with a thick steel cell door between them infuriated him. If only he could get his claws, or even his regular goddamn fists, on Dr. Cross, he would make short fucking work of him.

"What the fuck did you do to me? What did you do to Sean?" Jose caught himself and tried to calm down. He was mad and desperate, but he knew that he wasn't getting out of the cell of his own accord. He had to keep his aggression in check if he was going to plead his case for release.

"We'll get to those questions in a minute. Patience, please. As I was saying, from now on, prisoners being brought in for their, ahem, *vaccinations* will be housed in a separate unit. It's being prepared as we speak. No rest for the weary. Or is it wicked? Either way, there won't be any of the sort of commotion you caused going forward. I believe the next bus arrives in just a few short hours. To answer your eloquently posed questions, I have worked tirelessly for years at the very frontier of gene research, concentrating on the science of supplantation. I am so very, very close to perfecting a procedure that will allow me to insert multiple species' genes into a single human being. This is a double-blind study, so I cannot answer with complete certainty, but I would wager that your friend was in one of those groups. I am truly sorry about his fate. Don't worry, though. He was part of a larger cause." He swept his arm in a motion gesturing to the bodies on the examination tables.

Jose was tensing up to scream and assault the door like a wild man, but he remembered his goal. He had to get out of here before anything else. Dr. Cross seemed to notice his internal train of thought and paused for a moment before continuing.

"I have been administering different combinations of genes in different sequences to see which might work and which won't. All the computer simulations in the world cannot compete with real live human subjects. You, on the other hand, were likely in the control group, meaning you received one genetic trait from a single species. Judging from what you did to that poor corrections officer, I do believe you received genes from *Trichobatrachus robustus*. The hairy frog. It is a very unique species that is able to mold its bones into sharp objects and push them through the skin. Quite barbaric, I must say. Someone is going to be in big trouble for including that in the experiment's gene supply. There are some sick people in the world, aren't there, Mr. Gutierrez? Anyway, I digress. I will be keeping you here for observation until I find a way to dispose of you."

"You fucking murderer! Let me the fuck out of here! You—" But Dr. Cross had already turned and begun walking away.

CHAPTER 53
WHERE TO GO

They made excellent time getting out of the city. The roads were about as empty as they ever were, it being the very dead of night. It made them stick out like a sore thumb to anyone who might want to take notice, but they kept their speed unsuspiciously slightly over the limit. The engine purred on the highway leading south toward Crest Hill. Mik realized that despite what he may have said in the warehouse, he was definitely not about to see what this baby could do. Slow and steady was the key. It took them a shade over half an hour to arrive at their destination, a small car lot behind a ridge a couple of hundred yards away from the prison campus. They looked around, out from behind the windshield and side windows, and saw no people and no drones.

"Are you ready to do this?" Mik asked.

"I'm ready," Zen responded. "Let's get this over with. I want to get through this alive, so I can go back and see my parents again."

"Me too. We didn't go through all of this just for it all to end in a prison sewer system. Stay right on my tail, and tap me if you want my attention. We have to stay pin-drop silent."

Zen nodded. They exited the car and walked over to a cement staircase leading down to the left. The air was still cool, and it felt even cooler without the thermal shield blocking even the slightest hint of wind. They reached the bottom of the staircase and hastily crossed the street. At this time of night, there were no cars on the road, but they didn't want to take any unnecessary chances of being noticed by a passerby. Beyond the road was a half-mowed grassy field, the kind where young people would smoke weed and drink beers and leave all their trash behind. They walked steadily through it. They may have been within the distance of someone manning the guard towers, but anyone up there tended to look within the compound, not toward the outside. Even if they did, Mik and Zen were dressed in all black on a near-moonless night. It would take an eagle to spot them here. At the far end of the field was an aqueduct of sorts that collected excess water and re-directed it into the external sewer system leading away from the prison. Past that was the sewer gate. To Mik, it looked like a portal to hell, and he wasn't sure he was ever coming back, even with such a tight-knit plan. China was supposed to be in and out too, and look how that turned out.

It was a very good thing that they were wearing waterproof boots. They reached the aqueduct and gently stepped through the stagnant muddy water to the gate. Mik pulled on the rusty bars, but it was held shut by a large common padlock. He opened a satchel on his belt and took out a pair of undersized bolt cutters. He didn't want to bring attention by using the plasma torch he also possessed. He nodded at Zen and gestured for her to wait. She could tell that he was asking her to be patient. This might take a few goes to fully break the lock. After just under a minute, it snapped. He grabbed the lock, pulled it off, and slowly placed it in the dark water of the aqueduct. No one would notice it for quite some time. He nodded to Zen, and they stepped through the entrance into the darkness of the sewer tunnel.

Zen kept her hand on Mik's shoulder as the already meager light from outside slowly dissipated into total darkness. Mik could see everything ahead, and that was all that mattered. Zen closed her eyes, trying to envision the sewer map from the tablets they had looked at for hours. It was difficult enough to translate those diagrams into real life and that much harder when you couldn't see anything. She hoped that Mik could picture them in his mind as well as she could. She supposed that he would be good at real-time mapping from his time in the military. They headed deeper in until they reached a U-shaped intersection. They both knew where to go. They wound to the right and then forward again. There was no light here, but Zen could make out a slight glimmer ahead where the tunnel opened up into a service area. Beyond that was the staircase that led up to the guard station and specifically the electrical room that hopefully housed the transmitter system. The air was thick and heavy, and the smell, while not as overpowering as she expected, was anything but pleasant.

She tapped on Mik's shoulder, and he turned around. She pointed toward the lights in the distance, and he nodded, although she didn't see him do it. Mik waited for Zen to put her hand back onto his shoulder, and they continued forward toward the light. They moved slowly and quietly. There was little chance of anyone being down here since that only happened during scheduled maintenance or a total septic disaster, but they didn't want to risk being seen. They slid their boots through the low water, careful not to splash. Mik looked around. The light here was strong enough to see, but he also used his pit organ to check for heat signatures. The area was empty. A short set of stairs led up to a landing with three doors, two of which led to other parts of the sewer tunnels, while, according to the blueprints, the one on the far right led to the staircase up to their destination.

Mik used his plasma torch to sear off the lock this time. It was much more efficient. He pulled open the heavy steel door very slowly, as it creaked loudly when he went any faster. The staircase inside was a stark transition from the dankness of the sewers. The stairs were painted red, and the concrete walls were lined with bands of LED lights. It was almost blinding in comparison. The air seemed so much fresher here, although Mik wondered if that was just relative. Two floors up, there would be doors to the electrical room and the guard station. They headed up the stairs as silently as they could. They passed the first landing that had doors that were supposedly to other maintenance rooms and wings and continued up to the top. Just as predicted, there were two doors. Unmarked and otherwise identical, on opposite sides of the landing. The blueprints had shown them that the door on the left was to the electrical room, but the landing was circular. Mik couldn't be completely sure because it depended on which direction he was standing. *It was to the left once you reached the top, right?* He couldn't risk asking Zen verbally, so he shrugged and pointed questioningly at the door he thought was the one to the electrical room. Zen shrugged in response but nodded her head, mouthing the words I *think so. Maybe.* Mik closed his eyes and steadied his breath. Zen gritted her teeth and looked on intently as Mik put his hand on the door handle and pulled.

The electrical room. They simultaneously let out deep breaths as quietly as they could. Mik went in first and looked around. All sorts of screens and electrical hubs, but he had no idea what he was looking for. Zen followed and quickly scanned the room. She tapped him on the shoulder. She smiled widely and nodded. She mouthed *transmitter* and pointed to something near the back of the room. She walked over there and touched it. Just another strange block of metal and wiring; it seemed so innocuous and random. *This is the key to the whole plan? Completely absurd.*

Mik stood away from her and waited, wanting to give her enough time to concentrate and do her thing. He wondered if it worked like his pit organ, basically second nature, or if she needed to mentally and physically prepare to harness and deliver the electricity. He watched her place her hand on the object and closed her eyes. She was deep in concentration. Zen held onto the transmitter with an iron grip, her palm starting to become moist. She pressed her eyes shut as if the harder she did that, the more effective it would be. She felt a surge of nervous energy inside her, as if someone had jumped out to scare her, but it contained none of that fear. It built and built until she somehow knew that it was enough and then released it through her arm and her palm and fingers. It was a grand relief. She opened her eyes and watched as little lightning bolts danced on the surface of the transmitter system, sizzling and popping, then arced out onto the wiring and other units. She found herself surprisingly giddy. It was almost like the miniature fireworks her parents let her play with on a July 4 weekend during *one of the good years.*

She stepped back and joined Mik, who was also concentrating on the little light show. The tiny bolts fizzled along the wiring, leading through the walls and ceiling. When the last of them coursed along and out of the room, it seemed to get so dark and quiet, with the haze of smoke and the smell of ozone and burnt synthetic materials hanging in the air. They both coughed and waved their hands to push some of the smoke away. The whole place went dark. And they waited. And waited.

CHAPTER 54
POOR BASTARDS

Jose had calmed down, and he found that strange. He was always one to hold onto anger for longer than people usually did. He had started blaming it on his childhood, but that wasn't true. It was a culmination of everything that happened during years in the drug game and time paying for it. You couldn't just let things slide out there because kindness was weakness. The whole time he was subconsciously training himself to hold that anger in his heart. Sure, sometimes it burst out at inopportune times, like when his cousin burned the burgers at a family get-together and ended up with his face squashed against the hot propane grill. It was just a little thing, but all the big things had built up inside of him, and he let it out like a sudden storm, quick, random, and powerful. He remembered it taking two of his uncles pulling with all their strength before his hand left the back of his cousin's neck. The poor guy went through hell before they mostly fixed him up, although he still had the scars. After that, Jose learned to harness that anger, to let it simmer and release it out like hellfire on those deserving. Shit, it was scary when he did. It made people respect him. And it kept him honest to himself and his business dealings. No loan ever went unpaid, and every bag was accurate to the fucking milligram.

This morning, though, he was calm. The anger hadn't vanished like magic or anything, but it was energizing, not consuming. It gave him a warmness in his cold cell, not that it was outright pleasurable, but it kept him sharp and alert. He walked in patterns in the small square room, up and back, corner to corner. Every once in a while, he would peer out through the tiny window to the area where the people in white lab coats hurried about. Each time, he looked for Dr. Cross, hoping that he would pass by, that they would meet eyes, and

259

he could unleash the anger inside him again. But Dr. Cross hadn't been back since their previous conversation, and Jose figured he never would be, at least until it was time for disposal.

Maybe it was the peace that knowing his end was coming soon that allowed the anger to simmer and not boil over. He guessed there was a sort of peace that came to most people near the end. After all, it was the not knowing that drove people crazy. He thought that for the people who lived fast, put it out there, met danger head-on, it wasn't so bad when the curtains finally closed. But for the people who lived in fear, enjoying their creature comforts and blocking out the real world, it had to be pretty damn painful. When they realized that the lives in their movies and dreams never came to fruition and that they had spent their years simply waiting and wishing, oh man, the end must come hard and rough. For that, he counted himself lucky. Even if he made a truckload of bad decisions, at least he had the balls to make them. And no one could argue that he didn't truly live.

There was one thing, though. Ever since the fiasco with his cousin, he never once had let a personal slight go unanswered. And this was one mother of a personal slight. Dr. Cross had unceremoniously killed his best bud, Sean, for nothing except checking off a box on his supplantation study chart. The man had lived, too, like Jose, wild and careless, but alive as hell, and this motherfucker had the audacity to end it for nothing. Not even some street payback or a family grudge. Fucking nothing. Jose felt the anger growing. Sean wasn't ready to meet his end at the hands of this piece of shit, and neither was he. And he would roll over in his grave if he let an insult like killing his friend go unpunished. He had to live, if only to see that doctor look up at him, begging, as he squeezed his fucking eyeballs back into his skull. That would do the trick. Avenge his friend, and then he could go die peacefully in some ditch somewhere. But not here, and not now. He started to shake as the anger started pulsing in his temples. He walked over to the cell door and slammed on it again and again, and he started to scream, louder than he ever screamed before.

Into the void outside, filled with uncaring faces and nameless white coats, he slammed and screamed. He could swear he could hear loud thumps and zaps and crashes in the distance as if Thor or Zeus or some other god of thunder was answering his battle cries.

Then the craziest fucking thing happened that he had ever witnessed in his entire crazy fucking life. The cell door slid open.

He stepped outside, watching the people in their white lab coats run and stumble around like frightened rats in a subway tunnel. He was momentarily paralyzed. Just for a second, his anger was overwhelmed by his newfound sense of freedom. He could escape if he wanted to. All the other cell doors in the area were open, alarms were blaring, and people shouted desperate orders in a futile attempt to contain the situation. He could likely use the chaos and confusion to his advantage and head for the exits. The idea of it was very enticing, and his heart yearned for the outside, but he quickly regained his focus. He couldn't leave this horrible place without getting revenge for the death of his only friend in the whole system. He had to find Dr. Cross.

There were a small number of prisoners who were running for the entrance to the block. As he could see from the window in his cell, there were rows of solitary confinement cells, but it seemed that only a few were occupied. A man in a suit was yelling at the group of faceless white lab coats to *retrieve all data* or something like that. The dead bodies on the examination tables were immune to the whole scene, laying still and peaceful. Jose looked for Sean's body among them.

"You need to get back into your cell!" whined a small man in a lab coat. When Jose met his glance, the man lost all his nerve and ran away, joining the circus nearby. The rest of the inmates had vanished from the block, leaving him alone in a sea of research employees or doctors or lab assistants or whatever the hell they were, indistinguishable in their outfits. He resumed his search. Bodies of men who were unlucky enough to be chosen for this experiment and to get those two doses. Some of them were hooked up to machinery that was now partially disassembled and strewn about. Others were splayed open like Thanksgiving turkeys so their innards could be poked and prodded. *Poor bastards*. He even recognized a couple of them from back at Danville, shuttled over here with him and Sean back on that beautiful summer day. No sign of Sean, though. The place was starting to clear out. The people had *retrieved all data*, he guessed, and were heading for the doors. Only the man in the suit was still in the room, and he hadn't even seemed to notice Jose until now when they were the only two live people left. He looked at Jose and froze. The bodies on the tables were the only things separating them.

"Where's Dr. Cross?" Jose's voiced boomed and echoed in the large empty room. He didn't intend for it, but he was pleased. It made him sound more imposing.

The man hesitated at first. "How the hell should I know? What are you even still doing here? Don't you want to escape or something?"

"I need to find him. He killed my friend."

"I recommend you get the hell out of here while you can. All these alarms? They're gonna send everything they've got to this place any minute now. Local police, SWAT, maybe even the National Guard."

"You know where he is. Else you wouldn't be telling them to get all the data. I know who that's for. He was probably speaking directly into your goddamn HUDPhone. Where is he?"

"Look, you need to get outta here. Do you really want to be locked back up after all this? C'mon, think about it."

"Where's Dr. Cross? Where the fuck is he?" Jose walked through the corpses toward the man. The corpses didn't seem to notice.

"I can't tell you that! Just get outta here! Don't come any closer!"

"Tell me where he is!" Jose *knew* that the man knew. And he only had so much time to find Dr. Cross before he, too, escaped from the prison with all that data and research.

"Stop!" The man pulled out a pistol from his side holster and raised it toward Jose. "Last fucking chance! Turn around and get outta here, or I'll shoot!"

Jose concentrated. He felt the sensation in his forearms first, then his wrists, and finally his hands and fingers. In a final quick burst of sweet pain, the razor-sharp claws of bone pushed out of both his hands. His mouth formed a threatening snarl.

"What the fuck?!" the man screamed and pulled the trigger. Nothing happened. His face awash with panic, he pulled and pulled again in rapid succession.

"I never liked those smart guns," Jose said, the snarl slowly turning into a terrifying smile. "The biometrics tend to mess up when your hand's real sweaty."

"No—" the man screamed as the claws pierced through the soft tissue of his throat. Blood filled his mouth and flowed like lava from the holes in his neck onto his finely pressed suit.

There was no time to waste. Jose had a job to do.

CHAPTER 55
ONE MORE SHOT

"Get up, Mik! We have to go!"

Zen pulled on Mik's shirt-jacket. Her hand slipped off, and she grabbed his arm, hanging loosely on the ground. The electrical explosions set off by the initial charge had passed, followed by the quiet burn of plastic and silicon, and the alarms were now blaring, loud even in this room cut off from the rest of the prison. There was also some distant yelling and maybe even gunshots, but she couldn't be totally sure.

"C'mon, Mik! We have to leave *now*! They're gonna want to know what the hell went wrong!"

Mik was slumped against the metal grate in the electrical room. He stared at the opposite wall, lined with pipes and cables. The trees were bursting into flames inside his head. His squadmates were dying, bullets ripping through them, sending arcs of blood into the night, and fire consumed their bodies like match heads. Then nothing. His head pounded with the rhythm of his rapid heartbeat. His teeth felt cold and brittle. He could feel sweat trickling down his forehead, and it felt so cold against his burning skin. It dripped into his eyes, and it stung fiercely, but it broke his stare. He closed his eyes as the fire around him grew larger and hotter and—

Zen slapped him square in the face.

"What the fuck?" Mik looked at Zen with comically wide eyes and a fast-reddening cheek.

"We have to get the hell out of here, Mik! You were staring at the wall like you didn't even hear me!"

"I didn't. I was—"

"It's all right. It's okay; we just need to move."

Mik stood up, feeling a bit dizzy, and shook his head to clear it.

He let out a quick breath and nodded. "All right, let's get going." He shook his head again and headed back out into the stairwell from where they entered. Zen followed closely behind like a shadow.

"I don't usually thank someone for slapping me in the face, but I needed it," he said softly. There was still heavy commotion in the background, but no need to risk being heard.

"Anytime."

They walked down the stairs as quietly as they could, but their footsteps clanged against the steel regardless. They approached the door leading back into the sewer system, and Mik pushed it open. They were immediately met with the familiar stench, but any smell was worth getting out of here in one piece. As they passed the doorway, a loud bang echoed from above them.

"Who's *down there?*" The voice boomed through the cavernous stairwell.

"Shit," Mik whispered under his breath. He and Zen ran down from the landing toward the tunnel. Footsteps echoed above them, the drumming of steel. At least two people were coming down those stairs, and fast.

"Who's there?" The voice called again. They didn't feel much like answering back. If they were caught, who knows what would happen. They ran through the tunnel, darkness slowly enveloping them. Mik could see the walls and rails and the low water meandering underneath. He wanted nothing more than to break into an all-out sprint, but he was worried about slipping and falling since the floor was slimy, and Zen was relying on him for navigation. He refused to leave her behind, knowing they'd still be in that electrical room if it wasn't for her. They reached the U-intersection and were just about to start heading down the next tunnel when lights burst forward from behind them. They were bright and intense, and they reflected off the dirty water onto the walls like shimmering starlight.

"There they are! Get them!" It was a different voice this time. There were at least two. Zen couldn't help but turn her head to look. The lights were nearly blinding, but she could make out three figures at the entrance to the tunnel. The gunshot was deafening in the enclosed space. While Zen still had her head turned, Mik could see the bullet hole appear on the wall just to the right of his head.

"Get down!" Mik yelled, and Zen responded by rapidly ducking. "Move!" They sped into the next tunnel as two more bullets ricocheted off the wall only inches from their heads. The slipperiness of the ground be damned; they sprinted down the tunnel toward the sewer entrance, the early morning sun shining beyond the barred gate. Another gunshot roared through the tunnel. Mik crashed into the gate, causing it to spin outward and slam into the concrete wall outside. Another gunshot reverberated through the tunnel as they exited into the fresh open air.

"You need to keep running," Mik said breathlessly. "Trust me. Just keep running toward the street." Zen nodded, the adrenaline pumping through her, almost happy to have any sort of plan. She ran across the field. But Mik didn't follow. He stood against the wall outside the tunnel and pulled out the 1911 pistol that Filip had gifted to him. He held it by his side and waited. Not five seconds later, three men in suits burst through the opening. *Suits? Since when did prison guards wear suits? They're private security. And those suits are probably bulletproof.* They yelled and fired at Zen, once, twice, the bullets creating puffs of dirt near her feet. But Mik was still against the wall, and they hadn't seen him. He raised the 1911 and matched the sights. His military training allowed him to instantly focus on the front sight and allow his target to blur. He felt the beautifully light travel of the trigger until it met resistance. Then, with an artist's touch, he pulled. The first man shuddered and fell as the bullet hit its mark. Mik moved his hands like the steady head of a snake. The second man was farther away now, but he hadn't even noticed that his colleague had been hit by the time Mik pulled the trigger a second time. His head leaked red as he crumpled to the ground in a heap. The third man turned around and fired. The bullet crashed into Mik's left thigh. Mik's focus was obliterated as he fell to his knees. He had to regain his composure. It hurt like a son of a bitch, but he had to eliminate the threat before he could worry about the wound. He realigned the sights. His hands were shaking, but he willed them to steady. One more shot. He found the target. He relaxed his eyes and pulled ever so gently. The fire roared, and the man danced for a moment and then fell under his own weight. With one last leg twitch, the man was dead on the ground.

Mik collapsed mere seconds after and bellowed in pain. He placed his hand over the wound and gritted his teeth. He couldn't help but cry out when he put pressure on it. Zen noticed that the gunfire had ceased and turned to look. She had almost made it to the street when she heard the agonizing moans drifting on the morning wind. She walked back slowly and cautiously. She saw no one at first glance, but she kept going. They might be waiting for her, but she couldn't leave Mik if he was the one crying out. As she got closer, she could make out the bodies of the men in suits, almost hiding in the tall grass. Then she heard another moan and saw him. Mik was propped against the wall, holding his hands on his thigh. Blood flowed out of the hole beneath them and pooled on the ground. He could feel the slick wetness of his pant leg. He grimaced with every microscopic motion.

Zen ran over to him. "Mik! Are you okay? You've been shot!"

"I'm okay." He grimaced again and moaned. "We just need to get back to the Haven so I can get some medical attention."

"What about a hospital? The Haven is at least a half-hour away!"

"We can't risk that. Not now. I'll be okay till then. It missed the artery. Barely. Zen?"

"Yeah?"

"Find the shells. Black casing. They should be around here somewhere. Can't have it traced back to Filip. There should be three of them."

"Okay, I'll look for them, but we have to get you outta here." As soon as she said it, they could hear sirens in the distance.

"I know. We have to go. Please look quickly. Bet the whole state's coming down here after what we did."

The sirens, still distant, slowly grew louder. Zen looked through the grass and dirt. She picked up one casing, black with a silver rim. She looked again and found two more next to each other against the concrete wall. "I got 'em!"

"Good. Help me up."

Zen took Mik's hand in hers and pulled. Mik yelled out again, cursing under his breath, but he got to his feet. She took his arm and draped it over her shoulders. Mik steadied himself with his right leg and put some of his weight gently on her. He limped gingerly as she helped him across the field. He moaned with every step but smiled reassuringly whenever she looked concerned. The stairs up to the lot where their car was parked were difficult going, but she managed to take the extra impact without much wear and tear. The sirens got louder. The streets would be swarming within minutes.

"Can you drive?" Mik asked.

"It's been a while," Zen responded. "But I think I can manage. It's just like riding a bike, right?"

"I don't know how to ride a bike."

"Well, shit. Me neither." She helped Mik into the passenger's seat, closed the door, and entered the driver's side. It had been years since she was behind a steering wheel, and she had never driven a gas-powered vehicle before. Mik handed her the keys and pointed to the ignition. She put the key in and turned. The engine roared like a beast. She felt a shiver down her spine, but her face was beaming with excitement.

CHAPTER 56
A LONG SHADOW

Jose burst out of the entrance to the solitary block. It was already almost empty outside. He guessed most of the prisoners had sprinted their way out of the complex, at least the ones who could make it through the intake building without being stopped. Down a cement path lined with newly planted trees, he saw that the people in white lab coats were already running toward the entrance. Regular prison guards were nowhere to be seen. Perhaps he had been damn lucky to be in the solitary block with so few other prisoners. They hadn't even had an official guard detail, just white lab coats and the odd man-in-a-suit. Dr. Cross had to be headed toward the entrance and the parking lots beyond, that is, if he wasn't already there. He had seen him bright and early this morning, or last night, whatever he'd call it, so he doubted he went home. If he had, he could never get his revenge for Sean.

He waited a short while as the claws jutting out of his knuckles slowly began to retract into his hand. Aside from what looked like small incisions, no one would have a clue about what just happened. He started to walk down the path. He was itching to run, to find Dr. Cross as soon as possible, but he had to be smart. Guards or those fuckers in suits could be around here anywhere. Was that—damn, gunshots. Gunshots and screams. Ladies and gentlemen, they had a full-on riot on their hands. But that insanity was happening in Cell Block A to the right. And Block C off to the left, where he and Sean had been held. He might have ended up dead in one of those buildings. Or dead like Sean, on some examination table or cart somewhere, tossed out like garbage. He was lucky, all things considered, but he sure as hell didn't feel it. He had to find Dr. Cross and make him pay. For everything.

Jose's head was on a swivel. The altercations in the cell blocks could spill outside at any second. He walked slowly and carefully around the main command building in the middle of the campus. The white coats were already inside the intake building at the entrance or at the parking lots by now. He had to hurry. From here, it was a straight shot. He started to jog. He had passed most of the cell blocks by now, so he figured he was free of that danger. Then he heard the shot. It thudded against the cement next to him, sending up a cloud of white dust. He broke into a sprint. He looked ahead and scanned the horizon. There he was. A guard in the tower to the left of the intake building. The sunrise reflected off his rifle scope. Another shot. He felt a pinching sensation; then, he felt the warmness of the blood on his neck. He reflexively put his hand there while he was running. The bullet had just grazed him and took off the top layers of his skin. Nothing that would cause any real harm, but he was completely out in the open. There was no cover at all. He was flanked by buildings to his right, and to his left was just the prison lawn and—the corpses. He was running too fast to count, but there were three, maybe four dead bodies out there, no doubt victims of this sniper fire. Shit, maybe the prisoners never got out after all. He regained his focus, having lost it only momentarily. He had to make it to the intake building to cut off the line of sight. The gunshot rang out again, this time making a hole in the side of his loose prison jersey. He was getting close. He could see the open doors from here. He felt his legs churning beneath him and the breath rushing out of his lungs. Only a few more steps then—the bullet hammered into his arm. He felt his feet tangle up. As he slipped, his momentum sent him spinning and tumbling onto the steps of the building. Any breath he had left was taken from him as the concrete met his ribs.

Jose tried to take in air, but every attempt was met with wracking, scorching pain. He raised his head, peering through the doors of the intake building. From his point of view, it looked entirely empty. All those white coats must have left already, along with Dr. Cross. He started to get angry, but the dull, crushing sensation of his wounds took any unrelated emotion away in a hurry. He slowly turned over until he was sitting on the lowest step. He was out of view of the tower guard, but he was far from safe. He looked down and saw the dark redness of his sleeve. He painfully raised and turned his arm and saw that the bullet had made a clean exit. It missed the bone, then, but he wasn't sure if it hit an artery or something. Either way, he had to keep going. It was only a matter of time until that guard or someone else found him and put him away for good. Plus, if he wanted any chance, however small, of catching Dr. Cross, he had to get himself up and to the parking lots.

He tried to steady himself with both hands, but he immediately noticed it was a bad idea as his injured left arm buckled under the pressure. He turned and slowly propped himself up into a squat position, and with the help of his right arm, found his feet. His ribs sent ribbons of pain through him with every movement, but he had no choice. He walked up the steps and into the intake building. It was strangely quiet in here. Yes, it was empty, but it felt so far removed from the chaos that enveloped the place that he could see himself walking through here on his day of release. But that isn't quite realistic anymore, is it? He sneered at the thought. He either got out today somehow, or God knows what would happen, back into the system or worse. He killed two men, that guy in the suit with the sweaty hands and the moron who decided to get all up close and personal at the bars of his cell.

The entrance door to the building was also open, and he could see the path leading out to the front parking lot. It was nearly cleared out. If Dr. Cross had been parked there, he was surely gone now. Only a few cars remained, and there were no white coats or anyone scrambling about. The other parking lot was more off to the side of the complex to his left. This was a good thing if that guard was still in the tower. If Jose ran out to the front parking lot, he would be in his sights, but if he skirted the wall to his left and then went out to the side lot, that guard would never see him. He still exited the building cautiously. Enough insanity had already happened that his mind and body anticipated the worst. He jogged along the outside of the wall. It towered over him, casting a long shadow that blocked out the rising sun. The wind blew against his face, gently and pleasantly, and it energized him. Sticking close to the wall, he reached the corner of the complex. As soon as he got there, he began to hear sirens in the far distance, almost imperceptibly. He had to hurry. If Dr. Cross and everyone else were in a rush before, they absolutely would be now.

The side lot was in view, and it was packed. White coats and suits scrambled about. Cars skidded and peeled out. Jose scanned carefully. They were mobbed around an SUV in the far corner. People in white coats ran to and fro and two men in suits stood guard like statues. There he was. Dr. Cross was leaning over into the back seat of the SUV, fussing with what looked like data cards that were being delivered by the employees. Jose carefully moved forward, crouching behind the nearest row of cars. If he were seen now, it would all be for nothing. There were far too many people, and there was too much distance to cover. He was lucky that the outer row of parking spots was filled save for one or two. He slinked forward and around the corner of the lot, and then again, completing somewhat of a semi-circle so that he was now facing Dr. Cross and the men from the other direction, from the side nearest the road leading away from the prison. And freedom. He looked behind for just a second at the open field beyond the road, and the urge to run swelled up in him like a rumbling volcano from underground. But he turned back toward the lot just before the urge got too great. No one there had seemed to notice anything. The guards still stood there rigidly. And about fifty feet away was Dr. Cross, who was busy yelling at one of the white coats about missing data. Through the chaos, it was difficult to pick up any coherent lines of conversation.

It was now or never. At any minute, Dr. Cross could decide to enter the vehicle and head out, never to return. The sirens were getting louder. The roads would soon be filled with cops and who knows what else. He figured they brought the whole kitchen sink if there was even a rumor of a massive prison riot. He didn't have to concentrate very hard this time. He only had to look down at his hands for the process to begin. It stung. It always stung, but he was getting used to the sensation. The bony claws started to protrude from his knuckles, and within seconds, those violent talons were ready. And so was he.

He snuck alongside a black van, its height concealing him. When he reached the front, where the windshield sloped down and would expose him, he charged. For the first split second, they didn't react. He was coming from the opposite direction as would be expected, but as he got close, they turned. The two men in suits drew their guns in a quick, professionally trained fashion, but Jose was already on top of them when they readied their aim. His left arm still hurt spectacularly, so he swung with his right. His claws raked against the face of the nearest man. The claws had no sensation, but he could feel the change in motion when one of them entered the eye socket. The man screamed and screamed, dropping his gun and clawing at his own eviscerated face. The cartilage of his nose hung loosely, and blood poured from the four deep slashes. Jose tried to bring his left arm up to swing at the other man, but it responded weakly, and it couldn't reach him. He felt the bullet from the man's gun slam into his gut with a shudder of excruciating pain. His breath came in ragged gasps, the air seemingly always just out of reach.

Dr. Cross was yelling. He could make it out above the sound of the blood pumping desperately in his head. "Protect me! Protect the data!" Dr. Cross jumped into the driver's seat of the SUV and slammed the door shut behind him. The door to the passenger row was still open, and there were small computer hubs filled with input from various data cards.

Jose punched forward with his right hand and gave the man a touch of his own medicine, four deep holes in his abdomen courtesy of those wonderfully sharp talons. The man stared back at him, clearly too shocked and wounded to think about pulling the trigger again. He coughed, sending a sea of red droplets forward onto Jose's face and chest. As he fell to his knees, his eyes glazed over, staring into nothingness. Jose gasped again for breath. He felt like he was drowning. The blood pumped loudly and dully inside his skull, and his lungs burned viciously.

Dr. Cross was alone inside as far as Jose could see. The tires of the SUV screeched as Cross floored the pedal. He was so close. So damn close. If only his left arm would work, maybe he could swipe through the window. He tried and tried, but he could only muster a measly swing that scraped the metal on the door. As the vehicle peeled out and accelerated, he swung with his right hand. His claws cut through the data hubs like butter, causing electrical pops and sparks. He watched as Dr. Cross sped out of the parking spot and away, a fine line of smoke trailing from the back seat. Jose tried to yell, but he didn't have the breath, and he slumped down next to the two dead men in suits. He was so close. So damn close.

CHAPTER 57
FEELING'S MUTUAL

"Took you long enough." Ollie gave Mik a wry smile. He picked up a beer bottle that was on the table and placed it back down. "You need help?"

Mik shook his head. "I'll manage. It looks worse than it is." He steadied himself on one crutch as he pulled the chair out. Then he gingerly sat down.

"I think you sit down slower than Filip does. Here, have a cold one." He pushed the bottle across the table toward Mik. "You were in there for hours. What happened?"

"Corkscrew round. Doesn't shatter like a hollow point, but it really tears up the tissue inside. Still can't believe it missed the artery by less than a millimeter. Those nano-repair thingies are really something. Thank God for modern medicine, huh?"

"I'll take your word for it. Never been shot with *any* kind of bullet myself."

"Don't drink too much." The command came from Filip, who sauntered over to the table, his expression as serious as ever. "It slows the healing process."

Mik looked up. "I just sat down. This is my first."

"And you need to rest. You should head to bed early tonight."

"Give him a break, eh, Filip?" Ollie sipped on his beer and spat some of it back up in a fit of coughing. "It's all over the news. The cops found all those dead bodies. Mik and Zen helped stop that experiment before it got worse. A lot worse."

Mik put his hand up in a quieting gesture. "It's okay, Ollie. Filip's right. I just got out of surgery, and even with that nanotech, I have a long way to go. That just saved me from losing the leg. I gotta be careful. But one beer won't kill me, will it, Filip?"

"Hmm, I guess not." Filip shrugged dismissively.

"Come, sit down." Ollie waved Filip over to the table. "Join us!"

Filip pulled out a chair and sat down. Ollie was wrong. He was much quicker than Mik. "They're still investigating, but from the initial reports, you and Zen sent that place into total chaos before they continued the experiment on more prisoners."

Mik took a little swig of beer, savoring the taste as he swallowed. "I appreciate it. Both of you. Saying we stopped them. But we're the ones who caused that riot. What is it now, fifty-something dead so far, and that's not just the bodies they found on the exam tables? If we didn't do what we did, that wouldn't have happened."

Filip frowned and put his hand on Mik's shoulder. "Twenty-four bodies on those tables. And it would have been five times that if you didn't go when you did."

Mik shook his head. "I don't know. I guess maybe they'll find out. Anyway, where's Zen? She all right? She saved my ass back there, and I need to apologize to her. I put her in harm's way twice."

"She's over there with Jade and Caleb." He pointed in the general direction of the residential complex past the cafeteria. "They were waiting for you to get out of surgery."

"Want me to go get her?" Ollie asked. "Doesn't look like Filip's gonna offer."

"Would you mind? Bring 'em all over. Why not?"

Filip slowly stood up, stretching his back out in an absurdly dramatic fashion. "You know, Mikolaj, it's good to have you back. If only to temper my frustrations with having to deal with Ollie alone."

Ollie rolled his eyes and got up to go find the rest of the group. "Feeling's mutual, old man." He quickly returned with Zen, Jade, and Caleb in tow.

"Actually, I need to talk to Jade about something," Filip said. "Jade, would you mind, only for a couple of minutes?"

Ollie's jaw dropped incredulously. "What? You made me get up and—you know what, never mind."

Jade waved at the group. "Sure thing, Filip. Hey, Mik. Glad to see you're doing well. We'll be back soon, guys."

"Mike! Already up and about!" Caleb separated from Filip and Jade and walked over. He picked up Mik's crutches, trying them out for himself. "You won't need to get used to these, don't worry. My guys in medical have that nano stuff. It works lightning fast. You'll be good as new in a few days."

"Seriously?" Mik asked.

"No, I know your name's Mik. I was just joking around."

Mik smiled. "No, about how fast it works."

"Yeah, for real. As long as all the damage is muscle and skin, at least. It relies on your own blood flow, so tendons and ligaments take longer."

"Wow. Guess I'll have another beer then." Mik turned his head all the way to look at Zen, who was trailing behind. "Hey, Zen. Thank you."

Zen walked over so Mik had a better angle. "What do you mean?" She sat down next to Mik and pointed at his beer bottle. "Ollie, have any more of those?"

"Sure do!" Ollie reached into a cooler at his feet and pulled out a cold one. "I came prepared. Figured we would all get together after Mik got fixed up." He handed it to Zen.

Mik's face took on a serious expression. "Seriously, Zen. Thank you. If it wasn't for you, I never would have gotten out of there. You stayed with me and risked your own life. That's just—"

"Hey, if I didn't, I never would have found the entrance in the dark." She winked.

Mik started to smile, but it quickly vanished. "I mean it, Zen. I was paralyzed. I couldn't see anything. As soon as those transformers burst, or whatever it was, all I could see was fire. I was back in that forest in China, and the trees were exploding. It was—" He took a deep breath.

"It's fine, Mik."

"It's not. We could have been killed. And I put you in danger again when we got out of there."

"You did what you did because it was the only option. What if we both just ran?"

"We might have escaped just fine, and there wouldn't be any need to—"

"No, they would have shot us in the back eventually. You know that as well as I do. We had a long way to run."

"We were just lucky. I left you exposed."

"No, you stopped them. You didn't have time to formulate some complicated plan. It was the right move. We did what we needed to do, and we're alive. That's what matters."

"Uhh, you guys want to tell me what the hell you're talking about?" Ollie, who had been sitting there entranced, finally butted his head into their quiet conversation.

Mik politely shook his head. "Later, Ollie. Just know I'm sorry, Zen. And thanks again."

Zen beamed. "It's nothing. You're quite the shot. Give yourself some credit. Anyway, your beer's getting warm."

Mik nodded, finally smiling a little; his conscience satiated for a while. "Cheers, guys."

"Cheers!" Zen and Ollie responded in unison.

"Washburn will be on soon." Jade had returned, with Filip slowly following her.

"Huh?" Zen turned her head.

"*Windy City News*. They usually get all the updates before anyone else. They must have some shady backroom deals going on with everyone. Either way, we should know more any minute."

Filip returned and leaned over, placing both his hands on the table. "The good news is there have been no reports of drones in the area since this morning." He raised one hand to point at Mik and Zen. "However, I still think you two should stay put until we know exactly what's going on."

Jade nodded. "It looks like it's safe to start getting supplies for the Haven again, though, which is good news. We were running low on a lot of things, especially toilet paper. That and food."

Filip put his hand back on the table. "I want to say that I'm very proud of you two. And even Ollie, for that matter. You went above and beyond the call of duty. Zen, you've turned out to be a brave, selfless young woman, and I'm happy I opened the door to my butcher shop to you that day. Without your sacrifice and determination, this wouldn't have been possible." Filip paused and started to tear up just a little. He sat back down and turned his chair to face Mik. "And Mikolaj, my boy. I knew you were struggling when you got home. Your father had always looked after you, but no matter how much he tried, he couldn't do that any longer. You had to take care of him instead, and I never heard you complain. Not once. When he passed, I had to make sure you were all right. I never had children of my own, but I've always thought of you as my son. You've gone through so much, Mikolaj, but you never lost sight of what was right and wrong. Your sense of duty and responsibility. Maybe I've asked too much of you, especially with this mission, and for that, I'm sorry. But there is no one else in the world I trust more. From now on, I'll do my best to protect you. I'll do everything I can to make sure you don't have to live the rest of your life looking over your shoulder. I promise. I know we're not there yet, not by a long shot. But one day, I hope we'll find some peace."

CHAPTER 58
WASHBURN

"Available on all streaming providers in Illinois and the surrounding areas, this is *Windy City News*, and I'm Jeff Washburn. Ladies and gentlemen of the great city of Chicago and the world at large, we have some late-breaking news. It is of a very unsettling nature, so viewer and listener discretion is advised. There is a state of disaster at Stateville Correctional Center, where widespread prison riots occurred this morning as a result of what was thought to be an electrical storm of some kind. Upon initial investigation, local and state police found substantial evidence of an illegal experiment being conducted on prisoners.

"We at *Windy City News* pledge to go above and beyond the generalized information given to you by other news outlets, and what you are about to hear is completely exclusive. Police have combined forces with the Federal Bureau of Investigation and have launched a massive investigation into what exactly happened at Stateville. Authorities are still trying to figure out what caused the electrical surge at the penitentiary, but we have been told there is no evidence of any sort of storm or other weather event. The death toll now stands at sixty-seven, including seven prison guards and thirty prisoners, all victims of the riots, twenty-four other prisoners, unfortunate victims of the horrible experiment, and six private security operatives who, it has now been determined, were hired to help protect and conceal the experiment. All twenty-four experiment victims have been identified as inmates from Danville Correctional Center, who were bussed over to Stateville under the guise of annual vaccinations. Ten more of them died during the riots, leaving only two unaccounted for and remaining at large. Their names are Vitaly Poletov and Jose Gutierrez. Local and state police welcome any tips you may have as to their whereabouts.

"The disturbing information does not end there. There have been huge findings in the investigation of those clandestine human experiments. While most evidence and data had been hastily removed from the gymnasium and solitary confinement wing where the experiments were being conducted, laboratory assistants who took part in the experiment have since come forward. They have told authorities that both they and the prisoners were under the impression that they were giving out flu and COVID vaccinations and that when they found that most of the prisoners were dying, they had their own lives threatened. Most importantly, they revealed that the experiment was being directed by Dr. Isaac Cross, a disgraced former professor of genetic research at Johns Hopkins University. He oversaw a research team from Genovas, a company long known to be a player in the infant gene editing market. Dr. Cross also remains at large as a fugitive from the law, so police are welcoming any tips about him as well.

"Law enforcement wanted to know why Genovas would be involved in illegal human experiments, so they conducted a multi-agency large-scale raid only a few hours ago on their headquarters in downtown Chicago. What they found there shocked them.

"First, a quick shout-out to one of our amazing sponsors, Tem Tem. Tem Tem, improving lives through efficient and groundbreaking manufacturing.

"First, the task force found and arrested company CEO, James Colson. Then, in the actual basement of Genovas headquarters, locked in a laboratory storage area, they found none other than former deputy CFO Albert Murata, along with his wife and two children.

"Upon questioning, Mr. Murata revealed the true reason behind his sudden removal from the company last week. He told authorities that Genovas was indeed running a gene-supplantation experiment on unknowing prisoners. He said that he attended a meeting at the behest of CEO James Colson, where they went over the logistics of what he called 'Project Manticore,' a study that aimed to test multi-species supplantation in human hosts. Also allegedly attending the meeting were Dr. Isaac Cross, Correcticorp CEO Jane Witham,

United States Army General Terrance Fay, and Illinois Governor Bill Peters. Allegedly, Genovas partnered with Correcticorp, the private prison corporation that runs most of the state prisons in Illinois, in order to get access to the population needed for test subjects. A joint task force has brought Ms. Witham in for questioning, but, as of yet, we do not have any further details about her.

"Mr. Murata also told authorities that funding was received from the United States Army and the Illinois state treasury through General Fay and Governor Peters. Details are still hazy, but I have received word that General Fay has been summarily court marshaled. The charge is that he embezzled defense funds in exchange for potential research data that would allow him to have—this is mere speculation, mind you—the next generation of supplanted soldiers, much like the famous echolocation squad that captured Hans Schlemmer back in 2043.

"The task force was also sent out to bring in Governor Peters, but upon arriving at his mansion, they found Peters deceased on the back patio. The initial investigation found traces of BTX toxin on his body, the very same toxin used by the Killer Frog to paralyze and kill his victims. Authorities are still looking for any potential connections between Peters and the Killer Frog. A further investigation of the governor's home led to the discovery of a single printed document. True to former Genovas employee Albert Murata's word, this document detailed the personnel and logistics of the experiment dubiously titled 'Project Manticore.' Authorities are reviewing it as we speak.

"We will be sure to bring you any updates as they come in. It is my pleasure to inform you that there will be a very special edition of *The Power Hour* with Speedy Powers just two hours from now that you will not want to miss. Apparently, he has a surprise guest whose identity eludes even me. On behalf of *Windy City News*, I want to say that we are truly indebted to our loyal viewers and listeners for their continued support, and we will always pledge to give you the best, unfiltered information as soon as it arrives on our desks. For everyone at *Windy City News*, I'm Jeff Washburn. Stay safe out there, Chicago."

CHAPTER 59
NO MATTER

"No matter, no matter." Dr. Isaac Cross pressed a button, and the lone computer terminal in the room came to life. More a large tool shed than a room, it had outer walls of flattened steel, insulated with rows of fiberglass foam, and finally a polymer inner wall. It was located in the middle of a large, abandoned land lot quite away from any electrical grid and was powered by four solar generators outside.

"Those fools would have corrupted the data, regardless, what with their inconsistencies." He talked loudly, and the acoustics of the room fed that volume. "Now, let's see." He touched the screen with his finger and scrolled through. Although that disgusting wretch Jose Gutierrez had destroyed the data hubs with his absurd bone claws, Dr. Cross still had all his original research backed up here, off-site, away from the prying eyes of corporations or governments. It was true that it was stored in that labs at Genovas as well, but none of those idiots would ever know how to continue his work. No, it was the assistants that ruined it all, even before Gutierrez had a say. Maybe it was worth it in the end to sacrifice the pristine, state-of-the-art corporate lab. Here he could finalize his work without complications, red tape, and bureaucracy. The private security men who had guarded him in their final moments made a worthy sacrifice as well. Their lives were a pittance compared to the progress he could show the world with his research. Still, his experiment at the prison had failed where he entirely expected it to succeed. That meant something was wrong. Something was off.

"It has to be something. But I accounted for everything. Strand stability. Side effects. Immune response. Chromosomal mutations. Gene mutations. Silent. Missense. Nonsense. Nonsense indeed. It should have worked!" The last word echoed off the walls. "No, no, no. There is an elegant solution to this. I know it."

He exhaled forcefully and sat down in the chair in front of the monitor. He adjusted his glasses and leaned forward, inspecting every nucleic acid in detail. He slowly scrolled through, hardly blinking, until his eyes began to water. He let no minutiae slip past his vision until the burning overwhelmed him, and he squeezed his eyes shut, releasing tears from their corners to tumble down his cheeks. When he reopened his eyes, he looked away from the screen, stood up, and shook his head violently.

"Everything is perfect. I checked it a thousand times!" Dr. Cross paced around the room, still shaking his head and blinking rapidly to remove any lasting discomfort from his burning eyes. "There is no reason that it didn't work. None!" He brought his fist down on a metal table, causing the lab equipment on it to shiver and shake. A row of empty test tubes slid off and shattered on the floor. He growled in anger and was about to go grab a broom and dustpan when he suddenly froze in place. He looked down at his fist, still on the table, and the broken glass on the floor.

"That's it," he said, a smile slowly forming on his lips. "That's it. The supplantations are too close to one another. I should have known that from the beginning. Despite the rules of strand stability, there was no accounting for the ripple effect that each supplantation might have on the next. I almost feel like a fool, but no one else saw it. They would never have figured it out. Only I could. Those prisoners *had* to be sacrificed. The data *had* to be destroyed. It all led to this. I simply need to separate them farther apart, and the ripples will no longer destabilize them. It's not an elegant solution at all, but a simple one. I see it now, clear as day."

He dragged the chair back to the computer and sat down. Using both hands, he manipulated the DNA strands on the screen, deftly transitioning from two to three dimensions and back. After a few minutes, he was done. He stood up again, looked back down at the monitor, and initiated the formulation process. The computer fed information to another machine that created the supplantation formula and held it at immensely cold temperatures. As the machine did its work, Dr. Cross grabbed a sandwich and soda from a refrigerator on the far side of the room. After only a scant few minutes, the formulation was complete. Dr. Cross threw the remaining food in the trash can and walked over to the machine. He pressed a button, opening the top with a loud hiss and billowing vapors. He donned a thickly padded glove, then reached in and pulled out a vial. There it was, so innocuous, less than an ounce of light blue liquid. A single dose. And potentially the greatest achievement of his career. He placed it gently down on the table next to the machine. He took out a package of sterilized syringes from a drawer under the table, ripped it open, dipped one into the vial, and siphoned up the liquid.

In his hand, he held either his salvation or his destruction. But there would be no more mass experiments, no more controlled laboratory testing. Those times had passed, and here he was, holding what in another world could be the scientific leap that would win him a Nobel Prize. If it worked, maybe there was still that chance. Maybe he would finally get the recognition and respect that he deserved for all his long years of hard work. Yes, the world would learn to understand. And Dr. Isaac Cross would become a household name just like Dr. Larry Needleman, who created the first consumer supplantation, and all the other great scientists and inventors in history.

Dr. Cross swabbed his shoulder with an alcohol wipe. He held the syringe aloft, watching the bright ceiling lights through the translucent blue liquid. In one quick motion, he plunged it into his shoulder and pushed the solution into his body. And he waited. And waited.

Special thanks to:

Donna Soodalter
Courtenay Boland
Rich Parisi
Shoshana Smith
Marian Knapp
Tim O'Donnell